TROUBLE IN THE AIR

K. Patteson

To my son Will (Willopher):

As High as the sky,

As deep as the ocean,

To the Moon and Back.

1

Natasha, dressed in a black suit with her thick black hair tucked back into a bun, waited for the target of the biggest revenge killing she had ever been a part of. An earpiece in her ear and a government issued gun tucked into a holster at her side, a typical MP Grach. It was an absolute POS, and she had no intention of using it when the time came, but she couldn't refuse it. As part of her cover, she had been working this job for three weeks, the most she had ever invested in a cover story, but then the client was paying three times as much. Natasha specialized in up close and personal killings, high profile jobs. Creating detailed background stories for herself with plenty of documentation, she was able to get past most security checks. If you were looking to make a big show of the prey's death, Natasha was not afraid to kill in public places, even ones that seemed impossible to escape. This one had three layers of security. Snipers on the roofs of the surrounding buildings. Every officer in Moscow was on duty, along with parts of the military, and the SSA were manning checkpoints and doing crowd control.

The client had chosen her above the other Spartans because of Natasha's proven track record. It had been specifically requested that the prey be killed in the most public way possible. This event was going to be as public as possible. Aside from the prey's numerous entourage, several members of the public, as well as the press, hundreds of people would be in attendance today, which was abnormal for this target. There was a long list of people and nations who would like to see this prey dethroned, and for that reason, he normally did not make public appearances. However, by the prey's own request, the event today was being shown live throughout the nation, and he had requested a large number of the public be in attendance.

Within the kill zone there would be staff members, students, government agents, and the press. On the perimeter, there were thousands of the general public waiting to get a glimpse of their president. Natasha was going to have to get past all of them without being stopped if she was going to avoid being killed herself. Natasha's price had reflected this. In fact, it had been such a high price, she thought it would scare off the client. "I have heard the Spartans have a guarantee. Even if you are caught, you never tell who hired you."

"Never."

"Even under torture?"

"Never."

"I can not impress on you how important it is that no one ever suspects it is me."

"No one will ever know. And you still want to be present when it happens?"

"Are you kidding? That's the part I'm looking forward

to the most." Natasha could not remember the last time she killed a target while the client had watched. Natasha listened to the chatter on the radio in her ear, listening for the prey to arrive. No matter what happened, today was going to be interesting.

She cooly scanned the crowd, trying to look earnestly for threats. Several protesters had already been arrested and were currently being beaten back at headquarters. Nervous civilians scuffled around. Flags waved over their heads. The line of uniforms was already having a hard time keeping them back. It was now three in the afternoon, and they were getting impatient. She scanned the security perimeter to make sure there had been no changes. It was important to know how she was going to escape. Natasha knew which point had the least amount of security. It was in a built up area. While there would be snipers and the usual precautions, there were also lots of little places to hide in plain sight. Her heart rate was slow. She had calculated that this mission had a seventy-three percent chance of success. Natasha had worked under harsher odds.

"Godunov is pulling up now." The voice in her ear announced in Russian. It was time for Natasha to go to work. On the outside she was the picture of calm.

A black sedan pulled up on Natasha's left. She moved to make it look like she was at the ready. Another security agent ran up to the car as it came to a stop and opened the door. The president got out, waving to the crowd that had found a new voice. They were a sea of flying flags and the noise was almost deafening. Stepping out of the way, the president's wife also stepped out of the car and turned to wave to the crowd. Dressed as most politicians' wives seemed to, in a sensible brown skirt suit. Together they walked to the steps just below Natasha where a red carpet led them up the steps and into the building. They both paused on the top of the steps right in front of Natasha to turn back to the sea of people and wave. It would have been an excellent time to kill him, but the client had been very specific about where she wanted him killed.

Natasha kept a steady eye on the crowd and the couple. Having waved to the people, the President and his wife turned and made their way into the brand new ballet school they were there to open. The usual line of local dignitaries lined the hallway leading to the studio where the president was to be met by the school's ballet students. The press was numerous, and Natasha was nearly blinded by all the flashes. The president had been clear he wanted heavy press coverage and had even offered them a rare press conference afterwards. Shaking the hands of those lining the walk, President Godunov passed Natasha as she filed in behind him with the rest of the security team. Natasha looked out over the crowd, seemingly making sure there was no threat. In truth, it was so she could position herself where she wanted to be. The crowd of people was so thick, it was hard to ensure she was where she needed to be to make the kill shot.

Natasha thought it was rather brave (or trusting) of the President to allow so many people to get close to him. It had been clear at the many security meetings that had preceded this event, that the President was not a well liked man. Several attempts had previously been made on his life. Everytime the man left the residence, his life was in danger. To the point that his children were never seen in public and are forbidden to be seen with him. The children had been seen so little, many people in the country denied that he had any offspring.

The president had made his way to power by less than desirable means. Natasha had heard rumors connecting him to the Mafia. Connections he still used to get rid of his opponents. Disagreeing with the President could get you killed a number of different ways. Many of his enemies had fallen out of their own windows, gone down in planes, been found dead of radiation poisoning while out for a walk, and a few had simply disappeared. The rumor was there was a prison in Siberia where they were sent to starve and work to death.

So Natasha would have good reason to be worried, if she had been physically capable of such an emotion. Equally, she would have just as much reason to feel confident. Natasha had never failed at a killing in her career, having been trained since birth for exactly this purpose. It had been pressed upon her that creating a multi-layered background story that was well documented before taking on such a job would be more important than what weapon she used. Over the years, Natasha had found various ways to use human behavior patterns to allow her to escape from seemingly impossible situations.

The prey finished shaking the hands of the dignitaries and now made his way down the hallway where instructors and other school administrators were waiting with smiles at the entrance of the studio. He was presented with a large bouquet of white roses, which he kindly accepted and handed off to a security agent who then passed it off to someone else, and Natasha watched as it was passed out of the building. The time and location of Natasha's attack had been specific. Natasha looked ahead, the time for her to make her move was getting closer. Ballerina's dressed in their performance costumes lined the back wall, smiles plastered in place. When he entered the room, they all did a high kick and then rested in the classical ballerina pose.

"Kak fantasticheskie!" He said, clapping his hands. "You all look fantastic." Word went through to let the press off their leashes. The press went wild with the pictures. Flashes bounced all over the room and reflected off the mirrors. It was enough to give you a headache. Godunov shook the hand of each ballerina, making small talk here and there. The entire atmosphere of the room changed, becoming more relaxed. Natasha inched her way closer to him. No one paid her much attention.

"Once he is done here, they are going to make their way to the main theater where he will answer press questions." The voice in her ear went on with other instructions, but Natashsa paid no attention because she was going to upend the planned agenda. Slowly but steadily, Natasha inched her way closer to the prey, placing herself where she needed to be. By the time Godunov was halfway through the line of ballerinas, Natasha was directly behind him. With one last look around the room to make sure her escape was still clear, she tapped him on the shoulder and leaned in as if to pass a message.

"Good-bye." She whispered. Putting her ghost gun to his back, Natasha shot him once in the kidney from behind. The bullet went through, and blood splattered on the pink tutu of the ballerina in front of him. Godunov's face was full of confusion as it went white.The ballerina looked down at her costume in confusion. Not realizing what the red splatter was at first. Godunov's small, dark eyes went wide with shock and he looked at Natasha in astonishment. The room let out a scream, led by the ballerina who had figured out that she was covered in blood. Natasha had used a silencer, but there had still been an unmistakable noise. Godunov went limp and fell to the ground. Natasha supported him as he fell.

The screams grew louder as it became clear that something had gone very wrong. Easing her target to the ground, everyone still looking around to see what had happened, Natasha switched out the ghost gun and grabbed her government gun. She then turned and ran through the crowd. Speaking into her head set, "Godunov down, Godunov down. Need assistance. Medical, we need medical." She yelled into the headset as she ran out of the room, making sure to give it the right amount of panic. People parted to let her through as part of the President's security team.

A crush of people joined Natasha running out of the room. Once through the studio doors and back into the hallway, Natasha looked frightened and bounced from one side of the hallway to the other like she didn't know what to do. She stopped talking into her wire. Running her hands through her hair like she was in distress, she removed the wire and let it fall to the ground where it was almost immediately trampled on by panicking people running for the exits.

Ducking into a bathroom, Natasha locked the door and pulled off the black wig she had been wearing, throwing it into the trash can. She also disposed of the thick eyebrows that matched the ones on her ID badge and carefully removed the scar that had been under her right eye, which her back story said she had received while on a mission to

Afghanistan. Pulling a new ID out of her pocket, she was no longer a trusted member of Godunov's security team, but an administrator at the school. Natasha ruffled her tight bun that held her natural hair and pulled a pair of fake glasses out of her pocket. Then she splashed water under her eyes to look like tears. In a crisis, the one person NOT panicking will be noticeable. Leaving the bathroom with her previous disguise in the trash, she joined the crowd of people being ushered out of the building.

2

Godunov's wife stood there in genuine shock. Her husband had just been shot in front of her. Without knowing where he had been shot, she knew it was serious. The look on his face as he fell to the floor told her that. The room was chaotic, and she thought it interesting that after the shot was fired, everyone seemed to want to be as far away from Godunov as they could manage. The real security team was trying to control the screaming throng of people and get them out of the room. She ran to her husband. He had been left there on the floor, his blood coming through his shirt and starting to pool on the floor around him. She had seen enough death to know it was not far away. Kneeling behind him, she gently raised his head into her lap. He reached for her and she took his hand.

"Muzh, my Muzh." She said to him. He was a horrible shade of gray. His mouth was moving, but no words came out. "It's alright my Muzh, it will all be over soon." She stroked his head.

"Find them. Kill them." He managed to whisper. She

should have known his last words would be ones of revenge and hate.

"Oh my Muzh. I don't have to find them. It was me. I killed you." She said, to his shocked face. His eyes grew wider and he tried harder to form words. She didn't think it was possible for him to go another shade of gray, but he did. No words came out. The medics would be there soon. "I, your wife. The woman you thought was too stupid to know what you were, was the one who killed you. May you burn in hell for the things you have done." She had the great pleasure of seeing the horror in his eyes. Continuing to stroke his face and look at him with the love she had once felt for him, she waited for the end to come. It was not hard for her to pretend. Holding him close to her, she cried for all the hurt he had caused her. Her tears fell over him as he took his last raspy breath. The sob that escaped when his body went limp was genuine. She was free. Finally, she was free of the monster she had married.

The cameras that were recording every movement, capturing every tear, saw something completely different. Hearing the medics and security running down the hallway, she made them pull her off of him."We have to go. We have to get you to safety." They yelled at her. She let go. His limp body fell to the ground with a gratified thud. They half carried her out, his blood covering her dress and hands. He was left alone lying on the cold floor, his dead eyes looking back at him from the mirror he was facing. The bastard deserved nothing better.

It was all a bit of a blur as they walked out the back door of the school and placed her in a secure car.

"Are you injured? Were you shot?" They asked her.

"It's not my blood. I am not injured." She informed

them with an appropriately shaky voice. It was surprising how naturally it all came to her. *Maybe being a politician's wife has been useful after all.*

"Where are we going?" She asked.

"Back to the palace." She took a deep breath. They were taking her home.

"My children. Someone must get my children."

"Their security agents already have them on the way."

"I want that woman out by the time I get there."

"Who?"

"Don't play stupid with me. I know she is there, and if she is in the palace, then you know about her. She must be gone. Make sure the press doesn't see her leave. I will not have my husband's memory tarnished with scandal. Especially now." The agent nodded and radioed ahead. Her hands were shaking and that pleased her. Apparently, having your husband shot right in front of you was traumatic even if you were the one who arranged it.

"Who did this?" She asked, thinking it would be something the recently widowed wife of the president would ask.

"It's too early to know, but we are already investigating." They fell into silence, and by the time they had returned to the palace, she was able to walk in with her head held high, blood stains on her dress notwithstanding.

"Is it true?" Her daughter's face turned white as soon as she saw her mother. "Is he gone?"

"Yes, it's true." Her son and daughter fell into her arms. "He will never hurt you again, my loves." She whispered into their ears, followed by a kiss.

The reports would later comment on the widow's grief.

How she had comforted her husband in his final moments. Pictures of her hugging him and having to be pulled away from his lifeless body would cover the papers for days, followed by her stoically walking into the palace moments later. Head held high. They would comment on her strength. The nation would rally around her in a way she could never have suspected.

When Natasha ran out of the school, she, along with everyone else, was herded to a contained area. Natasha was held with the other witnesses. Through careful navigation of the buildings and allies that had the smallest amount of security, Natasha found herself calmly walking through an alleyway when someone yelled, "Freeze." Natasha did as she was told. The command had come from behind her. Her ghost gun was in her pocket and at this distance, the officer might get off a shot before she killed him, but she wasn't sure if they were alone yet. She scanned the rooftops. There weren't supposed to be snipers this far out, but no doubt things had changed quickly.

Not seeing anything, Natasha took a risk and turned to face the officer without being instructed. "I said, freeze. Keep your hands up." Natasha did as she was told and added in a meek, "I'm sorry." With just the right amount of fear mixed in. The officer kept his gun up, but his posture relaxed. Natasha now had him where she wanted him. Now able to scan this side of the rooftops, Natasha knew she had a lone officer. How he had spotted her she wasn't sure, but these things happen. The officer was carefully approaching her. Natasha waited.

"What are you doing out here?" The officer asked.

"I was in the crowd around the school. Something has happened, I wanted to go home." Natasha measured the amount of emotion in her voice carefully. Her plan had been to grab the officer's gun and use the butt of the gun to beat his head in. Shooting was also an option, but a last resort. While it would not be a problem to get away from here, shooting would bring unwanted attention to her escape route. Thankfully, it appeared she wasn't going to have to do either. Lowering his gun, but still keeping a ready hand on the weapon, he extended a hand and asked for her ID.

"You work at the school. Were you there?"

"I was going to try and get in with my ID, but they wouldn't let me, so I was in the crowd. I was hoping to see Godunov as he was leaving, but suddenly all these people were running, and then the security ran in. I don't know what happened, but I decided to get away from there."

"How far away is home?"

"A few blocks, not far." He handed her back her ID.

"Good, they have shut down all transport. Go home, and have a drink for our brave Godunov. May God rest his soul." Natasha took her ID back, not believing her luck. The officer stayed where he was while she walked out the other side of the alley.

The streets were empty by the time she got to the safe house. Businesses had closed early for the day and were unlikely to open tomorrow. The safe house was empty. While Russia was a lucrative place to do business, it was not a place you wanted to get caught. The winters were legendary, which Natasha suspected was why the Vodka was so good. With glass in hand, Natasha sat down in front of the TV and turned on the news. With the killing being done so publically and with so many cameras around, there was footage of Natasha shooting him. Though it was hard to tell it was Natasha. To Natasha's advantage, her black wig blended in with the hair of the person standing next to her. Camera footage of the back of her head had been enlarged to the point of uselessness and was being shown repeatedly.

"Considering the professionalism of the murder, authorities suspect the Spartans may be involved." The news anchor stated. "It is still unknown who hired them and what their motive is."

With the long list of potential governments, oligarchs, Russian Mafia members, freedom fighters, and champions of social justice, it was impossible to know who was responsible. Natasha would be long gone by the time they got anywhere near her. They wouldn't be able to keep the borders closed forever, and if no group took responsibility for the murder, then she should be able to make it to her next job in two week's time.

The existence of Spartans had only come to light within the last two years. Since their existence had become known, they had been blamed for just about everything. Natasha had not joined the younger generation of Spartans who had decided to take revenge on their creator and make their existence public. Despite the findings from the investigation going into great detail as to how Spartan's had come into being, most people thought a genetically altered human designed to kill was probably a conspiracy theory. And they certainly found it hard to believe these killing machines had been let out onto an unsuspecting public.

On the other hand, there was another portion of the populace who had embraced the existence of highly skilled and totally discrete killers for hire. Business had definitely picked up since their existence had become more widely known. Natasha held the great distinction of being the oldest Spartan, and also the first one made to order. Her ID number was nine-hundred and ninety-nine. After Natasha, the much larger order of the one thousand series was designed for the US military. They made up the bulk of the Spartans remaining. There had been a few custom orders afterwards, but nothing as large as the one thousand series. After their existence had become known, the Spartans that had gone into professional killings had joined forces and now shared resources. Natasha was lying low in one of the Spartans' several safe houses.

The borders opened back up a few weeks later, the day before the state funeral. They had to let the dignitaries coming to the funeral into the country. Examining her newest ghost gun, she carefully placed it in her coat pocket. The TV playing in the background, Natasha caught part of the speech given by the president's wife. She stopped to watch. Her client had done a fantastic job of playing the grieving widow. It would be a long time before the country forgot the image of her walking through the palace doors with the president's blood still wet on her clothes. The country had responded by demanding she take her husband's place in the palace. Today she was wearing a classy black skirt suit with a thick veil.

"Today marks the end of an era. There is no denying that. But as my husband said to me several times, 'the end makes room for

a new beginning'. This is a new beginning for Russia. For the Russian people. He would want us to move forward proudly." The crowd cheered. On that note, Natasha turned the TV off and left the safe house for her next job. There was still an increased presence on the street. Armed military stood at almost every street corner. People were still calling for the blood of whoever killed their president. The newspapers were still filled with demands to find the killer. The grainy picture of her still appeared almost everywhere she looked, but it was usually under the headline announcing no new leads. With her new ghost gun in her pocket, Natasha took her small rolling bag and one of her passports and headed for the train station and boarded the train headed for Slovakia and her next job. There was a virus that was spreading through the Americas and Europe. The talk around it was getting more urgent. Governments had started to talk about limiting air travel if it continued to spread. Natasha had a few more jobs to take care of before they locked everyone down. There was no time for delays now.

3

"What the hell are you doing up this late?" Jack said, coming into the galley and rubbing his head. He was shirtless, his sweat pants riding low on his hips. Ross was sitting at the table in the boat's galley, which was a common sight this last month.

"Working." Ross kept her eyes on her computer. If he caught her looking at him, it would only encourage him.

"Ross, you have been at it all day, Honey. You can't go at it all night as well. You need your rest."

"Jack, there is a worldwide pandemic going on. Your genius fiance has been asked to help design a test that will identify the virus in its earliest stages. You can't honestly expect me to sleep, can you? The world needs me."

"I thought you were just helping with the disposal of the waste from the machine? Besides, how much more work can there be? The thing launches next week doesn't it?" Ross looked up at him with a warning.

"This testing system is going to be used in a large number in every hospital in the world. It would be nice if the chemicals used to run it didn't contaminate the drinking water in the process. We have to be able to neutralize the virus as well as the chemicals used to run it, or this thing is going to cause more problems than it cures. We are still having a bit of a problem neutralizing the virus. Damn thing keeps adapting." Jack shrugged.

"Add more of the stuff that kills the virus." Ross looked up at him with a look he had come to fear since living with her.

"Thank you so much. Why hadn't I thought of that? Thank God you came in when you did."

"Ross…."

"If I add more of the 'virus killer' as you called it, then I have to add more of the 'virus killer neutralizer'. If we get the math wrong, I have either not added enough of the 'virus killer' which obviously isn't good. Or I've added too much of the neutralizer which will burn your eyeballs out of your head in too high a concentration."

"Sounds impossible." Jack slid into the bench seat next to her. "I'm simply arguing that you are going to be more likely to help if you have a good night's rest." Ross gave him a sideways glare.

"Jack, you and I both know the reason you are out here asking about me is not because you want me to come back to bed and *sleep*." She looked up at him again, bouncing her pen off her chin.

"Yes it is." He said, with his half grin.

"No it isn't, and I know it isn't because I have been working past this hour every night for the past four nights and you have not said a word." Jack continued to grin as he put his arm around her shoulders pulling her to him so that he could kiss the scar on her neck where she had been shot six months before.

"Can you blame me?" Ross let him do it for a moment, even leaning her head towards him before she shrugged him off. "Once we get to Boston, I will hardly see you. Your mother is going to have you off dress shopping, and Sam is going to be doing whatever it is women do before a wedding." Jack had stopped kissing her neck, but he was still leaning in, and his hot breath was doing more than he knew.

"No, they aren't." Ross said, bringing herself back to the topic at hand. "Again, there is a global pandemic going on. The dress shops are closed, as are the bars and whatever else people go for bachelorette parties. I'm wearing Mom's dress."

"Seriously?" Jack didn't know she had made a decision.

"Seriously. She's all upset because the alterations are going to have to happen quickly if they are going to be done in time for the wedding." A little flutter went through Ross at the word 'wedding'. The wedding in question was her wedding. Her wedding to Jack. She couldn't think too much about it or she started to doubt that it was actually happening. The thought of her marrying Jack, forever in holy matrimony, still seemed ridiculous. To say Ross had never spent time dreaming of her wedding day was an understatement. Receiving the Nobel Peace Prize for advances in chemistry? That she had envisioned herself doing several times. Marrying, absolutely never.

When the pandemic had started a few months ago, her lab back in Boston had reached out to her and asked for her help in designing a testing machine. In part to take her mind off the wedding, Ross had jumped at the chance. While engineering was very much not Ross's thing, they had specifically wanted her help with the fluids that ran the machine. They could not find a way of running the machine without using chemicals that would have to be disposed of in a controlled setting, and when you are dealing with a global pandemic, you just don't have the time for that sort of thing.

Ross was helping them neutralize the chemicals so they could be disposed of by pouring them down the drain. With technology being what it was, Ross had been able to work with her team back in the lab while still being on the boat in the middle of the Indian ocean. While the setting had been beautiful, it had also been frustrating more than once. Ross was rather looking forward to being on land, where she could go for a walk, have a pizza delivered, and enjoy decent bandwidth. While she had adapted amazingly well to living on a boat with two other people, men at that, Ross was very much looking forward to getting mad and storming off in a huff if she wanted to. Something she absolutely didn't want to do right now with Jack inching ever closer and doing everything BUT kissing her neck.

"You will look beautiful in whatever you wear." Jack said, into her hair. Ross had always been led to believe the woman was the one who went all romantic and soft at the mention of a wedding. Jack was getting more and more soft and romantic the closer they got to the wedding date. He got this soft puppy dog look whenever they talked about it. It had been suggested at one point that they elope. Ross had thought her mother and Sam would have been the disappointed ones. She had instantly retracted the idea because of the disappointed look on *Jack's* face.

"I want to see you walk down the aisle to me." He had said.

"What if I trip?" Ross had answered. It was truly the whole reason she wanted to elope. Jack had not answered. He knew as well as she did there was a decent chance of tripping.

"I want to see you walk or trip down the aisle to me." He had finally said.

"Jack, you were married before. You've done it already." She had pointed out in a last attempt to get him to join her side.

"But I haven't done it with you, Ross." At that point she gave up and resigned herself. Ross could not think about the wedding without her heart rate going up. If there was anything good that had come out of the pandemic, it was that most of the wedding guests had canceled. So if she tripped now, only ten people would be there to witness it.

"I'll cancel the dress then and we can walk down the aisle in our pajamas." Ross said, coming back to their current conversation.

"You do what you want, but I'll be dressing up. You deserve it." Jack winked at her.

Jack made one more attempt, blowing gently across her neck and brushing away her hair. A warm shiver went right through her. "Come on darling. In a few days we are going to be in civilization again. This might be our last chance out here in the wild." Ross closed her eyes and leaned in.

"Jack……this is important, honey." With it looking like his charms weren't going to be enough to pull her away from work, Jack kissed her forehead and scooted back out of the bench seat. "Okay, go save the world if you must, but don't stay up too late." He winked at her. Ross watched him walk away, and for a brief second, wondered if the world would forgive her for making it an early night.

4

Ross had been extremely hesitant to leave the world and come on board the boat in the beginning. Jack had been trying to convince her to join him on the boat when she agreed to go on the research trip instead. In fact, that decision had almost ended the relationship in more ways than one. Jack was angry, and she was too scared to commit. In the end, after being shot and nearly dying on that trip, she had been too weak to argue. As much as she hated to admit she was wrong, the last six months on the boat had been exactly what she had needed. Six months may have been a bit longer than was necessary, but she had healed beautifully. She had been able to heal in safety in the middle of nowhere with two men who would have done anything to protect her.

Inspector Dufort had wanted to lock her in her apartment with armed guards out front. The idea being that the Spartans would come and finish what they had started. Jack had convinced Dufort that the boat was safer. Since Jack and Si had a well documented history of fighting off Spartans, Dufort agreed, and Ross still exhaled with relief when she thought about it. Sitting in her apartment waiting for a Spartan to attack and no one but strangers to protect her still sent chills down her back. Ross trusted Jack and Si with her life because they had all fought off the Spartans before. There was no one else she would rather be with.

While Ross was looking forward to several things that land provided (for one thing it didn't rock when a storm hit), she had to admit she would miss the safety she felt here. There were no Spartans here. There wasn't anything. The pandemic was raging on land and yet, out here on the water, things went on much the way they had for thousands of years. Ross was both going to be glad and sad to say goodbye to the remoteness the boat offered. She consoled herself with the thought of being able to get 'fancy' coffee delivered whenever she wanted. Si made the coffee on the boat. No one would call it 'fancy'. In fact, very few would call it coffee. She had no idea how he made it because he never let anyone else do it, but Si's coffee was the thickest coffee she had ever seen and would render most people blind. The first time Ross had it, she thought she was having a panic attack after one sip.

"None of that hipster stuff served around here. This will put hair on your chest." Si had laughed over her while she had laid on the floor of the ship trying to get her heart rate to return to normal. Ross spent a few moments trying to remember what a caramel latte tastes like.

As she sat there in the kitchen, Si was in the wheelhouse steering them back towards Australia. The home of not only Si and Jack, but the boat they were sailing on. They had already been heading that way for a full twenty-four hours, and it would take a few more days before they hit land. Once they handed over the keys of the ship, they would fly to New York where Ross would reveal her research with the rest of the team to the medical world. From there, they would fly to Boston where she and Jack would become man and wife. They had yet to figure out where they would go from there. By the time they had gotten that far in the plans, the pandemic was starting to spread.

Six months had seemed like such a long time back when Jack had asked her to marry him. She had said yes after he promised they wouldn't have to get married right away, if ever. Unfortunately, Ross's mother had felt differently about the situation. Her best friend Sam had some strong feelings about it as well.

"Are you 'effing kidding me?" Sam had a small child at home, she was working on her language. "I have been secretly planning your bachelorette party for 'effing decades and you want to 'just live engaged'. I won't allow it Ross. The rest of us engaged people had to get married. You are getting married too."

"What's the difference if I....."

"Nope, sorry Honey. You said yes and put on the ring, you are obligated now."

"Sam, that's ridic...."

"Shmmm."

"Sam!"

"Shhhmmmmm. Your getting married and that's all there is to it." She had said, in her best mom voice. Ross had sighed deeply.

"My mother said pretty much the same thing."

"Ross, you've seen Jack. Why wouldn't you want to show him off? I mean, show your horrible cousin Janet that you CAN land a guy, and Jesus what a guy!"

"Janice, her name is Janice. She isn't coming because of the pandemic."

"Why not, that woman's too mean to catch anything? There will be pictures. Pictures of you and your smoking hot husband. Put the picture on your Christmas card. You should send the same Christmas card to Janice every year."

"Why would I do that?"

"Because of what she said about you when you got your doctorate. Stupid bi…..pig. I'm sorry, I know she worked hard to become realtor of the month, but she didn't need to rain on your parade." Ross had almost forgotten that. Janice had never really been nice and had often made fun of Ross's lack of a boyfriend.

"It seems like a lot of trouble to go through to prove a point."

"Ross, it is worth it. I mean, Phillip drives me insane half the time. But the man stood up in front of a church and before both of our parents, friends and preacher, said he loved me and wanted to spend the rest of his life with me. That means something." Ross remembered she had been there, once again worrying about tripping.

"I just never thought of myself as a bride, Sam. Someone's wife."

"Well, things change, babe. You will still be the amazing Dr. Ross Halloway. It will just change to the amazing Dr. Ross Halloway and her husband Jack." Ross wasn't sure why, but the whole sentence sounded wrong to her.

"That doesn't sound terrible."

"So, are you walking down the aisle, or am I dragging you."

"I'll walk I guess."

"That's my girl."

5

Natasha stepped out of the elevator at the basement level of a Slavakian government building. Leaving the harsh fluorescent lights of the elevator to enter the dark hallway in front of her lit by two lonely light bulbs. The cement walls were lined with forgotten boxes and office equipment. Damp was thick in the air. For some reason, humans seemed to think that bad lighting and poor air quality equaled secrecy. It was all very predictable. Natsha's heels made a clicking sound that echoed all the way down the hall. There was still snow from the outside dusting the top of her coat.

Obviously, the mousy looking woman sitting behind a desk at the end of the hallway had plenty of warning that Natasha was coming. Regardless of this, the creature still looked terrified when Natashsa stopped in front of her.

"Natasha, I'm here for the meeting. They are expecting me," she said, hardly looking at the creature who stared at her with wide eyes.

"Are you really one of them?" It was said in barely more than a whisper. While Natasha felt no emotions, she was very experienced with recognizing it in others. The woman was practically vibrating with fear. Natasha turned her cold, unfeeling eyes to the woman.

"What 'them' do you think I am?" Natasha said, leaning across the desk in a predatory way.

"A Spartan?"

"Yes. I am a Spartan." Natahsa said, standing back up.

"Are you as good as they say you are?"

Natasha shrugged. "I've had no complaints." The woman gave a quick look at the heavy iron door to her right and wondered what the mousy creature was up to.

"And you never tell anyone who hired you?"

"Never. Even under torture."

"How much do you charge to kill someone?" The mousy woman whispered. Natasha had rarely been approached like this. In a modern age, people usually like to hire her online.

"How far away is the target?" Natasha asked. The woman looked confused and then said, "In the next room."

"Ten thousand US dollars." The woman looked down at her hands.

"How much to shoot him in the knee?" Natasha had to stop and think about this. She had never been asked to wound anyone before. Spartans were known as killers. She couldn't remember shooting anyone anywhere other than a fatal location. Not that she was incapable of it.

"How much do you have?"

"Two thousand US dollars. Cash." The woman reached into her pocket with a shaking hand and pulled out a roll of money. "He raped me," the woman blurted out. "When my husband confronted him about it, he had him shot in the knee. My husband was a mechanic, he can't work like he used to. I have to stay working here to keep us fed."

Natasha didn't really care why. She took the cash and said, "Which one?"

"The short fat one, bald on top. He's usually smoking a cigar and sweating. He smells like boiled cabbage." Natasha nodded, she knew which one the mousy woman was talking about. In the next room were her regular clients, three government officials who specialized in making the nation's problems disappear. Taking the money, Natasha stuck it in her pocket. "Consider it done." The mousy woman smiled and buzzed her through.

Natasha was everything you wanted in a Slovakian assassin, and she was perfectly aware of it. Especially if you were a Slovakian man. She was tall, blonde, well built, with cold blue eyes and perfect aim. Natasha had learned a long time ago that men responded to her a certain way when they first met her. The three in the next room had met her several times as they were the ones who had ordered her creation from Gentix, and passed along her orders. Yet they still looked at her the same every time they saw her. Their eyes started at her legs and slowly moved upwards. Half smiles on their faces and approving nods until they got to her cold blue killer eyes. Then the smiles disappeared and they remembered she was a killer.

While the men did their usual assessment of her, Natasha found her target without a problem. The whole room smelled like boiled cabbage, but there was only one bald man sweating and smoking a cigar. He was so round, Natashsa thought he might roll off his chair. It would do no good to shoot him now, then she wouldn't find out what her next job was. He was to her left and she kept catching him leering at her when he thought she couldn't see. Natasha had every intention of shooting him regardless of what he had done to the mousy woman, but she had no trouble finding the truth in the woman's words.

"Won't you sit down?" A thin man to her right said, taking the cigarette out of his mouth and standing up, pulled a chair out for her. "We would like to congratulate you on your latest hunting trip. The government is very pleased with the results."

"You didn't hire me, why should you be pleased?"

"Let's just say, relations had grown strained between the countries. A problem that is now solved."

"You are assuming I was the one who did it." The thin man sat back with a knowing smile on his face he had absolutely no right to.

"Of course, I am making assumptions based only on your hunting grounds."

"Why am I here?" Natasha said, feeling no need for the small talk. She could not clearly see the man sitting across from her. Between the poor lighting and the cigarette smoke rising up in front of him, all she could make out was his chin. Her hand found her gun in her coat pocket. She had been brought into this room every time she had been called here. There was no reason to think these idiots wished her harm, and even three to one, Natasha had no doubt she could fight them off if she needed to. That being said, she kept her hand on her gun. Because of what had transpired in this room, she knew for certain these men could not be trusted.

Nothing was said for a while, and they all sat there in silence looking at one another. The fatty to her left cleared his throat. Out of all of them, he seemed to be the most nervous. He sat on the edge of his chair (that may have been because his fat ass couldn't fit otherwise), and his small eyes kept shifting from Natasha to the thin man who had offered her a seat.

Finally Mr. Chin, across from her, slid a folder in her direction.

"We need you to take care of these two men." Natasha slid the folder closer and opened it. There was information on both targets, but really all she was interested in right now was, what they looked like and where they were.

"Where is this?"

"The US. New York to be exact. They are the co-creators of a Parid-21 testing device. One of our labs is not far away from having their own machine. Whoever gets their machine to market first will make millions of dollars many times over." Mr. Chin informed her.

"I don't care." Natasha said, "A hundred and fifty thousand US dollars, plus travel."

"Done. Save your receipts." Fatty said.

"Of course." Natasha took the folder and tucked it into her coat. "Anything else?"

"Security will be extremely tight. The conference will be full of scientists from around the world. Will that be a problem?" Thin man to her right asked.

"I just assassinated the president of Russia in a room full of his security and civilians. I think I can handle a few unarmed scientists."

"Forgive me." Thin man said.

"Once the money has been deposited, I will make the arrangements. I would say you will be notified when the job is done, but since you want me to eliminate two of the world's leading scientists at a party in New York, I would say you will know without my telling you."

They all shook their heads. Standing,fatty to her left, grabbed her wrist with force and asked, "We are having a little get together this evening, if you would like to come." Natashsa stared him in the eye while she removed his hand from hers.

"I have plans." Quickly taking the gun out of her pocket, she shot fatty in the knee. Natasha wasn't used to shooting to injure, but judging from the amount of bone that exited the wound, and the way Fatty immediately fell to the ground, she hit his knee cap successfully. There was a brief look of shock before a loud scream of agony. Natasha had not bothered to use a silencer. They were in a soundproof room. The sound of the gunshot was deafening, quickly followed by Fatty's screams. Mr. Chin and Thin man jumped from their seats, and for a moment, stood there in silence while their colleague writhed around on the floor, blood spilling out. Natasha was not used to the noise Fatty was making,and almost shot him again in the head just to shut him up.

"He is so fat he can't even reach his knee." Natasha commented to nobody in particular.

"How in the hell did you get that in here?" The thin man to her right said. "This is a secure area." He had thought about restraining her, grabbing her arm, knocking the gun away. Fortunately for him, he had thought better of it. The smell of fear almost overwhelmed the smell of cheap cologne and cigar smoke in the room. Natasha held the gun up for him to see. Still debating on killing Fatty.

"Ghost gun." She said with calmness. "Made completely of plastic. Made it at home with a 3D printer. Very handy. Completely untraceable. No serial numbers.

You can use traditional bullets, but they are expensive and they set off metal detectors. I make the bullets as well. Since it's completely plastic, you can take it anywhere. Secure locations, airplanes. I can literally kill anywhere." The thin man seemed more terrified than impressed, so she put the gun back in her pocket.

Fatty had gone ghostly white. He let out another scream and yelled, "Get help you bastards." Risking that Natasha would have shot them already if she was going to, Mr. Chin kneeled next to him, offering a flask while the Thin man jumped into action and called out to the mousy woman.

"Get a doctor in here!"

"Have a nice day." Natasha walked out of the room.

"Who hired you?" Thin man asked, regaining some of his composure.

"Ah, you should know better than most that a Spartan never gives details."

"I demand to know!" Thin man's face was a terrible shade of red. A vein was pulsing in his temple. Their fear had turned to anger. People acted irrationally when they were angry. Natasha squared her shoulders and steadied her cold eyes on him.

"If I break the rule for you, I would have to break it for others. I'm sure you don't want me answering that question for anyone else. Do you?" Mr. Chin looked at the Thin man and shook his head. The room relaxed and Natasha walked out of the room without another word. The secretary smiled at her as she left. The mousy woman knew perfectly well her boss would be forced to suffer since no ambulance would be called. The bullet would be removed in the same room where they were now, by a doctor that could be paid off and nothing but vodka for anesthetic. The meeting had been listed as top security. No one could know. Under any circumstances. Mouthing the words 'thank you', the secretary closed her eyes and listened to the fat cabbage scream. He wouldn't be able to chase anyone ever again. It was well worth the money.

6

It was late at night. Ross looked at the clock and it was about one in the morning. They had about another day before they hit port. They had spent the day packing up some of their stuff and tidying the place up in anticipation of arriving in port. It was starting to sink in that they would be leaving the ship. Ross stretched and got up from the bench seat, left the kitchen, and went out on the deck. If she was honest, this was Ross's favorite time on the boat. She used to think it was the quiet, but out here it was rarely noisy. No, it was the stars. The stars were amazing. There were more than she had ever thought possible. The water took on a whole different level of mystery in the inky darkness. Ross made a point of soaking up as much of this as she could before they had to leave it. Ross liked to watch the moon dancing on the surface of the water, like the sea and the sky were continuing a conversation that had been going on long before man sailed these waters and would continue long after they had gone. It was rather a humbling thought.

The light was on in the wheelhouse. Si was steering the

boat back to land. Si tended to take the night shift, and Ross suspected he liked the night just as much as she did. They were so far out in the water they would have to sail night and day to get back to land in time to fly home. Not that this seemed to matter. Ross had thought you anchor a boat at night and everyone got a good night's rest. Si didn't trust anchors. Or so he said.

"Too much can happen when you aren't looking. That's why I sleep in the wheelhouse."

Part of Ross had expected Si to stay on the water while she and Jack went to Boston. Ross had never seen Si off the water and she knew he would be slightly uncomfortable until he returned to it. Si's willingness to come to Boston for the wedding had been the first real sign to Ross how much this wedding meant to other people. Si was still in the wheelhouse because he too was soaking up as much of the sea as he could. Ross leaned into the railing, letting the evening wind hit her face. She would leave him alone, let him get all he could.

Ross had been thinking a lot more about her apartment and home since they had turned the boat back to land. It was hard to think that soon the stars would be out shined by the city lights around her apartment. An apartment she would now be sharing with her husband. Jack. After their wedding. Earlier that day she had spent an hour measuring herself so she could send her measurements to her mother who was now having to alter the wedding dress herself. All the alterations shops had closed along with the wedding dress stores.

"You're twirling your hair again." Si informed her.

Coming out of the wheelhouse, coffee cup in hand. Ross let the hair go quickly. She hadn't even noticed she was doing it.

"Sorry." She said, as a reflex.

"No need to apologize to me, Love." Si answered patiently. "I get like that every time I head back to land as well." He took a sip of his coffee and made a face.

"You'd never know." Si seemed calm the past few days. He motioned for her to follow him so Ross entered the wheelhouse. Ross sat down on the stool next to him and looked out at the same black water. It looked like the stars were rising up from the ocean's surface. Si plunked himself down in the captain's chair and put a foot up on the controls.

"I've perfected the art of hiding it over the years. When you spend most of your married life on the water, the last thing your wife wants to see when you get home is a sour face."

"Care to share some tips?" Ross asked.

"One foot in front of the other." Si said, smiling. Ross was a little disappointed. They were on a two hundred foot boat. You could only put one foot in front of the other for so long before you fell into the water. "And this always helps a little." Si pulled out a Jack Daniels bottle from his overalls pocket. Ross seriously thought about it. Under normal circumstances she would have refused out right, but today she was seriously thinking about it.

"No thanks. I'll try putting one foot in front of the other for a while and see how that goes." Si shrugged and put the bottle back in his pocket. They both looked out over the water, the stars disappearing behind some clouds.

"Are we getting weather? I thought it was clear sailing

all the way into Perth?"

"Those aren't clouds. It's smoke. From the fires." Si said, with a grimace. It was easy out here on the water to forget that there was a whole life happening on land. Australia was on fire. Or at least a decent part of it. They had been following it closely, but the news of Parid-21 spreading had now replaced it on the news. Ross knew they were checking in with people in Perth. The family home was still there.

"Are you up late working on that machine of yours again? What's it called, Peter?"

"PAUL. Parid - 21- Analyzing- Ultrasonic- Lab Station. Yes. Just smoothing out the last details." At least her first social event back on land would be surrounded by her own people. She kept reminding herself of this. It was going to be a small affair since New York had essentially been shut down. Because of the importance of the event, some of the rules were being bent. Almost to the point of breaking. Ross had gone over her notes just that morning and they were in her pocket even now. They had not asked her to speak (thank God for small mercies), but Ross had a horrible habit of freezing when asked direct questions by people she thought were smarter than her, and there were going to be a lot of people who were top in their field. She had been quizzing herself on PAUL'S finer points for days.

"Any more word from your mother or Sam about the wedding?" Si asking, knowing the very mention of the wedding made Ross nervous. Sure enough, she picked up her hair and continued twirling it. Si took another swig of his Jack Daniels.

"Not really. Mom is disappointed we are so limited in who can come. She seemed to calm down a little after

Phillip suggested broadcasting it live online. I got a text this morning asking if we could make people RSVP to that. She's also worried because I won't be getting any wedding presents."

"Do you need wedding presents? You already have an apartment."

"No."

"What's really worrying you, Love?" Ross looked at him. Si was a crusty sea dog. In a former life he would have made a great pirate. Ross and Jack both respected Si's ability to see to the heart of the matter in an instant. However, Ross sometimes wished he wouldn't use it on people. She paused for a moment, considering whether she should actually answer him. He was Jack's father after all. Ross twirled her hair for a moment longer and then said, "I caught a glimpse of Jack's vows."

"Agh."

"I haven't written one word. I started at least twenty times, but I just can't make anything work. He's going to say something perfectly lovely. Then it's going to be my turn, and what am I going to say? Thank you? Ditto? Back atcha?"

"You haven't come up with anything?"

"So far all I have managed to come up with was something about being constantly amazed that he's in love with me. I even tried to make a joke about his abs. It sounded more like sexual harassment when I read it back to myself. I have no idea what I'm doing, Si. Most of my writing has been scientific papers. There is nothing scientific about love or marriage. Even if there was, it's hardly something you want to read out at your wedding. It's hardly going to get pulses racing. I can write a paper with easily repeatable facts. I can do that all day. Anything the average person would want to listen to…..no." Si looked confused and concerned at the same time.

"Is there no one you can ask? Sam maybe?"

"I don't want to. Jack isn't getting help with his….is he?" Ross asked him hopefully. Si shook his head no. "This has to come from me. There are a few apps I was using to help out, but they seemed to be confusing things more than helping."

"Ross, it will come to you. Just let it happen." Si said, offering her the Jack Daniels again. This time Ross took it. The wedding was now a week away and nothing much had been produced.

"You'll be alright, Love." Si said, interrupting her thoughts. "Jack knows how you feel."

"I only have one chance to get this right though."

"No you don't." This was said with such dismissal that Ross looked at him. "Ross, I barely remember my wedding. I remember being nervous as hell. I remember my mate having the ring and the liquid courage. I remember seeing Bev come down the aisle to me. After that I don't remember a thing about the day. You know what I do remember? Everything Bev did after that to let me know she loved me. Those vows are all well and good, but they are just words, darlin'. It's what you do every single day after that truly matters."

"What did Bev do? You know….to show you." Si smiled, as he often did when talking about his beloved wife.

"A thousand tiny things. She gave me Jack. She put up with me, fussed over me. Made sure I was clean, fed, had a home to come home to. Sent me cards for the dumbest holidays. Just to let me know that wherever I was in the world, she was thinking of me." Ross looked at the old salty sea dog and was suddenly filled with love. They had brought her out here to keep her safe. Ross had never underestimated what a huge gesture it was, but occasionally it hit her how much they must really care about her to offer such a thing. For all they knew, Spartans and Russian assassins were on her heels. When you boiled Si down to his core, he was a big 'ol softy.

"Thanks for letting me hide out here, Si." It had been six months and there had never been a threat. Nor was there likely to be one at this stage.

"I'm glad you had time to heal. And that you didn't get so annoyed with us that you poisoned our food." To all of their amazement, they really hadn't gotten on each other's nerves. All of them also agreed that if they stayed on the water for much longer, this streak would definitely come to an end.

"You do love him, don't you?"

"Of course. I wake up everyday amazed that I love him and more that he seems to love me back." Si shook his head.

"You are the strangest woman."

"So I've been told."

"How do you have no idea what a catch you are?" Ross just stood there blankly. "Ross, you have a brilliant mind, a kind heart, and you aren't bad on the eyes either. A woman with all those qualities is a rare find. I'm just glad that my son knew a treasure when he saw one. I tried to talk him out of you if I'm honest."

"When?" Ross had always gotten the impression Si

rather liked her.

"Right after you met. He was trying to figure out if he should go after you. I told him to forget you."

"Why?" Si shrugged.

"He was fresh out of a divorce, we were broke. The last thing I thought he needed was another woman mucking things up. To be fair, you've been nothing but trouble since we met you."

"I know I'm not very....womanly." Ross answered.

"What the hell does that mean?" Si laughed. Ross didn't really know. "I don't know how to put on makeup, wear the right clothes. Cook. My room is always a mess. My hair is always a mess no matter what I do with it." She shrugged. "I'm a mess."

"Jesus woman. What do those things have to do with actual life?" Again, Ross had nothing.

"I was told those things mattered." Ross said, Si waved her off.

"I was married for twenty-five years to the best woman this world has ever made. I can assure you, I didn't marry her because she always had the right outfit on, her hair was perfect and her eye shadow matched her lipstick. Listen, Jack was married to that woman already. I've met fish that were capable of deeper thought than Marta was. She was as cold as a fish too. I'm glad to say you are nothing like her." Ross smiled. Si put an arm around her and pulled her in for a half hug.

"Jack fell in love with you for the mess that you are. Remember that and calm the fuck down woman." Ross felt calmer already.

7

Jack came up into the wheelhouse and Si abruptly turned to face the wheel. Jack looked suspiciously at both of them.

"What are you two talking about?"

"Nothing." Si said.

"Nothing." Ross said. "Why are you up at this hour?"

"Can't sleep. I keep thinking of what kind of world we are going to become citizens of again."

"Been watching the news?" Jack nodded. Ross took his hand.

"We are getting close enough to land that the smoke is starting to black out the stars." Si said. The fires had hit him hard.

"Add in Parid and it hardly seems worth the trouble." Jack said.

"Should we stay on the boat? We could say we are isolating." Ross offered. Both Si and Jack looked at her with confusion.

"Ross, the experiment is over. The project's funding is all gone. We have to turn the boat in." Jack shook his head. "First, I couldn't get you on the boat, and now I can't get you off of it."

"If you've got the wheel son, I think I'm going to go use the head." That was Si's gentle way of getting out of the room.

"I am going to miss this." Ross said as Jack pulled her in close, and for a moment they were silent, looking out at the amazing view in front of them. Then Ross's phone rang.

"Who the hell would that be at this time of night?" Jack asked.

"My mother. Who else completely ignores the time change? Hello?"

"Ross, it's not good news honey." Belinda, her mother, said. Ross's heart froze.

"Is it Dad?" Frank had a stroke a little over a year ago. He had lost his ability to speak and walk for the most part.

"What? Oh, no, he's fine. It's the preacher. He has Parid. I wouldn't be surprised if he doesn't end up in the hospital. The man is almost eighty." Ross wasn't sure what was expected of her here.

"There are still other people who can marry us, right? A judge, other preachers. Boat captains." Belinda had wanted the preacher of the church where Belinda and Frank had been married.

"It's not going to be the same. Not to mention hardly anyone is going to be there to witness it. Ten people! What are your children going to think when they look at the pictures?"

"My hypothetical children will probably be learning about the Parid virus in school, and if they aren't, we will explain that there was a global pandemic going on. For God's sake mother. I thought something had happened to

Dad."

"Your Aunt Hilda is going to be so disappointed, but I think we are going to have to cut her." Belinda said, completely ignoring what Ross had said. That seemed to be the way their conversations went these days.

"Mom, Aunt Hilda is ninety-three years old and I've never met her. She lives in California."

"I know honey, but she dated that Australian during the war. She was looking forward to meeting Jack." Ross pinched her nose. Jack sat and smiled. He was so pleased that Ross loved him enough to put up with all of this. "Are you sure you two don't want to postpone, all the venues are offering free refunds on account of the pandemic." Ross's mouth opened and closed several times while she looked for the right words.

"I'm not sure Jack would be okay with that." Jack winked at her and gave her a thumbs up.

"You could sound a little more upset Ross. I mean a lot of people were going to stop what they were doing to come and celebrate the day."

"Mom, I have no control over the pandemic. I don't see much reason to get upset about things you have no control over. Also, you invited a ton of people I really don't even know, so it's hard to get extremely upset."

"It's a big deal Ross. A lot of them thought you were never going to get married. And the other half thought you were gay. Remember cousin Mark sent you that lovely message on Gay Pride day." Ross took a deep breath. This had been a sticking point with her since her mother had screamed from the nearest mountain top that her daughter was getting married. To a man. Half of these people didn't give a damn when she got her doctorate, published her first scientific paper (even though she sent out copies), or about the other scientific discoveries she had made during her career. But no, now she had landed herself a man, Ross had been declared 'normal' after all. Let's all fly in from the four corners of the earth to witness her marry him and make sure it's real.

Ross didn't say anything to her mother. A lot of these same people had reached out to her when she had nearly died the previous year (and the year before that). They were people who cared. Ross just couldn't understand why they cared so much about something 2.4 million people in the US do (get married) versus something only fifty-five thousand people in the US manage (get doctorates). "Maybe we can have a reception or something once this pandemic is over." Ross said, to make her mother feel better with absolutely no intention of following through with it.

"Oh, that's a good idea. I'll let Aunt Hilda know. I also wanted to let you know that your father and I won't be at the airport to greet you. They are only letting so many people in anyway, but the doctor said I shouldn't be out in crowds more than I can help since your father is so fragile these days. Sam and Philip have volunteered. Also, you are going to have to wear masks around us."

"That's fine."

"I made you a white mask with 'bride' spelled out in glitter." Belinda stated proudly.

"Thank you?"

"Well, I might as well tell you now," her mother sounded really dejected, "I had planned a big reception for you here when you got back." Ross's eyes opened wide. This was the first she was hearing of it. "I was going to combine a welcome party with a bridal shower." Jack didn't know what Belinda was saying, but Ross was having to put her head between her legs. "It doesn't look like we are going to be able to do that now honey, I'm sorry." Ross realized she was supposed to be upset about this. That her mother thought she was delivering *bad* news. With as much fake empathy as she could muster, Ross said, "Well, what are you going to do Mom? We have to keep this thing from spreading. The last thing we would want is one of us getting sick right before the wedding. There will be time when all this is over to celebrate."

"That is true. Oh honey, it's going to be so good to see you. I wish you were coming straight here. I hate the thought of you being in the country and me not being able to see you."

"I know Mom, this thing in New York won't take long and then we'll be home." Ross got off the phone with her mother. "I now get why you love it so much out here. The rest of the world…."

"Yep." Jack sat down next to her. "They love you honey, that's all. It's a good sign they are being so supportive. My first marriage my mother tried setting me up on dates."

"After you were engaged?"

"Right up until the week of the wedding. Even dug up my first girlfriend, hoping that we would rekindle the spark. At least your mother seems excited to have me in the family." Not for the first time Ross wondered how bad Jack's first wife was.

"It will be good to see them. It actually seems longer than six months." And it had. She couldn't remember having gone so long without seeing her parents and Sam. Ruby was now walking and saying her first words. Ross had planned on being there for all of it and had even started a solid "Aunt Ross" campaign to be Ruby's first word before she left for the research trip that would end with her being shot.

"Come on, let's go to bed." Jack took her hand and led her down into the belly of the boat. Ross paused to take one more look at the inky black sky filled with more stars than could ever be counted.

"How are you not constantly amazed by all this?" Ross said.

"Oh, I used to be, and really you never get used to it. But a little while ago, I found something that fascinated me more." Ross turned to look at him and asked, "What? What could be more fascinating than that?" Ross's answer lay in the way Jack looked at her. "Oh."

As they walked down the hall to their room, Jack banged on the bathroom door, "We are going to bed." The sound of the toilet flushing answered them.

8

The last time Inspector Dufort saw Ross and Jack they were leaving the hospital in Canada, and he was at least fifty percent sure they would be dead in three months. While it had been unconventional to let a civilian handle a security issue on their own, Dufort had let them go simply because he thought sending Dr. Halloway to her apartment to be guarded would have a similar outcome. That being said, he was neither surprised nor disappointed that he had been wrong. Which was not usually the case. Since the discovery of Spartans, they had become the focus of Dufort's work. Somewhat of an obsession. By proxy, Dr. Ross Halloway had become a bit of an obsession. Ross had escaped death at the hands of the Spartans twice. Something no one else on the planet had ever accomplished. Followed a close second by Jack, Si and Ross's friend Samantha. They had all escaped a Spartan once. Also something no other living person had done.

Now he was stuck in his office. With Parid making its presence known around the world, Interpol was sending its agents back to their home countries and slowing down operations. The problem was, the Spartans were ramping up theirs. As the new leader and founder of the Spartan Taskforce, he was now the one they came to when there was a Spartan killing. He had not gotten far with the murder of the Russian President when a murder in Turkey had been brought to him. Just that morning three more murders thought to have the hallmarks of the Spartans had been placed on his desk. With his agents being sent home and rumors that airports were going to start shutting down, there was very little chance that he was going to get any closer to figuring out where the Spartans were. Not that it mattered. All Dufort had been able to think about for most of the morning was Dr. Lillian Petrov.

Dufort had suffered losses in the field before. He could remember each and every one of them. Most had been fellow agents. Some informants, but all of them had known the risk of what they were doing. Then there was Lillian. A woman who had been trying to live her life in peace. To be who she was and, because she would not sell her soul to the Russian government, she had paid the highest price. Dufort leaned his aching head against the cold glass of his office window, remembering when he had gotten the phone call she had been killed along with her parents. Two more innocent bystanders that had gotten wrapped up in something bigger than themselves. The image of Lillian's mother lying in the entryway of her house. The one with the blue gate Lillian had told him so much about. Lillian and her father had been found in a nearby park. By the time Dufort had gotten there, they had both been pronounced dead and removed from the scene.

The Petrovs had not seen their daughter in many years when Dufort had pulled most of the strings he had available to get them out of Russia and had them waiting at Lillian's house when she got home from the hospital. There was not a day that went by that he didn't wonder if that had been the act that had sealed her fate. No doubt it had upset more than a few people that not only had Lillian survived, but her parents had escaped the country right under their noses. He wasn't sure he regretted it. Though sometimes he seriously wondered if regret was warranted. He remembered the look on Dr. Petrov's face when he had informed her that her parents would be there to greet her when she got home. What kept him wondering was, what else could he have done? What else could he have done that he didn't do? What had he missed? He should have known his actions would make them targets. He should have kept a sharper eye on them. What action could he have taken to ensure she would live safely in her little house with the blue gate that she loved so much. The door opened behind him, Dufort didn't move, he already knew what it was.

"Sir, three more cases." his assistant Rand said quietly.

"Just put them on the desk."

"Can I get you anything? Aspirin? Valium?"

"Find the Spartan headquarters phone number and tell them all to knock it off for a while."

"I left a voice message, but no one has called back yet." Rand said dryly.

"Probably for the best. Lord knows how much they would want for something like that." Dufort said, turning slightly to look at his assistant. "I doubt I could get budget approval." Dufort was not a natural administrator. Ever since he had started the Taskforce, it seemed he spent all his time administrating. His days were filled with meetings, and he was constantly being asked to justify his spending. What pissed him off more than anything was the fact that he had done all this to himself.

"How much do you think a Spartan gets paid?" Rand asked.

"No idea, why?"

"Well, if they send us home, I am going to need another source of income….." Rand answered. There had been many assistants before Rand. All had quit within a week. Rand had now been his assistant for three years. His slightly inappropriate sense of humor being the only reason he was tolerated.

"I'm not sure the Spartans would accept you as one of their own."

"I don't see why not." Dufort turned around with a lifted eyebrow.

"Spartans are emotionless, highly trained killers who feel a tenth of the pain normal humans do. Meaning they can get shot in the leg and keep running. You complained endlessly for a week because the lumbar support in your office chair wasn't where it needed to be. Also, you are one of the most dramatic people I have ever met, and you failed your department required shooting test. Maybe you should consider baking….or something." It was Rand's turn to raise his eyebrow.

"Just because I can't shoot doesn't mean I can't kill people. I think poison might be more my thing."

"That's comforting coming from the person who brings me my coffee every day." Dufort picked up one of the files Rand had brought in and started looking at it.

"Male, fifty-five, antiquities dealer. Shot with a high power rifle through the window of his hotel. One shot.

They can't even figure out which room across the road he was shot from. No apparent motive." Dufort tossed it back down on the desk with annoyance.

"Smolaian general killed while being driven to his office. Single shot while he was getting into the car. They think it was a Spartan because the bullet managed to miss the driver and the security guard standing directly behind him." Dufort closed and tossed that one down on the desk. Placing both hands on the desk he leaned over.

"Aren't you going to read the last one?" Rand asked.

"No point. It's going to be another unsolvable murder done with skill that makes it unlikely anyone else other than a Spartan committed the crime. I need to find them, Rand. I need to find their nest." Rand picked up one of the files and flipped through it.

"The Spartans, they operate all over the world right?"

"We have open cases in thirty different countries....and counting."

"What makes you think they have a nest?"

"They have to sleep somewhere. Occasionally, they work together on larger projects. We know that from the Hunter case. Stands to reason they would need some place to plan such a thing."

"These murders all happened in countries far away from one another, yet some of them are within hours of each other."

"What are you getting at Rand?"

"Well, there are a few hundred Spartans left right?"

"Right."

"They operate in several different countries seemingly at the same time, yet they leave no trace in travel expenses, hotel reservations or anything else."

"I know all this Rand." Growing tired of this conversation.

"What if there isn't one nest? What if there are several small nests spread out? I mean these Spartans were pretty much working independently before Ikan Hui, they only joined forces after. Is it possible that instead of creating one nest, one safe house, they simply turned their individual safe houses into safe houses for everyone? Creating a spread out network of safe houses." Dufort leaned back and looked at his assistant with new eyes.

"Aside from the fact that your theory makes tracking the Spartans a helluva lot harder, I think it is a very plausible idea. Any idea how many safe houses we are going to have to track down now?" Dufort almost asked as a joke, to his surprise Rand's face lit up.

"Actually, I've been working on that based on the cases that have been coming in, and I think I might have some ideas." Rand put up his hand to have Dufort wait, and he ran back to his desk in front of Dufort's office. When he came back, Rand had a smile on his face and a tablet Dufort often saw him carrying around. With one hand he pushed the contents of Dufort's desk out of the way and laid down the tablet with a detailed map of Europe. Red dots spread out over it.

"So, this has been a bit of a pet project of mine. For a while now I have been marking down on this map where the Spartan murders have occurred. With Parid closing things down, they have increased sharply, so my little red marks have increased over the last month. Combine that information with the fact that Spartans don't kill in their own backyard, and I think a pattern is starting to emerge." Rand hit a button on the screen and grayed out areas of various sizes appeared over several different cities, basically giving a radius around certain areas where no Spartan murders had been reported. Not that Dufort hadn't been listening before, but now Rand had Dufort's complete attention. Two things stood out to Dufort immediately. Just how many grayed out areas there were, and that they were all located in cities. This had long been a theory of his. That the only place Spartans would be able to move around with anonymity would be an urban area. Dufort studied the map closely. The gray rings around some of the locations were only a few blocks in radius. "With men on the ground, we could stake out these locations and potentially have our Spartan." Dufort said, mostly to himself.

Dufort turned around to face Rand, and held out his hand to shake. Rand looked at it as if he wasn't sure what it was. Dufort nodded to him, and Rand took his hand. Dufort shook it the way his father had taught him to shake a hand. With firmness and respect. "I don't know what they are paying you son, but it isn't enough. This is good work. Really good work. Keep it up, I want every new murder mapped like this. If they keep killing the way they have been, we will finally catch them." Rand was speechless.

"Thank you, sir."

"I'm just sorry I didn't think of it myself." Rand shrugged.

"If you weren't so busy with budget meetings, you probably would have." Dufort nodded. He appreciated the reasoning.

"Send me that file, I'm heading off to talk to the chiefs. Don't forget the other project I have you working on."

"I haven't, Sir."

"Good work Rand." Rand took a deep breath, smiled, and went back to his desk.

9

"What are you doing here?" Was Natasha's greeting when she entered the London safe house. Heather didn't even look away from the TV.

"I have a meeting with a client tomorrow." She answered, moving to the back room to claim a bed. There were plenty to choose from. Heather seemed to be the only other Spartan in the place.

"You are going to be staying here a while then because they are shutting everything down. You can only leave if you have already made arrangements and the place you are going to hasn't shut down." Heather was sitting on the couch in the living room, watching a baking program and taking notes.

"I'll be alright. Arrangements have already been made. It's how I'm getting to my next job actually."

"That's clever. Must be a job for someone high up then. Travis tried to get back here from South America and they wouldn't let him."

"Why did he want to come back here? Why not just stay there?"

"Well, for one, he did a job down there and he wanted to get out while things were still hot. The other is, if he was going to be locked down, he wanted to be able to order from the Indian restaurant around the corner from here. He loves their tandoori chicken and masala."

"Are the others locked down already?" Natasha sat down on the couch next to her, getting somewhat caught up in the baking show. The cakes did look amazing for amateur bakers.

"For the most part, from what I can tell. Some went ahead and got where they wanted to be. Others got caught where their last job was. It really depends on the country. So who is the job for? Has to be high up if you are so confident you are going to be able to get to the job." Heather said, not looking at Natasha, but instead watching the TV.

"Yeah, it's someone high up."

"Mmmm, government job then?"

"You could say that. It's going to get me to the US, and from there I can get to my next job in New York. After that I'm going to settle into the safe house there until this Parid stuff is over with. The money from my last three jobs should be more than enough." Heather was looking at her.

"High up….. government but not really? Has to be the royal family then." Natasha tapped her nose.

"You got it."

"I take it you aren't allowed to share?"

"I don't know the job yet. I'll find out tomorrow. If I had to guess though, I would say it has something to do with that American billionaire who was just arrested for operating a sex trafficking ring off his own private island."

"You might have competition then. That sounds very

much like the job Javier is going out on. Some American politician hired him." Natasha sat down on the couch next to Heather.

"I'll reach out to him tomorrow after my meeting. Maybe we can work together on this. How did he make a lion head out of bread?"

The next morning Natasha was standing in front of her client who was sweating more than was probably healthy. Natasha wanted to hand him a towel, but there wasn't one around. She knew who he was of course, it had been a surprise when he answered the door to the country estate himself.

"Come in. I gave the staff the day off. The family is in London on a shopping trip. We have the house to ourselves."

"I am not used to meeting directly with the client in situations like this. Usually I find they are handled by a third party or by other secure methods. This is usually done so that if something should come to light, the client can deny knowledge."

"I can't risk it. One more scandal, and I'll be cut off completely. No one can know you were here, and I don't want there to be any phone records. I've even turned off the security cameras."

"Secrecy is part of what the Spartans offer. They won't hear anything from us." The client was walking her into a sitting room at the back of the house and indicated that she should sit in one of the red plush chairs that looked like it was new a few hundred years ago.

"That's why I reached out to you. Spartans I mean. I

need this done quickly, and it can't come back on me. Do you understand? No one can ever know it was me." Natasha grew bored with the pleading. She was tempted to shoot the man and put him out of his misery. While she had been invited to sit down, he was still pacing the room drying his sweaty hands on his pants before wringing them again.

"You said he's in prison? Do you know which one?"

"Yes, in New York. The Metropolitan."

"Security level?"

"What?"

"Maximum, minimum?"

"Maximum. How soon can you get there? I've already been contacted by his attorney and told that if I speak to authorities, his associates intend to release photos. I didn't even know they had any photos." The man was practically crying.

"I can recommend a colleague to retrieve these photos and any other evidence." Her client's eyes lit up.

"That would be helpful, thank you. I don't suppose you offer a discount to repeat clients? It's just I'm having to pay for this myself. Mummy, that is, I'm not able to use official funds for this."

"The price for my colleagues' services are up to him." Her client nodded. "I should mention that my own fee will be considerable. With travel and then the intel that is going to be required to to get into a maximum security prison, not to mention having to make it look like an accident. All of this will cost."

"I'll sell the bloody house if I have to. You can make it look like an accident?"

"That will not be a problem." Her client nodded.

"And you guarantee your work?"

"Of course." The client sat there, staring at her not knowing what to say for a while. Natasha did nothing to help him.

"Would you like a tour of the grounds? Do you like horses?"

"No, I'll send you an encrypted email with the payment instructions. Follow those. Once the full amount has been paid, I'll get to work."

"Right." Natasha got up and showed herself out. Leaving the sweaty man drinking his whiskey.

Taking the train back to London, Natasha called Javier.

"Entiendo que vamos a trabajar juntos." *I understand we will be working together.* Natasha said when he answered.

"Como es Que?" *How's that?*

"We have been hired for the same job from what I understand. Target is a billionaire in prison." Natasha continued in spanish.

"Is your client afraid that his dirty little secret will be revealed?" Javier asked.

"Terrified, it would have been kinder to shoot him in the head."

"I would imagine there are several out there like them. What do you want to do? We can't both kill him."

"No, but we can work on it together. It is a maximum security prison after all." Natasha pointed out.

"You once broke into a prison camp in Siberia and extracted three prisoners in broad daylight. A maximum security prison should be nothing for you."

"I have been asked to make it look like an accident. I have a plan, but I think I could use some help." The rest of the train ride back to London they laid out their plan. By the time Natasha got back to the safe house with Heather, it was all laid out, all she needed was her fake documents. Heather made dinner, Cornish pasties. "I made the dough myself." She stated. They ate their dinner while watching the finale of the baking show and making her fake identity for the prison. Natasha's phone dinged.

"He's made the deposit and there is a charter flight arranged for tomorrow."

"Too bad, I was going to bake a cake tomorrow and make my own strawberry cream cheese icing." If Heather's pastry was anything to go by, the cake would be worth waiting for.

"I can't delay it, I've arranged to meet Javier at the prison. He was going to fly in today. I'm hoping to get this taken care of in the next week. I have another job to prepare for. I liked the jalapeno bread they made last week, I thought I might try and make that once I've settled into the safe house in New York."

"Send me a picture of the final product. I might try to make it here." Natasha thought it might be best if she didn't spend the lock down with Heather. It would take her a full year to get back into shape.

10

It wasn't as hard to get into a maximum security prison as Natasha had thought. "They are hiring." Javier said when they showed up at the meeting point to start their intel gathering. He handed Natasha her Chai Latte that he had gotten her.

"And here I thought we were going to need specialized equipment to get in. Turns out, I just need decent references."

"Well, I say we scratch this and go back to the safe house to work on our resumes." Which they did. Javier applied first to see what it would take to get placed on the same floor as their target. Turns out, all they needed to do was ask for the third shift. A few days later, when Natasha handed over her resume, she was hired on the spot. "You worked at Guantanamo? I bet you saw some shit there." The shift lead said. Natasha smiled. "I really can't say, Sir." The shift lead smacked his hand on the desk and laughed.

"I bet you can't. Come on, I'll show you around. As you may know, our fair prison is currently being blessed with a VIP guest."

"I saw the press outside." Natasha said.

"Keep in mind, leaking any information to the press is grounds for immediate dismissal. While he may be a sick bastard who deserves to fry in hell, we will treat him like any other prisoner and that includes not talking to the outside world about what happens inside these walls. Understood?"

"Understood, Sir." Natasha could tell the shift lead liked it when she acted like she was still in the military, especially when she called him 'Sir'. They went up to the fourth floor, which was more enclosed than the other floors. Every other floor had the familiar open floor plan where the cells surrounded a common area. The secure floor where the VIP was staying had a central guard station with single occupancy cells. Their doors were solid with only a small square window to look into. These guests were only allowed out of their cells for an hour a day. It was still considered prime real estate because they didn't have to share their cell with three other people. The shift lead walked her up to the guard station and introduced her.

"You'll be working with Jose, he just signed on a few days before you did. He also had a strong background in the military." The shift lead informed her. Javier was waiting at the guard station when she got there.

"Jose, this is Ellen. Don't let his stern look scare you, Ellen, Jose's nice enough. I wouldn't give her too much crap guys, she was a guard at Guantanamo. I doubt there is anything you can throw at her she hasn't seen before." The shift lead left Natasha there with Javier (Jose) and one other guard that looked like he was nearing retirement. The man was drinking coffee from a thermos the size of a gallon jug and was carrying about fifty pounds of extra weight.

"I'm afraid it's rather quiet here these days. Not much to keep you from falling asleep. Most of the prisoners have been moved to other locations on account of our VIP." Randel informed her. He walked at a snail's pace as he showed her the rounds. "He's on suicide watch. We are to put eyes on him every hour." Randel showed her the cell he was in and had her look.

"If he's on suicide watch, he shouldn't have a sheet." Natasha pointed out. Randel shrugged his shoulders.

"We didn't give one to him the first night. Those are the rules. Princess called his lawyer the next day. It was cruel to make him sleep on a bare cot, so they gave him a damn sheet." Randel shrugged. There were three other prisoners who they hadn't been able to relocate. One had another trial coming up and the two others were so bad, no one else wanted them.

"Everyone is having a hard time finding the staff to deal with who they have, much less babysitting more." Randel explained. "It used to be this was a good job. A hard job, but the pay was good and the benefits were great. I haven't had a raise in fifteen years. Every year they come at you talking about budget problems. Now, the benefits aren't worth what we pay for them. They cut our vision, they cut our dental. It's pretty bad when the criminals you're guarding have better medical care than you." Randel shook his head as he walked back to the swivel chair with the busted springs and picked up his crossword puzzle. That's where he would be until it was time to do another round in an hour.

The first few nights she had shadowed Randel while

Javier manned the guard station. On her fourth night, Randel called in sick. This was not a surprise since Javier had added a laxative to his gallon of coffee the night before. Natasha would be surprised if he was able to get off the bathroom floor, much less drive to work. The fifth night it was just her and Javier. On the hour, just like she always did, Natasha got up and did her rounds, making sure to stop by the VIP's cell and check he hadn't killed himself while no one was watching. Javier stayed at the guard station and watched the monitors. Instead of looking in the little window on the door, Natasha slipped on rubber gloves, and unlocked the cell turning the light on as she entered.

"What are you doing here?" The VIP said, using his hand to shield his eyes from the sudden light. Natasha made no secret of closing the door behind her and locking it.

"I'm here to change your sheets."

"What?" The target sat up off his cot and looked at her confused, and then he smiled.

"Oh, I see. You heard I'm rich and a sex addict. You figure I'm probably getting a little desperate by now and you can take advantage." A grin slid across his face and he leaned back in his bed. "I don't blame you. The media will probably pay you more than you'll make here in a year for a story like that. Hate to disappoint you, you're a little old for me. " Natasha stayed where she was, back against the door. Her target got off his cot and took slow steps towards her. "You see, I just can't perform with anyone out of their teens. Now, if you have a younger sister you'd like to bring by..." A few more and he would be within striking distance.

"....now I could really go for that." The VIP raised his hand to stroke her cheek. Natasha shortened the distance in one stride and had the cable tie around his neck in a swift move. His air cut off immediately, the VIP stumbled and grabbed for her. Natasha stayed directly behind him to avoid his hands. Within a minute, he had gone down on his knees and she stuck her knee in his back to stabilize him while maintaining pressure. The gurgling sound he made let her know the cable was in the right place. Looking down at him, the VIP's face was now purple, his protruding tongue already swollen. His hands were still reaching for her, but he was only able to get them out in front of him. Natasha kept her arms tight and her eyes on the VIP's movements.

His movements were growing slower, like his arms were getting heavy until they no longer grabbed for her. The mistake most people made when strangling a person was, they stopped too soon. You can't let the fact that your victim has stopped struggling make you think the job is done. It takes approximately two minutes for a person to die of strangulation. Natasha always made it a point to hold her victims for a solid two minutes, counting it off in her head. If she had to readjust her garotte for any reason, she would add another minute. Sixty seconds left to go. The VIP had gone limp, his weight now working with her. Javier appeared at the door.

"The security cameras are off." He said, going behind Natasha and pulling the bed sheets off. Natsha's arm muscles are starting to shake.

"It would have been easier to shoot him." She pointed out.

"The clients both wanted it to look like an accident."

Javier stood on the toilet to get the sheet over the piping. Natasha counted off until the end and then let him go, checking his pulse to make sure the job was done, and leaning back to catch her breath.

"Damn. I'm just saying. There are several easier ways of killing a man." Her arms were burning.

"I offered to do it for you." Javier saw her check the VIP's pulse and said, "Double check, we don't want another repeat like last year. That was just embarrassing." Natasha knew he was referring to the disastrous attack on a research boat where two scientists had been left ALMOST dead because the Spartan who shot them hadn't double checked they had no pulse. Natasha had given the Spartan some slack. Doing most of her work in colder countries, it can be hard sometimes for your cold hands to feel a pulse. The incident remained one of the few times the Spartans have had to make good on their warranty. Natasha stood opening and closing her cramped hands before rechecking.

"No he's definitely dead. I'm glad I charged extra. I wish you hadn't talked me out of poisoning him. We could have just watched him die on camera."

"As I said before, poisons leave a trace and then there is the dosing problem. Too much and it can make a poison obvious, too little and you end up having to strangle them anyway." Javier said, coming down from placing the sheet on the pipes and placing the other end around the VIP's neck, making a slip not.

"Alright, pull." Javier and Natasha pulled the VIP up. "He's heavier than he looks." The VIP's body rose limply off the ground.

"One more pull and his feet are off the ground." They

both pulled, the VIP's limp feet were now hovering just above the floor. Javier held the sheet steady while Natasha tied it to the metal bar that anchored the bed to the wall.

The weight of the body had tightened the sheet around the VIP's neck. With all the bruising, it would be almost impossible to tell that the sheet had not been what killed him. Taking a few deep breaths to normalize their breathing, Javier left the room and went back to the guard's station where he started the security cameras again. Natasha went out into the hallway and used the walkie talkie to inform the staff what was happening.

"I need a medic. I repeat, I need a medic. VIP is hanging in his cell. I'm going to cut him down." Following procedure, Javier called the hospital wing and requested a medic. The shift lead had heard the call go out on the walkie talkie and was just coming on the floor when Javier hung up.

"Medic is on the way." He informed the lead. They both ran to the VIP's cell where Natasha was found giving CPR to the freshly cut down body of the VIP.

"Fuck." The lead said when he saw what had happened.

"You stupid fucker, he was on suicide watch. You let him have a sheet?" The medic said when he got there. Natasha stayed focused on her completely pointless CPR until the medic pushed her out of the way. "Let me check for a pulse, get those paddles ready." He yelled. They tried for thirty minutes to resuscitate the VIP to no avail. Natasha and Javier watched the next day from the safe house as the headlines splashed across the news. The VIP's death was being called a suicide and an official investigation had been started. Their final payments from their clients hit almost at the same time.

11

They had said a teary good-bye to Si. Ross was feeling a little naked without him around and she wasn't entirely sure what to do with that feeling.

"Stop looking at me like that. I was sailing the seven seas before you were born. I can manage a flight to Boston." Si had said to them fussing over him. Ross had been surprised at how emotional she had become at them splitting up. "He'll be alright, love." Jack had reassured her as Si had walked away.

"It's like we are breaking up the band." Ross said, wiping the tears away from her face.

"Maybe let's not have any wine on this next flight." Jack suggested even though he was enjoying the way Ross was hanging onto him.

"He's going to be alright though, right?" Ross asked as Si disappeared into the crowd.

"Si? He'll be just fine honey. Si has gotten himself out of more trouble than you've ever imagined. He once lost a boat off the coast of Tasmania. He floated in the life raft for a few days before waving down a fishing boat. When he got back home he was sunburned all to hell, drunk as a skunk and had four new friends. Last I checked he was still writing them Christmas cards."

"Si was lost at sea?"

"You and I would call it lost at sea. Si thinks of it as a slight detour." Jack and Ross went to find their own gate and settled in for the two hour wait before they took off. It might have been the two glasses of wine and the little sip she had stolen from Si's Jack Daniels, but now that they were on their way to get married, Ross had to admit she was starting to feel less like a scientist and more like a bride. It was terrifying if she stopped and thought about it, but taking Sam's advice, Ross had decided to not think about it, and just go with it. Not for the first time, Sam had been right. Going off to marry Jack felt weird but right all at the same time. Which could pretty much be the motto for their relationship. Ross nuzzled up to Jack and they looked all the world like a couple in love. "You're going to get someone upset with us for being closer than six feet." Jack said.

"Shut up. When was the last time we were alone together?"

"We aren't alone now, we are in a crowded airport. There is a guy asleep in the chair next to you."

"You know what I mean. Also, could you please look less attractive in a mask? It highlights your hazel eyes."

"Worried Ivy might see me?" Jack answered with a smile on his face. When Jack had proposed, Ross had lost her mind a little. To the point where she had argued there was no point in them getting married because eventually Jack would meet a model named Ivy who would fulfill all his fantasies of what a woman was. Obviously with a woman like Ivy, Ross would fade into the background and he would forget about her. Jack had pointed out that Ivy was a figment of Ross's imagination. That as far as either one of them knew, there was no such person and therefore it was impossible that he could leave Ross for Ivy. Ivy had been the source of many jokes since Ross had regained control of her senses.

"Statistically speaking, sixty percent of households....."

"Aren't us. Statistically speaking, the Spartans should have killed us back on Ikan Hui." Jack pointed out. Ross had been throwing out marital statistics quite a lot the past few days. Reasons why marriages don't work, how many marriages end in divorce, the amount spent on weddings versus how long the marriage lasts.

"Point taken." Again, it was probably the wine, but Ross looked at Jack and was suddenly filled with love and contentment. "I love you." Ross said. Jack looked at her out of curiosity. "What was that for?"

"For some reason, right at this moment, I need you to know I love you. That's all." The smile under his mask was visible in his eyes.

"Back atcha."

The voice came over the speaker calling their flight. "That's us." Jack said.

"I really am going to miss the quiet of the boat after all this." Ross said.

"You were always going to miss the quiet of the boat. Wait until we go to bed tonight and there are no waves gently rocking you to sleep. You won't realize how good you had it."

"Thank you again for getting me out there. On the boat."

"You're welcome. Next time, it would be nice if you skipped the getting shot part." They both stood up and started gathering their things.

"I'll do my best. Jack?"

"Hmmm?" Jack looked at the departure board again.

"What are we going to do after the wedding?" Ross had thought about it, but there had never seemed to be a good time to discuss it. Jack and Si had taken the job on the boat to get seed money for their shark diving business in Australia, which was a very long way away from Ross's job at the lab and her apartment in Boston. Jack looked around him like he was looking for someone in the crowd to give him an answer.

"We'll figure it out Ross."

"What does that mean Jack? Why can't we figure it out now?" They were walking to their gate.

"It doesn't really seem to matter at the moment." Ross opened her mouth to argue, but Jack cut her off. "For the foreseeable future, we will be staying at yours if for no other reason than I won't be able to fly anywhere else." He couldn't see her face between the mask and now the glasses, but Ross wasn't saying anything which wasn't always a good thing. "What?"

"You were going to start the business back up when this job was over." Ross was choosing to not point out that he had not mentioned that her job was in Boston.

"Yeah, well that is looking less likely with every passing day. The business ran on tourism, and there isn't going to be very much of that for a while is there?"

"Jack...."

"We'll figure it out Ross." Jack said with a confidence that Ross didn't feel.

"How can you say that? We are literally days away from getting married, and we haven't figured out where we are going to live." Ross was getting mad. How could he be so nonchalant? It was starting to piss her off.

"Ross, I simply don't see what the point is of having this conversion when we are going to have to have it again because the pandemic has changed things." Damn it, he was making sense. "I think we should go and get married, plan on living in your apartment for the immediate future, and when we figure out what is happening with the pandemic, we will sit down and have a serious conversation about where to live."

"You wouldn't feel better figuring it out now?" Ross said, somewhat calmer than she had been.

"Not really."

"Why not?" She narrowed her eyes (not that he could see it).

"Because this is a serious decision and I don't want to make it while I'm walking through an airport."

"So, you don't know where you want to live?" It was hard to tell with the mask, but Ross was pretty sure he was giving her a stinky side eye. This was a change from the last time they had this conversation. Albeit a lot had changed. The conversation had happened before she left for her research trip on *The Hunter*.

"Ross, wherever we end up living, it will be a place that we both agree on. I'm not going to force you to live wherever I want without taking what you want into consideration. Likewise, I would expect you to do the same for me. We are rational adults after all, we can do this together." Ross peaked an eyebrow and looked away from him. She doubted very seriously it would be a rational conversation when it came down to it. " Y o u ' r e right. Of course you are. There is no point in making this decision now. I will, however, point out to you that while my mother absolutely loves you, and Sam is fond of you as well, I will not be responsible for their actions if you tell them we are moving far away." Ross pointed out. Jack's eyebrows furrowed. He could see her point.

"What would they consider far?"

"More than ten miles."

"Ten miles! That's no distance at all. Your apartment now is more than ten miles away from your mother."

"I know. That's how I know we will have hell to pay. You would have thought I was moving to Alaska when I signed the lease on that place. She made it sound like it would be a three day walk to get to me." If Ross had wanted Jack to feel as anxious about where they would live as she did, that statement had done it.

"I don't think Si would ever have cared where I lived in the world as long as there was water attached to it. That's our flight now, last call."   Jack's brow still furrowed with Ross's last statement. He had never considered living in Boston long term. It had been a fine place when he had visited her last Christmas. But to live there for the rest of his life? To see the sea and never take off on it again? Was he ready for a stagnant life? He was ready for the wife, he even thought he was ready for the two point three children. But was he ready for the nine to five job?

"Come on, what are you waiting for?" Ross was saying to him. Jack put one foot in front of the other but he felt sick. He saw himself in a suit and tie, waiting at the bus stop, and it made him feel ill. "You okay? You look pale." Ross said with real concern.

"Fine, I'm fine."

"Well, could you look it? People are starting to stare."
Jack straightened his back and forced his mind to focus on
what was in front of him. One thing at a time.

12

Dufort was looking out the window in the office he hated. He was finding himself in it more and more these days with the world shutting down. The streets were empty, and he could no longer distract himself by watching the people below hustling from one end of the street to the other. Today there was a lone, white plastic bag flying in a breeze. Dufort watched it make its lazy way down the street, thinking about all the things he should be doing, but just couldn't bring himself to at the moment. The higher ups were talking of shutting everything down, and there was a stack of papers on his desk that would somehow help that. He couldn't believe that out of all the things he could be doing right now, his choices were watching a plastic bag flow in the wind or filling out paperwork. Rand started to come into the office and saw Dufort standing at the damn window again. Men like Dufort were not meant to be kept in captivity. They were meant to be out chasing criminals. Rand thought he might have something that would help.

"Inspector?" His assistant Rand interrupted his

thoughts.

"Hmm?"

"More files. They are concerned about the large amount of killings happening in New York."

"Why should they worry about that? Like any other big city, the Spartans are more active there. It's where the people with the money live." Dufort said without taking his head off the glass.

"They are worried a Spartan has joined up with a family there....if you know what I mean." Dufort took a deep breath.

"Again, we know the Spartans have from time to time joined with the Mafia. They have for the most part stopped doing it though."

"Why? Seems perfect. You get the guy you want whacked and your cousin doesn't have to go to prison for it." Dufort turned to look at him.

"The Mafia is mostly run by a family because they rely heavily on loyalty. Spartans aren't loyal. They follow the money. It was a huge disaster last year. An Italian family hired a Spartan, put him on contract. The Spartan did all their killings. As you said, a good arrangement. Then the Mexican gang finds out what they've done and reached out to the same Spartan and hired him. Now you have this Spartan who can basically walk into the inner circle of the Italian Mafia because he's known, he works for them and kill them all, which is exactly what happened. He got six high ranking members of the Gibali family before they managed to injure the Spartan enough that he stopped."

"They didn't kill him?"

"Oh, most of them wanted to, but one of them saw the potential. They waited until the Spartan was healed and then sent him back to the Mexicans. He got ten of them, but they made sure he was dead. As far as I know, no other gangs or such have hired them for the same reason."

"What do the Spartan's do with their money? I mean after they die." Rand asked, sitting on the corner of Dufort's desk.

"Rand, we can't even figure out where their money is, much less what they do with it once they die."

"It's just a lot of money to leave behind." Dufort looked at him in a way that let Rand know he was tired of their current conversation. "What did they say in the meeting about the maps? Possible locations of where the Spartans' nest are." Rand said, changing the subject. Dufort turned around and rested his back on the window where he had been leaning his head.

"They were very impressed, Rand. That is saying something. They don't impress easily. You are to continue to mark down locations as you have been."

"And then what?"

"They will be using satellite imaging to monitor the areas where there is no activity to see if known Spartans can be identified coming and going. They are going to use some new technology to take the pictures from the Spartans' files so the computer can identify the Spartans." This seemed like remarkable progress. Dufort's dark mood did not reflect this. Rand was used to Dufort's dark moods, they were getting worse the longer he was behind a desk. Rand was partial to dark moods himself, which he credited as one of the reasons he was able to tolerate Dufort where others had failed. As long as they didn't get in a dark mood together, everything would be fine.

"So, they identify the Spartan's and now we know where

their nest is. Then what?" Rand asked. Dufort twirled a cigarette between his fingers.

"Nothing. They are sending agents home. There is no time frame for when they will be brought back."

"It will take months for all the data to come together. There is a chance we wouldn't have all the information before the pandemic is over anyway. There is a chance it won't affect things." Rand offered, as a possibility. Dufort looked at Rand and nodded. There was a chance the boy was right, of course. These things would take time. Months. Years even. Dufort might be stuck in this office pouring over satellite images and adding little red dots to a map for years before he was able to put boots on the ground and raid a Spartan nest.

"And that is if the Spartans don't catch wind of what we are doing and move safe houses. Who knows? Maybe they move safe houses regularly anyway." Dufort waved his hand around. "It doesn't matter, it is very clear that while this group wants nothing more than to get Spartans off the streets, they have no idea what to do with them once they are captured." Dufort spat out. The whole meeting had left him angry and wondering what the point of it all was.

"You could do what a lot of people are doing. Instead of working from home, they are just retiring. You could, I don't know, get a personal life." Rand said. Dufort often wondered how Rand knew some of the things he knew. Dufort had been thinking more about having a personal life of late. Out of the twenty years he had worked for Interpol, he had been without a personal life for seventeen of them. His wife had left him after three years, stating that he was never home. Dufort hadn't fought it. He was never home and loved the job more than he had ever loved her.

Before the conversation turned any darker, Rand brought up the reason he had come in to begin with.

"Speaking of ongoing projects, Dr. Halloway looks like she is heading to New York. They left the international airport in Perth headed for San Fran. From there they are flying to JFK at two forty-five local time."

"They've left?"

"It looks like it, sir. I confirmed they handed in the boat keys to the harbormaster yesterday."

"New York? Why the hell is she going there? I thought she was from Boston?"

"I thought you might ask that, so I emailed a report to you with a full listing of her movements for the next two weeks." Rand turned to leave.

"You're standing right there, just tell me." Rand rolled his eyes.

"She's heading to New York to launch PAUL, an early detection device for Parid-21."

"What does she have to do with that? She's a chemist."

"She was contacted by her lab a few months ago to help with waste disposal issues. Then she is flying to Boston to get married." Dufort smiled. So getting her on the boat had done the trick. Dufort was happy for them. He had rarely seen a man more tortured than Jack was when Ross had first been injured.

"When is the wedding?" Rand made a point of looking at his iPad.

"According to my *report*, this coming Saturday. Four in the afternoon. Hill Street Methodist Church."

"How are they managing all that traveling with the airports shutting down?" Dufort wasn't looking at Rand now, but he was well aware of the annoyance pouring off of him. Rand prided himself on his detailed reports. Dufort rather enjoyed them as well, but annoying Rand was one of the small pleasures in his life. Nothing annoyed Rand more than ignoring his reports.

"As of yet, none of the airports they are planning on using have announced shut downs, though they will be lucky if they don't run into trouble somewhere. London Heathrow says they are shutting down in seventy-two hours. Other major airports are expected to do the same, including JFK. As you can imagine, this has caused a bit of chaos. People are scrambling to get home before they no longer can." Dufort snorted.

"When are they due to land in New York?" Dufort was already gathering his things.

"I put her flight information in the *report*. Including flight numbers." Rand tried again. Just once, Rand wanted Dufort to acknowledge his detailed reports. Instead, Dufort grunted and hunted around for the cigarettes that were hidden in his top right hand drawer.

"She lands at 07:45 pm tomorrow evening. The event launching PAUL is hosted by the New York Society for Scientific Advancement in their main hall for eleven the following morning." Rand added, anticipating his next question. "A buffet lunch to follow." Rand thought about reminding him to grab his lighter, but didn't out of spite.

"Get me on a flight to New York. I don't care when I get there as long as it's in time to see Dr. Halloway at the event."

"What about the airports shutting down? The flights will be packed." Dufort shrugged his shoulders.

"If you can't get me there through official channels, go through the unofficial ones." Rand rolled his eyes again and went off to make the arrangements. Dufort went back to looking at the empty streets twirling an unlit cigarette between his fingers. "Rand?"

"Yes sir?"

"After you get me to New York, use the unofficial channels to get me to headquarters in England. Let them know to expect myself and two others."

"Sir?"

"That's all I can give you right now. I don't want to go through customs and all that.

"Consider it done."

Dufort threw on his jacket and a few things he would need. Tooth brush, deodorant, cigarettes, vape for when he couldn't smoke, patches and nicotine gum for when he could neither smoke nor vape. Pulled a clean shirt he kept as spare from his desk drawer, put them into a backpack and headed out the door. If he needed anything else, he would buy it on the way. His phone pinged. Dufort stopped midwalk to pull it out of his pocket. Rand watched him with curiosity. He had never known the inspector to give a crap about his phone until a few months ago. Now the man dropped everything like a teenager to see who had texted him. Rand had no idea which way the inspector leaned. He had never seen him involved with another person either male or female, but whoever this person was had the grumbly inspector looking at his phone with a childish grin on his face that would have been adorable to watch if it hadn't been for the man's persistence in ignoring Rand's perfect reports.

LP: Might have had a bit of a breakthrough here. When can

```
we talk?
D:Heading your way soon.  Can it wait a few days?  Might
bring you a surprise.
LP:  I suppose it can wait.  I'm busting to tell you
though. A surprise?  Should I be worried?
D: It's a good surprise. I'll let you know more when I
can. X
LP: X
```

Continuing where he had left off, Dufort stomped out of his office in a hurry. Rand looked up at him with the phone to his ear.

"I can get you to New York commercial, but there is nothing to London."

"Unofficial then?"

"They'll have a jet waiting for you on the runway at three o'clock tomorrow. They were rather stern, they wanted me to make it clear they would not wait for you."

"Or what? They will fly an empty airplane to the UK?" Dufort took the information Rand had printed off for him.

"Sir? Have you seen the email?"

"What email?" Rand rolled his eyes.

"The internal email." Rand looked up into Dufort's blank face. "They are sending all the office staff home. The pandemic." Dufort paused at that. He couldn't turn on his own computer without Rand. He never said it, but they were both perfectly aware of it. "I'll do what I can for you from home, but things aren't secure there. They might try to set something up, but for a while, you will be on your own." Rand almost felt sorry for telling him. Dufort stuck out his hand. Rand blinked, and then took it. Dufort gave his assistant a firm handshake. Two handshakes so close together, Rand was touched.

"Take care of yourself, Rand. If you need anything, please let me know." It was said with all the honesty and intention Dufort could manage. Rand almost choked up. Dufort was a grump from the previous age, but he was good to his word.

"You too, sir." They locked eyes for a moment and then Dufort took off to catch his flight.

13

"Guess what? I am no longer calling you from another time zone." Ross smiled into the phone as she was attempting to put on makeup.

"I'm not salty at all that you are going to a science thing before you are coming home to see me. I just want you to know that." Sam said. "Because I'm a big person like that. Not to brag, but so far I have successfully resisted the urge to run from here to New York just so I can give you a hug."

"You hate running. You always told me if I saw you running to shoot the person chasing you." Ross said, now wiping away the eyeliner that was obviously too thick.

"That's how much I've missed you. You are causing me to have an urge to run."

" I'm so glad we have matured and no longer throw around passive aggressive hints that we're upset with one another. Motherhood has really changed you." Ross gave it another try and then decided to forget the eyeliner.

"Oh God, I've missed your smart ass."

"We'll be home tomorrow."

"You have to be enjoying some alone time with Jack

before you get here. Must be different without the motion in the ocean...." Said with a suggestive tone.

"Sam....!"

"I guess I am going to have to get used to him coming first now that he is going to be your *husband*." Ross rolled her eyes knowing that if Sam saw her, it would have earned her a pinch. Sam was joking. For the most part.

"I don't love you any less Sam, just because Jack is in my life now. You are just as important to me."

"Damn right. You should see the trouble I'm going through to make sure you have the best bachelorette party ever." Ross's eyes shot open. *Oh hell.*

"Are you sure we should do that? There's the pandemic and everything. I don't want to get anyone sick."

"Nice try sweetheart. That line may have worked on your mother, but I have gone out of my way to have the safest bachelorette party there ever was. We are staying in. Everyone is going to come over here. I have only invited six people, so don't panic too much."

"Everyone? Who is everyone? You are like the only person I know."

"I called your boss and invited some people from your lab." Ross's blood went cold.

"People from my lab? Sam, did you meet any of these people?"

"No."

"Search them on Facebook?"

"No, should I have?"

"It depends on what you have planned. The people I work with are all more socially awkward than I am. I'm the cool one. I've actually been to a cowboy bar."

"The only reason you have been to a cowboy bar is

because I made you go." Sam pointed out.

"It doesn't matter...."

"They all seemed very excited about it, which is good. The guys are putting the poles up in the living room as we speak."

"Poles?"

"Well, pole. Phillip would only allow the one. He doesn't know whether to be thrilled or scared."

"I know the feeling."

"Well I tried to get a stripper, but they aren't sending people out right now, so I got a pole. We can be strippers."

"Jesus Sam, you know I would die if you got a stripper. Not pretend die. Actual death. What the hell are you going to do with the pole after the bachelorette party?" Ross glanced over the 'being strippers' part because no one could make her do something she didn't want to. Sam was very good at getting her to do things she would have previously said she didn't want to do, but no one.....absolutely no one.... was going to make her get on a strippers pole.

"Ross, honey, I know you would be perfectly happy to have some sangria and watch some old movies with dead movie stars, but you can do that any night of the week. I want your bachelorette party to be so good that when we are old and sitting in our rocking chairs, I can turn to you and say, 'Remember your bachelorette party?' and we both just start laughing." Ross wanted that too. She just wasn't sure she needed a stripper pole to make that dream come true. The silence from the other end of the phone didn't go unnoticed.

"Ross, you are getting married, which is a huge big deal. Bigger than it is for most people. We are doing this right.

Stop arguing and go with it. We are going to make memories for a lifetime." Ross looked for a viable argument, but found none. Actually, she thought of several viable arguments, but none that would convince Sam.

"I asked for a doctor, you know, since you have a doctorate. I thought it would be funny with the pandemic and everything. Oh god, I really wanted to see your face when that doctor stripper came in. Oh well, maybe I can get one for your fortieth or something." Ross had her head in her hands, trying to massage the headache that was coming on. Turns out finding the right man may not have been the only reason she had never gotten married. "Then I tried to get someone out here to do something like a striptease class. Show us all how to spin on a pole without killing ourselves. But that is a no go as well. Theeeennnnn, I thought about just putting on YouTube, you know, like an instructional video. Thankfully, I researched that. Have you ever searched for 'stripper how to' videos?"

"I can't say that I have." Ross said.

"DON'T DO IT. I mean, unless you are into that sort of thing." Sam said. Jack had no idea what Sam was saying, but Ross had her eyes closed, was rubbing her forehead, and rocking back and forth. Ross was reminding herself that Sam was almost solely responsible for every 'interesting' evening out she had ever had. While some of them had gone drastically wrong, Ross had survived those, she would survive this. It might actually be fun even if it promised to be the most undignified evening she had ever had.

"You are going to make me dress up like a stripper, aren't you?" Ross asked, fairly confident in the answer.

"I mean, I can't make you. I may have gotten us

matching stripper outfits though. And fake money."

"Why can't we use real money?"

"I love ya honey, but I'm not sure I want to use the money that has been tucked in your g-string."

"Nevermind."

"Then I thought you could do that thing you do when you get really drunk and list the periodic table alphabetically. Do you think you could do it while upside down on a pole? Oh, and I got beakers for us to mix the drinks in. One of your co-workers actually suggested that." Now Ross thought that was clever. "They even came up with some chemistry themed drinks we could have." Sam was getting more animated with every word.

"I'm having a chemistry themed bachelorette party?" Ross said, thinking she might want to show up for this disaster after all.

"With a stripper pole!"

"Has Jack told you what Si has planned for his bachelor party?" Sam asked.

"No, Jack hasn't told me what Si is planning for his bachelor party." Ross repeated for Jack's benefit. A devilish smile crossed her face.

"Si planned a stag night?" Jack asked, his face going red. "He didn't say anything. I spoke to him right before we left."

"Surprise! He didn't want to tell you too soon because he knew you would talk him out of it. He's been texting me for two weeks now making plans." Sam was yelling into the phone so Jack could hear her. Ross put it on speaker.

"Who the hell is he inviting? We don't know anyone."

"Well, Philip and some of his friends. Si's your best man, Jack, so he wanted to mark the occasion. Your outfit arrived yesterday."

"Shit!" Jack said, his mind reeling as to what his father had planned while sitting on a boat thousands of miles away from Boston in the outbreak of a pandemic.

"What if you and Si are also going to be using the stripper pole?" Ross asked. This did bring a smile to Ross's face.

"I can't even think about that." Jack suddenly looked sick.

"He did ask what size lingerie I thought you wore. I thought it was a very strange question at the time, and coming from anyone else, I would have felt uncomfortable answering it." Sam said. Jack put both his hands through his hair. There was a sharp cry in the background.

"That's Ruby, gotta go." Sam said.

"Give her a kiss for me." Sam hung up in a hurry. Their goodbyes used to take almost as long as their conversations. Now they came to an abrupt end. Ross and Jack stood there looking at the silent phone for a moment.

"It's not too late. We can still elope." Ross pointed out.

"I would seriously think about it, but I promised your mother she would get to see you walk down the aisle in a white dress."

"You did? She made you promise?" Jack smiled his sideways grin.

"Yeah. I think she knew there was a strong chance you were going to avoid a family wedding."

"And now you know why. I guess there is nothing we can do then."

"I can't believe Si is going to throw me a stag party. I figured I was safe with there being a pandemic and not knowing another living soul in Boston. I should have known."

"It is the traditional thing for the man of honor to do."

"Ross, the tradition at home is for the groom to be dressed in lingerie while doing a pub crawl. Heels, stockings, the whole thing. I did it once before, and I have accompanied a few mates doing it, but at my age, I don't really fancy walking around unknown streets in fishnets and heels. Not to mention with Si in charge of the arrangements, there is a decent chance we will end up in jail. I would say better than fifty percent. Dad threw a bachelor party for a friend of his when I was ten. They called two days later from New Zealand. They had no memory of how they got there. They didn't have a penny between them. Mum had to wire the money to get them back. She was furious for days."

"Then you better be nice to me. I can only afford to bail one of you out, just keep that in mind." Jack gave her one of his best smiles that made promises Ross knew he would make good on.

"Stop looking at me like that and get dressed. We have a fancy event to go to."

"Yes ma'am." Jack got up and smacked her bum on the way to the bathroom.

14

"I am not entirely happy with how good you look in a mask." Ross said. They had left the hotel all dressed up for the event, and Ross had watched in shock as the head of every woman (and a few men) had turned to watch Jack pass. There were few people on the street, a lot less than the last time Ross had been to New York for a symposium. Jack was wearing a tan suit with an open collared light blue shirt. It was doing an amazing job of highlighting his tan. The suit was fitted well enough that his toned biceps were pulling the fabric of his jacket sleeve tight. How he had managed to find a face mask that was the same color as his shirt was beyond her.

"Would you believe they sold them as a set?" Jack had answered her.

Ross was wearing a cream pants suit. The cream color of her outfit was also showing off her tan. They both looked like they had just spent all summer on the Riviera. A pale pink silk scarf tied nicely around her neck hid the massive scar from where she had been shot. Sam had suggested it. Ross had just about accepted that the scar was a part of her now. She even loved how it felt when Jack kissed it. Something he was all too aware of. Ross had not gotten used to people staring at it and had absolutely no idea what to do if people asked how she got it. Telling the truth got a variety of reactions, none of them nice. Her hair was braided and over her shoulder adding extra protection. She felt very elegant walking down an almost empty New York street, her heels clicking on the sidewalk.

"We could not look more different than we did on the boat." She said, smiling under her mask.

"We scrub up well, don't we? I'm actually rather excited for all of this." Jack said.

"Really? I would have thought you would be bored to tears. I helped build the thing, and I'm planning on being bored."

"I get to see the great Dr. Ross Halloway in action at last."

"You've seen me work."

"On the boat, yes. But this will be you in your natural habitat. Surrounded by your own people. It's going to be great." His smile went all the way to his eyes.

"These people are going to be more like me than you. Get ready for an afternoon of awkward conversation and obscure references."

"I can handle it."

"Okay, but if they start the mating dance, we are out of there."

"Deal." He kissed her hand. "Remind me, what time do we fly out tonight?"

"Nine. So we aren't going to have a lot of time after leaving here to get back to the hotel. Keep an eye on the time."

"It might be difficult with all the stimulating conversation you are anticipating."

"These are my people, they are going to stay just long enough to be polite and then they will leave."

"I'm glad to hear it, I planned a little something for us."

"Jack, we have to be at the airport two hours before the flight, and I was going to suggest we get there even earlier since they are showing long wait times...."

"It's a carriage ride through Central Park." Jack said, holding up a hand to stop her. Ross stopped walking and looked at him in confusion. "We should have time to leave here, check out of the hotel, the carriage ride people said they could keep our luggage, they even have lockers. I will book us an Uber about halfway through the drive that can take us to the airport. It's all figured out."

"Why a carriage ride?" was all Ross could think to ask.

"I wanted to do something for just you and me on this short trip. Once we get to Boston, we will be in the hands of those who love us." He tugged on her hand and looked into her eyes, "I wanted something for just the two of us." Ross went all wobbly in the knees when he looked at her like that.

"Okay." She said, as her mind raced to figure out something equally romantic she could do in the short time they had.

"Why do you have that look? I can't tell what you are thinking with the mask on."

"It's just so damned romantic."

"Why are you making that sound like a bad thing?"

"Because, I didn't think of anything romantic for us to do."

"Ross, I didn't do this because I expected you to do

something in return. This is for us. To make a memory that doesn't have violence or boats in it."

"I know, it's just I feel like you make all the grand gestures. I've been trying to be better about doing grand gestures myself, but I keep forgetting." Jack tipped her chin up at him.

"Listen, you've got all the brains. You aren't short on having beauty either. Let my 'thing' be grand gestures."

"Okay." Ross said, blushing. He said she was pretty.

"Good." He started walking again. But Ross continued to get after herself. *You don't do romance. It is a complete fluke that you are getting married. It is nothing short of a miracle, really. You can break down chemical equations with the best of them. You can apparently figure out how to neutralize viruses in wastewater. You have your talents, but romance just isn't one of them. Be happy.* Ross smiled at Jack.

"Besides, you'll have plenty of time while we are in lock down to romance me." Ross almost reversed and walked back to the hotel out of reaction. Old Ross would have run a mile at the idea of being locked in a closed space with another human being. Instead, she gave a nervous laugh and kept walking. Jack was different. She had already been confined on a boat with Jack, and they had survived. It still sent a shiver through her though. If they were honest, the past six months had not been enough to erase the trauma that had preceded Ross coming onto the boat. Jack was more than happy to have a reason to hide her away for a bit longer. Likewise, Ross was pretty sure that after this event and the wedding, it would be some time before she felt the urge to see other people.

"Maybe. I haven't had a lot of experience with romance. Other than movies. How do you feel about rose petals on the bed?" She asked.

"Well, given what you are then supposed to do on the bed, it seems like they would end up in some strange places."

"Yeah, that does seem possible. You don't really strike me as the champagne and bubble bath type."

"No." Ross's mind was spinning. Romance definitely seemed to be geared more towards women than men. It wasn't fair. Jack gently took her hand from where it was twirling her hair and held it.

"Ross, don't worry about it. You are putting too much pressure on yourself." But Ross wouldn't be letting it go. Words seemed lacking somehow. She couldn't just keep going around saying 'I love you'. Gestures were needed. Big, big gestures.

Jack held the door open for her as they entered the event. It had only been a few blocks from their hotel. There was staff there checking everyone's temperatures. A box of masks ready for those who needed it on the table next to the name tags. The name tags not only had their name, but their picture. Ross didn't know where they had gotten hers, but it looked very much like a mug shot. Everyone was then ushered into a large conference room filled with people wearing masks, which still looked a bit strange. Models of PAUL were in a few different locations throughout the room. They looked more like works of art on display rather than pieces of medical equipment. Ross had never been to an event like this, and if she was honest, she was nervous. It would be the first time she had been seen professionally since the shooting. What if she had forgotten how to behave? Ross turned and looked at the people in the room while she put on her name tag.

"Can you tell which ones are scientists and who the hospital executives are?" Ross asked Jack, trying to relieve some of the tension. It was a game she and Sam often played. Jack surveyed the crowd. There was a mixture of people. Soon, he saw the difference Ross was referencing. Everyone was dressed well, but when he looked closer, he could see that the suits and dresses on some didn't fit as well as the others. Some had expensive hair cuts while others had more natural hair. The longer he looked, the more he could tell who had the money and who had the brains.

"Ross!" A small group of women waved to her.

"Oh my god, Christy and Marie are here."

"Never heard of them." Jack said.

"They work in my lab. I haven't seen them in forever." Jack followed as Ross went over to speak to Christy and Marie. Ross introduced Jack with a small amount of pride.

"The notorious Jack." Christy said. "We've heard a few things about you." Christy poked her finger into Jack's chest and let it stay there a little longer than Ross was happy with.

"All good I hope." Jack answered, making sure his smile went to his eyes. Christy looked him up and down and said.

"Not bad. Not bad at all." Ross felt herself hating Christy with a great passion all of a sudden.

"You are coming back to the lab after the wedding?" Marie asked.

"That's the plan." Ross said, not taking her eyes off Christy. "I guess a lot will depend on what happens with the pandemic."

"Yeah, we are waiting to see if they shut us down. Ralph

is trying to make us essential. That's one of the reasons we took the PAUL project. It certainly bought us some time. He is trying to grab a contract for vaccine development, but with our background, there are too many labs who have more experience. We'll just have to wait and see. We already can't get gloves or white suits. Everything is being sent to the hospitals." Ross tried to keep smiling while Marie essentially informed her that she might not have a job to come back to for the foreseeable future. Ross had been so happy to see the both of them and now she wanted nothing more than to get away from them. Jack offered the opportunity, tugging on Ross's arm because a very nicely dressed woman was waving them over.

"Excuse me." Ross left Christy and Marie. Once they were out of hearing range, Ross said, "Under no circumstance will you go around Christy alone." Jack smiled.

"Yes ma'am."

"Hello, Dr. Halloway, I'm Terresa Mattingly from Seascape Diagnostics. We are distributing PAUL in the United States. Thank you so much for your help in these difficult times." The woman was feigning sincerity. "Since you have been working remotely, I thought you would like to meet the rest of the team." Jack heard Ross take a sharp intake of breath.

"I would love to." Ross almost whispered. The fake blonde disappeared.

"What's the big deal?" Jack asked.

"The rest of the team includes Dr. Victor Montizant of the Hildabrand Association. He, along with Dr. Junta Montoya, are up for Nobel Prizes for advancements in science, specifically for their work on creating PAUL. They not only came up with PAUL, but brought together a team so that it went from conception to market in five short months. Why are you looking at me like that?"

"Nothing." Jack said. He was having a blast watching her freak out.

"Dr. Halloway, I would like to introduce you to…."

"Dr. Montizant and Dr. Montoya, it is so nice to meet you. I'm a big fan of your work." Ross shook their hands a little too hard and then stood there with a smile on her face that went from ear to ear.

"And who is this gentleman?" Dr. Montizant asked with his thick accent.

"Oh, um, this is my…..fiance. Jack." Ross still hated the word 'fiance'.

"Nice to meet you Jack. We would like to thank you for all of your work on the system, Dr. Halloway. We were really struggling with the waste issue." Dr. Montoya said. Ross was practically vibrating.

"It was very much my pleasure." Was all she managed to say. "I'm glad I was able to help."

"I was rather impressed with your work. Specifically your discovery a few years ago. Finding a way of using organic material to reduce ocean plastic. Very impressive." Dr. Montizant said. Ross was stunned. They shook Ross's hand and went to leave. "Do you mind if I get a picture?" Ross blurted out before they could go. Jack knew his roll here and pulled his phone out of his pocket.

"Okay, one for fun." Jack said. Three extremely professional and well respected scientists pulled funny faces. Laughing, they all said their good-byes, and the two Nobel Prize winners continued to make their rounds. Despite the mask, Jack could tell Ross was smiling from ear to ear. Her eyes were sparkling.

"I can't believe that. They are two of the leading minds in science right now. Send me that picture. That is getting framed." Ross was fan-girling hard, and Jack was loving every minute of it.

"They seemed to know who you were." Jack said. Ross grabbed his arm.

"I know, right! How amazing is that? They knew about my work with ocean plastic!" There was a clinking of glass as a woman at the head table announced it was time to take their seats. The two gentlemen were sitting at the head table. The room filled with shuffling as everyone moved around to find their tables. Jack and Ross had found their names at one of the tables, almost at the back of the room. Once everyone had settled down, the rounder of the two, Dr. Montizant stood up, and the room erupted in applause. He gestured for them to quiet down.

"I would like to thank you all for being here. The way things are going, you may not be able to get back home. So I appreciate your sacrifice." There was light laughter throughout the room. "This project is like no other we have ever worked on in terms of the scope of its use. One of my graduate students did the math, and if PAUL is used the way we think it will be used, half the population of the planet will have come in contact with PAUL in three years." The room applauded again. "I speak for the entire team when I say it has been an honor to be a part of this. That we will be able to help humanity in such a way is a great honor. Now, a few words from some of my colleagues." There was another round of light applause. "Good afternoon, the team and myself at Seascape Diagnostics are also very honored to be a part of such a tremendous project….." Jack pulled out his phone. Ross leaned back and sent Sam the picture of her and the nobel prize winners. She knew Sam wouldn't care who they were, but other than Jack, she was the only other person Ross knew who would pretend to be as impressed as Ross.

The doors at the back of the room opened quietly. Catering made their way in to arrange some of the tables to make room for the lunch that was to follow. They moved in silence, all dressed in black, no one paid them much attention. Ross looked at them only because they came right by their table and she wanted to make sure they wouldn't run into her. They were dressed in black with black masks on. *They look like catering ninjas.* She thought to herself. Ross had not looked at the menu for the luncheon. Being far more interested in who was speaking, but whatever they were serving, it smelled *amazing*. Ross placed a hand over her stomach as it gave out a low growl.

"I told you to eat this morning." Jack said, not looking up from the game he was playing on his phone.

"My stomach doesn't know what time zone we are in." Ross said. The thought of food that morning had made her sick. "Hopefully they will keep the speeches short and we can get to lunch."

15

Forty-five minutes later, Dr. Donegal, who was chief of medicine at some hospital, was discussing how PAUL would be a great benefit to his team in their attempt to slow the progression of Parid-21. As Ross had promised, the event had taken a rather boring turn. While she wanted to be respectful, this man was trying to stop a global pandemic from killing people, yet her stomach had gotten louder as the smell of food had gotten stronger. People from other tables were starting to look at her. One woman had already handed her a mint, which had done nothing at all to stop her stomach.

As if to make the situation worse, the caterers were now bringing out the food and carrying it right past Ross's table. Ross was trying to figure out what they were having by smelling the trays as they passed her. Jack reached out and grabbed her hand, "You look like one of those sniffer dogs at the airport."

"There was a lovely meat smell coming from that one. Maybe meatloaf, maybe……" Ross looked over while she was talking because one of the caterers had screeched the legs of the table along the floor and something caught her eye. Something that made her heart stop. What had it been?

She kept looking and she couldn't find it again. Ross looked back up front and then turned to look again, and it hit her. Everyone was wearing masks, which accentuates a person's eyes since that was all you could see of their face. Standing along the wall, waiting to serve them lunch, was a tall blonde woman with blue emotionless eyes that looked out on the world without caring. No doubt sensing she was being looked at, the woman turned, and for a brief second, locked eyes with Ross. Quickly, the blond looked back to the front of the room while Ross's hand grabbed Jack's thigh under the table. Her nails digging into his skin.

"Oiw, what the hell?" Jack said loud enough to make the people around them turn their heads.

"Spartan." Ross whispered.

"What?"

"There is a Spartan over there." Ross answered, turning it up a notch.

"Where?" Jack scanned the people immediately around them.

"Catering." Ross whispered. Jack scanned the faces of the caterers and froze. Staring back at him were the unmistakable eyes of a Spartan. Natasha looked at him and pulled a gun from inside her vest. She had been planning on waiting until they broke up for the buffet, but it seemed at least two people in the crowd knew what she was. A problem she hadn't had before, but not one she intended to let get the advantage of her.

Pulling her gun out of her jacket, she took aim at the target on the main stage and pulled the trigger. Jack threw

Ross to the ground. Ross hit the ground and opened her eyes just in time to see Dr. Montoya's lifeless body fall behind the head table. Jack barely registered that it was Dr. Montoya. All he cared about was that it hadn't been Ross. There were screams all around the room. People hit the ground around them. A second round went off, this one sounding closer, and the security guard behind them fell to the floor, his gun falling a few feet in front of him. Ross looked back and saw the life leave his young eyes. Jack pushed Ross's head to the ground and covered her completely with his body. He didn't know if this Spartan knew that Ross was there. He had absolutely no idea if the Spartans still had an interest in getting rid of her, but he wasn't risking it. Looking around, Jack frantically looked for the nearest door for them to run out of.

Natasha took a few steps towards the head table. A few people who had been close to the exits were starting to flee. Most of the humans had hit the floor, including her second target. He was trying to hide under the table. Natasha came up behind the table, kicking the chairs out of her way. He was not the only one under the table. It was a stupid place to hide. It offered no protection against bullets. They would cut right through the plastic. Yet it never failed as a hiding place.

In a few seconds, it would occur to one of the people who had just fled to the room to call the police. Natasha ran through the times in her head. For a mass shooting, the response time would be slower. First on the scene in four minutes. Probably another ten to secure the scene. Natasha estimated that she would need another two minutes to complete her mission and then she could start her escape. By the time the first team entered the building, Natasha would be leaving it.

Having found which table he was hidden under, Natasha had to flip it to get a clear shot of him. Being a rather round man, his bum had been sticking up in the air. The sound of the table falling to the ground with all the glasses and silverware on it let Jack know where the Spartan was. He looked around them and saw that there was a back door that led into the main part of the building. Rolling off of Ross, he pulled her in that direction.

The others under the table scurried away like rats. Natasha stood over the target, and Dr. Montizant looked up at her, saw her gun pointed at him, and immediately rolled over, raising his hands to protect himself. Natasha shot him in the head. His body went limp, raised arms falling to the ground instantly. Ross and Jack were half standing when the second shot went off. Ross turned her head out of reflex and saw Dr. Montizant go limp, the Spartan standing over him. Without a moment to take in what she had done, the Spartan leaned down next to him and busied herself changing her disguise. Ross took one more step before she pulled her hand away from Jack's grip.

Natasha moved with steady, quick hands, not paying any attention to the few remaining people in the room. Pulling a security badge out of her pocket, she placed it on her black dress shirt, and out of her other pocket, she pulled a clip on tie.

Ross saw what she was doing and yelled, "No! No!" Pulling herself away from Jack, Ross ran for one of the walls.

"Ross!" Jack yelled, he had the door open, they were that close to making it to safety. Jack let the door close and he hit the ground wondering what the hell Ross was doing. She pulled a fire extinguisher off the wall and pulled the pin. Jack looked at the Spartan, sure that she was going to see Ross killed right in front of him. Instead, the woman was busy changing into a clip on tie. Her gun lay next to her.

"Ross, come one." Jack whisper-yelled, but Ross had already started spraying the contents of the extinguisher into the room. Natasha picked up her gun and shot over Jack's head. Jack went flat on the ground. Natasha then pointed the gun where the woman had been, but she could no longer see her. Ross saw the bullet go into the wall over Jack's head and something snapped in her. She had been mad, now she was fucking furious.

"Don't be stupid." Natasha said, to the smokey room. Jack looked up and couldn't see Ross either. What the hell was she doing? The white mist surrounded him as well. Jack could see nothing. Feeling along the wall and then out in front of him, he went in the direction Ross had been in. "Ross!" He whispered again.

"Do I have the pleasure of being in the presence of Dr. Ross Halloway?" Natasha said, her gun at the ready. Eyes scanning the room for the first sign of her. Jack's heart froze when he heard Natasha.

"Come out, come out wherever you are." There was silence. Jack stood still. He had no idea where Ross was, but he also had no idea where the Spartan was. "You have a bit of a reputation amongst us Spartans. I see it is well deserved. You aren't stupid like the rest of them are you?" The Spartan was to his right. Jack prayed that Ross didn't give her whereabouts away by answering. "You don't panic. You keep a calm head." There was silence for a moment. Jack looked around him and listened for any sounds of movement. He thought he saw something move off to his right, ducking to the ground, the bullet went over his head. Almost immediately followed by two gunshots.

16

"ROSS!" Jack yelled into the white mist. He was on his feet now and fumbled in the white haze. "ROSS!" The panic was clear in his voice. He didn't care if the Spartan heard him. He had to find Ross. This couldn't happen. She had agreed to marry him. They were just days away from the wedding. He expected another shot. The one for him, since he was no longer concerned with hiding. Running blind through the mist, Jack ran into tables and chairs. With the noise he was making, the Spartan would have no trouble figuring out where he was. It didn't matter. He had to find Ross. "Ross, honey, answer me. Please answer me, for the love of god."

"Over here." The voice was Ross's. Jack couldn't register it. She didn't sound scared or hurt. If anything she sounded annoyed. "Ross?"

"Get down." She instructed him. Her voice was coming from in front of him. Jack squatted down on the floor but kept moving towards the sound of her voice.

"Are you alright?" Jack said, the desperation still in his voice.

"Shhhhh….I don't know where she is." Jack did as she said. Crawling on his hands and knees, the air was clearer down there. "Move towards my voice." There was another sound as well. Something was moving in the room, but all Jack could focus on was the fact that Ross was okay.

"Ross, are you alright?" Her hand was the first thing he saw. He reached out for it, and much to his relief, she gripped his hand in return. The rest of Ross appeared out of the mist. In her other hand was a gun.

"Are you okay?" Jack asked, pulling her close to him. She felt solid. Jack looked her over and saw no blood from anywhere. If he could have seen an exit, he would have pulled her out of there. Ross never took her eyes off of the room in front of them, or lowered the gun.

"I'm alright Jack." Ross whispered. The white mist was climbing towards the ceiling. The tops of the tables were now visible. Ross was holding the gun and pointing it out in front of her, taking one slow step at a time. The white mist from the extinguisher apparently hit the ceiling, setting off the sprinklers. With the addition of water, the mist dissipated quickly, and the source of the groaning became clear. The Spartan was laying halfway down the stairs that lead up to the head table. There was a door right in front of her, though at the speed she was moving, it would take hours for her to get there. The reason for the groaning and her inability to walk was clear. There were gunshot wounds in both of her legs. A trail of thick blood marking her slow progress.

Jack looked at Ross in amazement. He had assumed the gunshots had come from the Spartan. Ross carried the gun in front of her like she had been training her whole life for this. Jack followed her. Despite being painfully wounded, her weapon nowhere to be found, and both of her hands occupied with pulling herself towards the door, Ross and Jack approached the Spartan slowly.

Even with less nerves, and therefore, the inability to feel pain on the same scale as a normal human, Natasha was still in a considerable amount of discomfort. If she was right, her left femur was broken and her right leg had a shattered ankle. Neither one was lethal, but it was going to make escaping rather more difficult since it was physically impossible for her to walk. Unfortunately, her body had gone into shock, and she was finding it difficult to regulate her heart rate and keep her focus.

"Come on, let's get out of here." Jack said, he took Ross's arm heading towards the door in front of the spartan.

"Freeze." Ross said, to the back of Natasha's head. Natasha did not freeze. Instead she pulled herself forward another half and inch.

"Ross, honey, let's get out of here. Leave her."

"Shoot me." The Spartan yelled with amazing strength.

"Shoot yourself." Ross said, taking a step closer. Natasha stopped and rolled over so she could see her killer. She would have shot herself, except she was out of bullets. Her gun was tucked into her waist band, but it was useless. Natasha had given herself enough bullets to kill the targets and a few more just in case she missed or someone put up a fight.

"So I have the pleasure of speaking with Dr. Ross Halloway? I saw your name on the guest list. I should have planned better. And Jack, I assume? Where is the third? I thought there were three of you?" Ross firmed up her grip on the gun. She was glad that her hand didn't shake and give away how nervous she was to be looking a Spartan in the face….again. Natasha was speaking the truth. She had seen Ross's name in the guest list. While she was, in fact, getting a reputation for surviving Spartans, she was still just a human. Not even one with a particular skill set that would warrant her a credible threat.

"You really are a more worthy opponent than most. I mean that as a compliment." Natasha grimaced as she pulled herself backwards on her elbows and sat up to face Ross and Jack more squarely. There was very little chance of her escaping in her current state. Ross shooting her was her only option.

"Ross, come on." Jack said, trying to get Ross's attention. She was completely focused on the Spartan.

"Why did you do it? They were two of the greatest minds in the world."

"Because I was paid to." The Spartan raised her gun at Jack and a fourth round went off. A hole appeared in the Spartan's forehead as she fell backwards. Her ghost gun falling to her side.

"Jesus…" Jack half screamed. He looked from the Spartan to Ross, who was frozen with an equally shocked look on her face.

"Ahh." Ross dropped the gun like it had burned her. "Shit. Shit. I killed her. I killed her. She's dead, isn't she?" Ross asked, looking at Jack. Jack went up and kicked the Spartan's gun away.

"Um, yeah." Jack said, looking, but not wanting to get any closer. Jack noticed the gun was not like a normal gun and bent down to look at it before going back to Ross. The mist had now cleared the room almost completely.

"She was going to shoot you. She raised her gun." Ross said, half statement, half question. Jack looked at the gun.

"She pointed it at me, but it's empty. There aren't any bullets." Ross couldn't breathe. Jack looked at her in amazement.

"You thought she was going to kill me?" Ross shrugged.

"Yeah."

Jack and Ross were the only two standing up in the room. There were tables and chairs overturned. Napkins and other litter spread out over the room. Jack made a point of not looking at the men the Spartan had been sent to kill. He couldn't help but notice how young the security guard had been. Ross tucked up next to him, and he put his arms around her.

"Shit Jack, what have I done?" If he was honest, Jack wasn't sure what had happened. He kept replaying the scene that had just happened in his head to convince himself it hadn't happened that way. There was no getting around the fact that the woman he loved, who he wanted to spend the rest of his life with, had just shot a woman in the head with pinpoint accuracy.

A door opened behind them, Jack and Ross jumped, and Ross bent down for the gun she had just dropped. The gun was half raised when she realized the nicely dressed woman crawling out of a supply closet was no threat.

"Is she dead?" The woman asked, in a shaky voice.

"Yeah." Ross said. There was a loud bang, followed by yelling. Ross and Jack froze her grip on the gun in her hand tightened, but she didn't raise it. There was a lot of yelling and between the commotion and the yelling, it took them a while to figure out what was being said, "What are they yelling?" Ross asked Jack.

"I don't know." One of the police dressed head to toe in tactical gear stepped ahead of the others. Ross was surprisingly calm considering there were at least twenty guns pointed at her. Feeling safe in the knowledge that they were there to save them, she was extremely surprised to find Jack had several red laser dots on him dancing around. They exchanged questioning looks. Jack was equally as confused as to why Ross had the same red dots dancing on her chest.

"HANDS UP!" The lead policeman yelled. All three of them complied. "PUT YOUR WEAPON DOWN." With a start, Ross dropped the gun she had almost forgotten she was holding. "KICK IT OVER HERE." Ross did as she was told. "LAY DOWN, FACE DOWN." Once again, Jack and Ross exchanged confused looks, but did as they were told. As soon as they had complied, the sea of police were upon them. Ross's hands were yanked from behind her head and placed behind her back where they were cuffed. She was then hauled to her feet with amazing strength.

"I think there has been a mistake." She said to the police that was half carrying, half pushing her out of the conference room. "Save it." Was the reply she got.

Jack and Ross were seated on the curb handcuffed. A man in a suit stood in front of them and identified himself as Detective Stevens.

"So what happened Dr. Halloway? Why did the two doctors, a security guard, and a caterer have to die today?" Ross's mouth opened and shut several times. Her brain did not know where to start in explaining.

"Detective…." Jack started.

"I'll get to you in a second Crocodile hunter. Right now I

would like to know what the lady has to say."

"I was invited as part of the team who created PAUL." Ross lamely offered a way of explanation. "I never would have killed anyone."

"Then why were you seen holding a firearm, pointed at a recently killed caterer? We have a witness who said you were the one who shot her."

"That's not a caterer…..that's a Spartan."

"So you wouldn't kill anyone, but you did kill a caterer who is a Spartan?"

"Well yes, I guess I would kill, as long as they were a Spartan."

"Who was trying to kill her…." Jack tried to inject.

"What did I tell you?" The detective snapped at him.

"Dr. Halloway, help me try to understand, okay?" The detective leaned over to look her face to face. Ross's eyes couldn't help but notice the spot on his neck where he had missed when shaving that morning and though she knew she should really be focused on the fact that they thought she had killed all the dead people in that room, but it was all she could focus on in the moment. *Some master criminal you would make.* "What happened today? Did you snap? The pressure of trying to get this PAUL thing out quickly get to ya? Were they not paying you what you deserved? I get that. I do." Ross squinted, trying to figure out if he thought he was coming across as sympathetic. "I think most people would understand that in these difficult times, you had just reached your breaking point. There is only so much a person can take. Right?" Ross had to stop this before she started laughing.

"Detective Stevens, I think a lot of your questions could be answered if you reached out to Inspector Dufort with

Interpol. I did not kill anyone in that room other than a Spartan who was disguised as a caterer. The Spartan killed the others, as I'm sure the other witnesses will tell you."

"Inspector Dufort at Interpol, ha?" Detective Stevens leaned up. "Is this some secret agent shit?" The detective was already taking his phone out of his pocket.

"Yes, that is exactly what this is. Some secret agent shit." Ross looked at Jack and shook her head in exasperation. Jack wondered who the hell this woman was.

Dufort had not let the local authorities know he was coming, but the news report on his rental car radio told him where to find Jack and Ross, the Center for Scientific Advancement. The shooting was breaking news. His ID in his breast pocket, Dufort made for the radius, getting as close as he could. Not bothering to look for a parking spot, Dufort parked the car in the middle of the road and grabbed his backpack. Walking to the two blocks to the police line, he pulled out his ID and asked to speak with Dr. Ross Halloway.

"Interpol." The cop whistled. "News travels fast."

"Bad news travels faster." The cop let him in.

For a split second, Dufort was concerned that whatever had happened, Dr. Halloway might be injured. Again. Or worse.

His phone distracted him, buzzing to life in his pocket.

"Inspector Dufort speaking." The surprise was clear on Detective Steven's face when Dufort answered. He had done what Dr. Halloway had asked simply to poke a hole in her lies.

"Are you familiar with a Dr. Ross Halloway?"

"I am. What about her?" Dufort walked as he spoke, heading to the inner circle of emergency vehicles. He spotted Jack and Dr. Halloway sitting on the curb with plain clothes standing on the phone in front of them. It was clear from how they were sitting that both Jack and Dr. Halloway were handcuffed.

"We have her in custody, she was caught with a firearm in her hand at the scene of a mass shooting." Dufort put his phone down and said to the detective's back, "Then I suggest you let them go as soon as possible." The detective spun around and Ross took no small amount of joy in seeing the startled look on his face. Dufort pulled out his ID card and showed it to the detective.

"So, this is some secret agent shit." Jack said. A uniform police was told to unlock their cuffs.

"I would like an explanation." The detective said.

"And I will be happy to give you one if you will just come with me to some place a little more private." Ross and Jack watched them leave.

"I'm glad that is going to get sorted out. Being associated with someone involved in a mass shooting wasn't going to do me any favors with getting a visa." Jack said.

"Do you think they have a food truck around here? I was hungry before all this started, now I'm absolutely starving."

17

It did not take long to explain the Spartan and Dr. Halloway to the detective. "They all have a microchip and a tattoo with their identification number on it. That is all you will need to confirm that the person Dr. Halloway killed was a Spartan. If there was a Spartan on the scene, then they were there to kill someone. My guess is the two lead scientists for PAUL."

"The security guard?" Dufort shrugged his shoulders.

"Most likely taken out because he was the only other person in the room with a gun. Poor man was doing his job." Dufort suggested even though he had only the barest idea of what had happened.

"So, you want me to believe that a Spartan breaks up a convention of scientists, kills a security guard and then the main guests. While this is going on, Dr. Halloway over there, instead of running away and hiding like everyone else in the room, comes up with a way of getting a firearm and then kills this Spartan chick by first blowing out her knee caps and then putting one between her eyes? Inspector, I don't know how things are where you come from, but I've seen gang killings that showed more mercy." That one was harder for Dufort to explain. He would have to ask Dr. Halloway about that. Dufort gave one of his knowing smiles and simply said, "Dr. Halloway has been singled out by my task force because she shows a high aptitude for such situations."

"I'll need a signed statement." Stevens said, suddenly seeming bored with the situation.

"And you shall have one." Dufort answered. The detective went to focus on his other witnesses, shaking his head as he walked away.

Before he returned to Dr. Halloway and Jack, Dufort pulled his phone out and called Rand.

"Inspector Dufort's office." Rand answered.

"Please don't call your living room my office." Rand of course knew it was Dufort calling. Caller ID.

"Stop complaining or I'll tell you what I'm wearing."

"Our conversations have gotten very casual since you were sent home to work."

"Not for the first time, I will remind you, I wasn't sent home to WORK. I answer your calls out of the kindness of my heart." Dufort grumbled. He kept forgetting that.

"There's been a big blow up at the event in New York. Our Dr. Halloway managed to kill a Spartan and almost get herself arrested in the process."

"She really needs to see my Reiki healer. A few well placed crystals could change her world for the better." Dufort ignored this statement.

"Find out what they are doing with the Spartan. I want a tattoo and chip number as soon as one is available. Also, I need a statement from my office stating that we are aware of Dr. Halloway and we are confident she was acting in the interest of the safety of others when she killed the Spartan."

"She killed a Spartan? I thought that was impossible for mortals to do."

"I'll call you when I know more."

"You are so frustrat....." Dufort hung up. The scene around him was still chaotic. The curb where he had left Dr. Halloway and Jack was now empty. It didn't take long to find them, he just had to listen for the distressed ramblings of Jack.

"Jack, for the last time, I'm fine." Jack was pulling the silver thermal wrap around Ross's shoulders. Having been cleared of a mass killing, the detective had insisted they be looked at by EMT's with the other survivors. Jack was convinced something was wrong with Ross. How could they be fine?

"You're in shock."

"I'm not."

"Alright, then I'm in shock."

"That I believe. Maybe they should look at you."

"What in the hell possessed you?" Jack blurted out. Ross had never seen Jack like this. His neck was red, he was running his hands continuously through his hair and pacing in front of her.

"I got mad." Ross offered meekly. If Ross was honest, she didn't know what had possessed her. Now that she was sitting there, after the event, she had no idea why she hadn't run as far and as fast as she could.

"You got mad? You got mad, so you jump up and announce yourself to a Spartan? This is why you scare the hell outta me Ross? You keep on telling me about this quiet life you used to lead, but ever since I met you, it has been one near death experience after another. We were almost out of the room. You went back in."

"She killed two of the leading minds in the world, not to mention an innocent man who was just doing his job. Who knows what else they could have accomplished." Jack just looked at her, his jaw clenched and growled. "Then she shot at you." Ross couldn't control her voice when she said it. "That bullet missed you by three inches….give or take." Ross regained the shakiness in her voice as she spoke and wiped the tear away from her eye. Jack looked at her, he knew what she had felt. He had felt the same. In a calmer voice he said, "And where did you learn how to handle a gun like that? Did they cover that at university? Right after 'How to conceal yourself from a gunman using household items'?"

"I told you, my father took me to the gun range before I went to college."

"You didn't say he took you for tactical training as well…Blimey!"

"What are you so upset about? It worked didn't it?" Ross could honestly not figure out why Jack was yelling at her.

"Yes, yes it did work. I am upset because I thought I was marrying a chemist. A quiet nerdy chemist who would make jokes I wouldn't understand and outsmart me. Now, I find out you can handle a gun better than Dirty Harry. " Ross could feel herself getting mad again and stood up, the silver blanket flowing after her like a cape.

"You listen to me….this is the second time I have pieced my life back together after a damn Spartan has ripped it apart. The last time I managed to talk myself into going somewhere after a Spartan attack and bam…I get shot in the neck." Ross was gesturing wildly and raising her voice.

"I almost died. I piece myself back together after that, I venture out and bam….another fucking Spartan shows up. This time, she doesn't just kill two scientists who literally changed the world for the better, but the bitch tried to kill you Jack. I don't know who sent her, or what the hell, but that bitch literally attacked everything I love today. So excuse the hell out of me if I refuse to lay there and let myself be a victim. AGAIN." Jack took a deep breath.

"We were out of there, Ross! I had the door open. I almost had you to safety. Keeping you safe Ross, that's what is most important to me, and you didn't let me." Jack's voice was calmer. There was a ring of desperation about it even. Ross took her own deep breath.

"I got mad Jack. I got really fucking mad." Neither one said anything for a moment. Jack looked around as if an explanation he would like better would be out in the crowd somewhere.

"How did you know to do half of that? Like the fire extinguisher?"

"I wanted to cover myself while I grabbed the guard's gun." Jack waved his hands around.

"This is what I'm saying. I haven't been around many chemists, but out of all the people I have met, most would just want to get out of the room. Not be looking around for things that could give them cover while they grab the dead security guard's gun."

"I don't know what to tell you, Jack. I did what I did." Ross said, exasperated. Hell, she didn't know where she got half of what she had done in there. It was like she was two different people. One could sit all day figuring out the gaseous state of the ozone. The other could shoot someone dead in the center of their forehead without thinking.

"Hello, you two." Dufort decided to interrupt their argument. As amusing as he was finding it. " I hope I'm not interrupting something." Inspector Dufort came up behind Jack. He looked very much the part of a secret agent. He lifted his Ray Bans as he walked up to them with his hand casually tucked into his dark blue dress pants, slightly pulling back the matching blazer. His white shirt was open at the collar, and he sported a smile, which made him look slightly menacing to Ross.

"Not that I'm upset considering the circumstances, but how in the hell are you here right now?" Jack said, exhausted with the whole situation. "Jack, it's good to see you too. You are looking a lot better than the last time I saw you. Being engaged must agree with you." Jack gave him a half smile. Seeing their masks, Dufort pulled his own out of his pocket and put it on. "I'm still getting used to this. I hate them don't you? They pull on my ears.   D r . Halloway. You are looking very well. I take it you were not injured today?" He took her hand and kissed it in that old world way he had.

"No. Thankfully, I wasn't the one injured today."

Jack pointedly looked at Ross and then back at Dufort. "Go on, tell him what happened."

"You don't have to. I know most of what happened, and what I don't know, I will eventually find out. What I would like to know, however, is how you managed to shoot a Spartan twice in the legs and then once between the eyes and walk away without a scratch?"

"That's what I've been trying to figure out." Jack added.

"Potassium Bicarbonate. It's the main ingredient in fire extinguishers. It causes lightheadedness and disorientation. Aside from essentially hiding me, so she couldn't shoot me, it would slow her reaction time." Dufort was smiling from ear to ear. Jack was standing in silent shock.

"I applaud your fast thinking."

"It can not be normal for a regular human being to react that way while under fire." Jack said, shoving his hands in his pockets and looking away.

"Ah, well, I think you will agree with me that Dr. Halloway is not an ordinary human being." Jack cut Dufort a glaring side eye.

"Yeah." Ross answered meekly. Even though they were going to get married, she didn't really feel like telling him about her teenage love of finding out the chemical composition of everyday objects.

Dufort stood there expectantly. Ross didn't feel like going through the whole thing again, especially since Jack was still bouncing around. "I got mad. I used the fire extinguisher to hide myself. Grabbed the security guard's gun and aimed before it obscured my view, and I shot. I was lucky that I hit her in the legs. I had no idea if I had hit her at all." Ross left out the part where she glared at the woman in her expressionless eyes before shooting her in the head. She was with Jack on that one. It was both impressive and scary that she had been able to do such a thing.

"Dr. Halloway, I certainly hope I never upset you."

"Amen to that." Jack added. He had taken several deep breaths and they had done nothing to bring his adrenaline back down to normal levels. Like Ross, he was tired of the Spartans following them around. Not for the first time, he had been absolutely convinced Ross was dead. He was getting really tired of thinking Ross was dead.

"Why are you here? Do you have an update on my case?" Ross asked.

"How would you like to get out of here? Find someplace quiet to talk." Dufort asked.

"Are we allowed to leave?" Ross asked.

"They said we had to stay and give a statement. They might have some further questions." Jack said, also ready to be out of there, but not wanting to get deported.

"I will take care of it." Dufort assured them. That was all they needed. Ross ditched the thermal wrap and followed Dufort through the seemingly endless sea of cop cars, SWAT vehicles, and firetrucks. Dufort made his way through the crowd with authority, and no one asked them where they were going. Ross couldn't help but think what they looked like in their wet and dirty fancy clothes walking behind a very crisp Dufort.

"Why am I getting a sense of deja vu'?" Jack asked. Ross knew what he meant. It seemed like every time they went anywhere, emergency services were soon to follow.

18

Leaving the chaos and sirens behind them, Dufort led them to a nondescript black sedan parked in the middle of the road in a residential neighborhood. Dufort did some questionable driving through the streets of the city then entered the highway.

"Our hotel is on…." Ross started to tell him.

"I'm afraid we won't be going back to your hotel."

"Then where are we going?" Jack asked.

"I told you, someplace quiet so we can talk. When is the wedding?" Dufort asked, changing the subject.

"We get married in three days." Ross said, doing a very good job of covering the lump that formed in her throat when she said 'wedding'.

"I promise I will have you back by then." Dufort said. Jack leaned back in the seat, realizing what should have occurred to him before now. Dufort's presence had nothing to do with the day's events. For Dufort to have materialized out of thin air, he had to have been on his way already.

"Inspector, I feel I should warn you that I have had a

helluva day, and I am in no mood to be messed around. Now, tell me where we are going and tell me now, or I will call 911 and tell them I have been kidnapped, and you can explain yourself then." Ross said. Dufort lifted an eyebrow in the rearview mirror.

"I am having a member of the NYPD stop by your hotel and gather your things. They are going to meet us at the airport where we will fly out." Jack wouldn't mind if they paid the bill as well, but he said nothing.

"Inspector….where are we going?"

"I can't tell you that. But I can tell you that in addition to going over what happened today, I can fill you in on your case and go over something new that I was hoping to talk to you two about."

"What 'something new'?" Ross asked, leaning forward in the seat a little.

"I can't tell you unless we are in a secure place."

"Are you serious? Look at us, do we look like we are in the mood for this?" Jack said. "Just tell us what it is you want." Dufort was beginning to regret this.

"To tell you that would be in violation of international law since the information I have to impart to you is classified, and there are only four people in the world that know about it. So you would not be able to make it back to Boston for your wedding because you will be in prison."

"I vote we get out of the car." Jack said, thinking the day had already been interesting enough.

"I take it since you came to New York to look for us, whatever this top secret thing is, it involves Spartans. Can you confirm that?" Dufort nodded his head.

"I agree with Jack. I think we should get out of the car." Ross said. Dufort of course ignored them, but made sure to keep the doors locked all the same. When they reached the airport, Dufort drove right up onto the tarmac where there was a plane waiting. Dufort stopped the car and turned around.

"I can't make you get on that plane. That would also be illegal, but I do think that you would very much like to know what it is I have to tell you." Ross looked at Jack who was looking more tense by the moment.

"Will we be back by the wedding?" Ross asked. Jack's eyes got big.

"I promise, I will have you back in time for the wedding."

"Can you tell me how far we are going?" Ross said.

"You are going to need your passports." Was all Dufort would say before getting out of the car.

"What do you say?" Ross asked Jack.

"There isn't a secure location nearer than this mysterious place? I mean this is New York. There isn't somewhere here, or D.C.?" Jack asked.

"Of course there are. Very secure locations in both of those places, however, there are things I need to show you that I can not show you there."

"And I suppose these things are vital to whatever it is you need to tell us?"

"I wouldn't have gone through all this trouble if they weren't." Dufort replied, looking at his watch. Jack sucked in his lip and thought of all his options. While every bone in him wanted to leave, it was very clear that Ross would not go with him.

"I have to say my Love, life with you has never been boring." Jack said. "I can't believe you are up for this after today. I would think you would want to go home and stay put."

"Of course I do, but I also want to see what this new information is." If Ross was completely honest with herself, like super honest, she loved all the world's secrets she was now privy to. No, she didn't like all the shooting and the killing. Yes, she still fantasized about working in her lab again, but Dufort seemed to know things that no one else knew, and right now, he was willing to share those things. If they were going to be back in time for the wedding, what was the harm?

"I'm just not sure I want to fly to wherever it is he wants to take us during a pandemic, just to find out."

"Jack, he has information about my case."

"That isn't classified. He could tell us that." And he was right.

"I could go with Dufort, and you could go on to Boston. I'll meet you there." Jack's eyes grew large.

"There is no way in hell I am letting you fly off with that guy."

"I'm going Jack, I completely understand if you don't want to come with me." Jack opened and closed his mouth a few times, trying to think of an argument that would change Ross's mind, but came up with nothing. "Don't look so glum. We are with an agent from Interpol getting on a private plane, what could go wrong?"

"Actually, I'm MI6 for the purposes of this mission." Dufort said, leaning into the car to grab his backpack. Ross gave Jack a smile and then hopped out of the car. Jack sat there for a moment thinking about what he was about to do. Everything about this seemed like a bad idea. Yet, here he was about to get out of the car and go and do it. Love makes you do crazy things.

"Come on Jack, I want to get a picture of us in front of the jet before we take off." Jack paused, putting his mask back on. They all posed for pictures, Dufort doing so begrudgingly before waving his arms around and saying, "Would you hurry up? We were already running late, they are going to cancel the flight." Dufort's Belgian accent came out more when he was aggravated. He hadn't been kidding. As soon as they were aboard, the stairs were lifted and the engines kicked up. Jack and Ross both stood there in the middle of the aisle in shock. Dufort scooted past them and took a seat in a swivel chair with a table in front of it.

"You still have to sit down and buckle up for take off and landing." Dufort informed them. Since they clearly didn't know how to behave on a private plane. Jack and Ross sat down and buckled up. The plane they were in could not be more different than flying commercial.

"We are going to be ruined for life after this." Jack said.

"I know a chemist like me could never do it, but any chance you could get a form of employment that would allow us to travel this way all the time?" Ross asked.

"Not unless Si found hidden pirate treasure on one of his voyages and he has successfully hidden his wealth all this time." The engines revved, and they kicked back in their seats as the plane took off. Jack had never been a nervous flier, but at this particular moment, his stomach was doing summersaults. Every other time he had flown, he had known where he was going. He looked over at Ross to see if she was feeling the same. Ross buckled herself in and then looked at Jack with a giant grin on her face. Jack made sure he was buckled in properly. It appeared they were going on another one of their adventures.

19

Once they had reached a cruising altitude, Dufort invited them over to a table where he opened a laptop.

"I still can't tell you where we are going…" Dufort said, seeing Ross open her mouth to talk.

"Can you tell us which country?" Ross asked, determined to figure out what the hell was going on.

"England." Dufort said, meeting her challenge. Ross looked around and then her eyes lit up.

"Oh. I think I know where we are going. Oh, that's interesting. Why are we going there?" Jack sat there still clueless. Dufort smiled again.

"I have no doubt that you are correct, Dr. Halloway, but this trip is top secret. I can't confirm where we are going until we land."

"I'm less interested in where we are going and more interested in how you are planning on getting us back when all the airports are closing." Jack said.

"Yes, while that might complicate matters, we have a security clearance that I am sure will negate those issues." Dufort informed him. I have been given an update on the events in New York, and I have to say Dr. Halloway, you never cease to amaze me."

"I'll second that." Jack said.

"I ordered an immediate autopsy of the Spartan you neutralized, and if I didn't know better, I would accuse you of being one of them. The Spartan's human name was Natasha. She was registered to the Slavakians, so you may have caused a slight international problem there. She was shot once in the femur, which broke a bone. The second shot hit just below her ankle, shattering it. I am going to assume that is why she was slowed down enough for you to shoot her in the head with such accuracy." An image appeared in Ross's mind of Natasha crawling away, and she leaned over and threw up in a nearby trash can. Jack rubbed her back and handed her a napkin.

"I am sorry, Dr. Halloway, I consider it something to be proud of even though I would have preferred the Spartan alive as I am about to explain."

"I'm sorry. I've never killed anyone before."

"Really, you wouldn't know." Ross vomited again. Dufort's phone rang and he let Ross get herself together while he went to answer it.

"You okay?" Jack asked.

"I have no idea. Is this a normal reaction for killing someone?" Ross asked.

"I shouldn't have agreed to this. We should have just gone home to Boston like we planned."

"I want to know what is going on Jack. I'll be alright. Eventually it was going to hit me that I killed someone. It doesn't really matter where it hits me, does it?"

"You think you know where we are going?" Jack said. He was getting a feeling in his stomach that he was going to regret getting in the car with Dufort.

"I think we are headed to Porton Downs." Ross said, leaning her head back and taking the water Jack offered.

"Why does that sound familiar?"

"It's the United Kingdom's area fifty-one. It's a military base where a bunch of classified shit happens. I only know about it because some of the best advances in chemistry in the last twenty years have come out of there." Jack rubbed her back some more.

"Any idea what might be at Porton Downs that is worth kidnapping us?"

"Not a clue." Ross was running through the possibilities in her head. "They work on curing some of the world's nastier viruses. Maybe there is something Parid related."

"Would Dufort be working on that?" Ross shrugged. They stopped talking when Dufort came back and sat down across from them again.

"Sorry, I had to make some arrangements for our landing. If you are feeling better, Dr. Halloway, I would like to explain to you what I have been up to since we last met."

"Hopefully finding out who ordered the hit on *The Hunter*." Jack said, with no small amount of bite.

"Well, I'm afraid we have hit a roadblock there."

"Just about everyone involved is dead?" Ross asked. Her mind went to Dr. Lillian Patrov who she had grown close to on *The Hunter* as they had been the only women and then the only two to survive. Dr. Petrov had later been killed on order of the Russian government. Along with her parents.

"In the end, yes. As you may have heard, the Russian President was killed while touring a new ballet school. I had just traced the order for the hit on *The Hunter* to his office when all this unfolded. Not that we were likely to get any satisfaction out of it, but understandably, all investigating in that area has stopped. Interestingly, we think the Spartan you killed today was connected to the killing of the Russian President."

"What? How?"

"Natasha mostly worked in that area. It seemed her specialty was high profile killings. A lot of her work involves killings happening in a public area. Her file says she has a particular knack for getting out of impossible situations. The question is, who ordered it?" A stewardess brought around a tray with coffee and tea. "Have some tea, Dr. Halloway. It will settle your stomach." He poured a cup for her without waiting for her response and poured a coffee for himself. Jack also had tea.

"Another government?" Jack asked seemingly stating the obvious. Spartan's had been in high demand from some of the less scrupulous countries since their existence had become known.

"We thought the same thing. Goodness knows there was no shortage of people in the world, within Russia even, who had reason to want the man dead. The truth, as it usually is, turns out to be more interesting. I am only telling you this because I trust you. This is not classified, but not exactly something we want in the press. You understand?" Jack and Ross nodded their heads. "To explain, I will have to give you some background. Around the time we believe the order to eliminate *The Hunter* was being given, the Russian President announced to parliament and other dignitaries at a state dinner that he was divorcing his wife." Ross shrugged, there wasn't anything newsworthy about that. "The problem was, that was the first time his wife had heard the news."

"Charming." Ross said.

"At the same time he was making the announcement, staff at the Kremlin were moving the wife's belongings out and moving in the President's twenty-eight year old pregnant girlfriend. You may recognize her as she won gold a few years ago for gymnastics." Dufort said, showing them a picture on his tablet.

"What a bastard." Ross said.

"Hm. Well, as was expected. The wife moved out dutifully. I personally believe he would have found a way of killing her. She knew too much. Her father was well connected to the right people when the president was up and coming in local government. As you would have to be if you want to become president in Russia, he had stepped over a lot of people to get where he was, and she knew about every single skeleton in his closet. Not to mention birthing all five of his children."

"So you think she hired the Spatans to kill him?" Ross asked.

"Yes, I do." Dufort said, point blank. "There is some proof, though not enough to stand up in court."

"Like what?"

"She had the Spartan's number. We know that because the defector that gave us information around your case, indicated that the number was handed off to the secretary and then the president's wife. So while she obviously passed it along, it was in her hands and there is no reason to think she didn't use it. We also know that she wasn't too pleased with the situation. According to our informant when she arrived at her new residence, Madam President was livid. She had been around politicians enough to know exactly what was happening. There is also some indication she was worried not only for her life, but those of her children. They were sent away to study in different countries. A month later the president was dead. Our source says the opening of the ballet school was meant to be their last public outing together. The president was going to announce to the country their split. "

"Imagine his surprise."

"Hmmm..she managed what no one else had before. And within a tight timeframe." Dufort said, taking a sip of his coffee.

"Maybe you should have hired a woman for the job in the first place." Ross said, smiling. Dufort winked at her.

"She's taken over though hasn't she?" Jack asked.

"She has. In a way no one, even her I don't think, could have predicted. As you may know, she was elected in a special election after his funeral. Are either of you hungry?" Dufort asked.

"Starved." Ross said. Aside from barfing up whatever had been on her stomach, she had been hungry when the whole horrible evening had started. Dufort nodded to the stewardess.

"The food is actually very good. Nothing like that stuff they feed you on commercial."

"No offense, but what does this have to do with us?" Jack said. While the smooth cream leather seats and absolutely fantastic tea was helping calm his nerves a little, he was still uneasy about this situation.

"Not much, other than with the lead suspect dead, the investigation has more or less come to a close." Dufort said. "I was coming to New York with the express purpose of seeing you Dr. Halloway. While I haven't made much headway on your case, I assure you I have been busy."

"I never doubted it." The conversation stopped while the stewardess brought out their meals including a bottle of champagne.

"To mark your wedding." Dufort said when they both eyeballed the bottle. Ross dug into her food with little regard for how she looked.

"Before we get into new information, I would like to stay on the topic of *The Hunter* for a moment" She asked. "There is something that happened today that has me wondering."

"What is that?"

"This Natasha, she knew who I was. She recognized my name from the guest list." Jack leaned forward.

"The Spartan even said Ross was getting a bit of a reputation amongst the Spartans."

"I'm sure she is. They have built their reputation on leaving no survivors. Dr. Halloway and yourself along with your father Si are the only people to upset their perfect record. Dr. Halloway has now managed it twice." Dufort said, cutting his chicken delicately.

"Three times, if you count today. My fear is that there might be a mark on me." Ross said.

"What if they start to look for revenge?" Jack added his own fear in.

"I can't say for sure that isn't the case, but I don't think so. We have no intel that would indicate that."

"Do you have decent intel on the Spartans?" Jack asked, thinking that if Dufort had decent intel on the Spartans then he would have them in custody.

"Not really, no." Jack's fleeting sense of hope

immediately vanished. "I wouldn't worry too much about it though. The Spartans don't seem to kill if they haven't been hired to, and as far as we can tell, there is no one interested in killing you."

"What about this international incident Ross may have caused?" Jack asked.

"The Spartan you…neutralized today was one that had been commissioned by the Slavakian government. We have suspected they had one for some time. People kept dying at convenient times in situations that benefited them. Today was their attempt at getting rid of PAUL. They have their own system, similar to PAUL, that is not nearly as reliable. They felt it would take the place of PAUL if they were able to cause enough of a scene. They aren't very happy to now have a finger pointing at them for the murders." Dufort waved his fork dismissively. "They are starting to beat their chest a little, it's nothing that can't be handled. I wouldn't worry about it."

"They shot two of the world's leading scientists and a security guard over a machine that has already been bought by most of the hospitals in first world countries?" Ross asked.

"Yes. They thought the disruption would make people step away from PAUL. Allowing their machine to come in." Ross threw down her fork.

"That is the dumbest thing I have ever heard."

"The deal was worth billions of dollars, Dr. Halloway. People have killed for less."

"How much does a Spartan cost?" Jack asked, trying to gage the Slavakian's anger.

"To make or to hire?" Dufort asked.

"Make…I guess."

"At the time of Natasha's purchase, it would set you back about half a million." Dufort said.

"Jeez, how much for a whole army of them?" Ross asked, referring to the fact that most of the Spartans had been created for the United States Military.

"Let's just say you could buy a small country for the same amount." The fact that Genetix was pulling in that amount of money for the Spartans raised more questions than answers. Ross knew nothing about how to make a human from scratch, but she knew the cost of running a facility that could create many at the same time would be incredibly expensive to run. They must be talking in the billions of dollars. "How did no one notice that amount of money missing from the defense fund?" Ross wondered aloud. Dufort laughed.

"Oh, believe me, that question has been asked several times over since the Spartans were discovered and Mother's records backed up the claims that the military had paid for their creation. It's all been kept very quiet, but there are some meetings happening that I would love to be a fly on the wall to." Dufort laughed to himself.

20

Ross's mouth was incredibly full of creamy mashed potatoes when Dufort opened a file on the laptop that showed a map of Europe. Hitting another button, red lines spread out over the map like a web.

"Since the discovery of the Spartans, I, along with others like me, have been combing through open murder cases making links to various Spartans. On my own, I have closed over twenty cases since their discovery almost two years ago. The last time I paid attention, there were over a hundred murders thought to have been committed by Spartans." Dufort hit another button and several pages of data flashed by.

"How many murders do you normally solve?" Jack asked.

"Myself, as an Interpol agent, usually helps in the resolution of about five a year." Dufort noted the disappointment in Jack's face at the relatively low number. "Keeping in mind that if Interpol is being brought in, something about the case is unusual or complicated." Jack nodded, but Dufort knew he still wasn't all that impressed.

"While I and others have been solving those problems, another team has been trolling through the information from the Genetex's records Mother left behind. The thought being that we can now figure out the true scope of the Spartan's crimes. There is some thought they were even used in other crimes like espionage and complicated thefts. However, up until now, all this information had been spread out over several different agencies. Four months ago, I started a task force with the purpose of being Spartan Headquarters. I want to know everything there is about Spartans, and compile the data in one area."

"Do you have any idea how long the Spartans have been active? Did no one notice an increase in really well executed crimes?" Ross asked.

"Yes, we did. Before I was moved to tracking down Spartans and closing cold murder cases, I was on a team trying to track down an extremely secretive, but well organized group specializing in guns for hire. We thought there was a gang out there specializing in assassinations. Understandably, genetically altered super humans had never occurred to us, but the professionalism with which they killed had been noticed." Dufort was slightly disappointed that neither of them asked about his task force, so he continued. "The task force is still in its early days, and what we have been doing for the most part is trying to track down exactly how many Spartans there are at the moment. Recently the focus has been shifted slightly to trying to figure out where the Spartans are located." Dufort brought up Rand's red dot map. " Up until recently, it was thought that there was one, maybe two headquarters. Some place where the Spartans went to lay low, organize and strategize." Dufort pointed out the gray areas in the sea of red dots. "Now we think there are several safe houses spread out all over the world. Using the information that the Spartans never hunt in their own backyard, combined with the increase in killings going into the pandemic, we think we will soon be able to find their nests." Ross was leaning in, studying the maps. Jack sat leaned back, wondering what the hell this all had to do with them.

"The pandemic might help with that if they have to stay in one place for a while." Jack offered.

"I had the same thought, but unfortunately, my teams are being called back home, so there goes that thought. We are going to have to rely on satellite imagery for a while."

"You don't know how many there are?" Ross asked.

"So far we have just over a hundred. With this new information, my dream of catching all of them at once is shattered."

"You are cross referencing the information from Genetix with what?" Ross asked. Dufort smiled. He found intelligent women much more fun to talk to.

"It turns out that Mother tattooed the Spartans. It's not a perfect process, but we are trolling through death and medical records looking for numeric tattoos. Thankfully, Mother also kept records of each Spartan's death, so in terms of backtracking, she saved us a lot of time and trouble. Another thing working in our favor is the fact that they can not reproduce. So there is no threat of new Spartans popping up."

"They can't?" Jack asked.

"Mother wanted the money for her creation. You wanted a Spartan, you were going to have to pay for it. No getting two Spartans and hoping for the best. We are still learning a great deal about what went into the Spartans, what would help us more than anything would be to get a live one."

"You want DNA. Can't you get it from a recently deceased one?" Ross didn't want to mention the one she had killed specifically. Dufort raised his eyebrows and said, "Yes. And we do have a small collection of DNA from deceased Spartans. What I would love more than anything is to talk to one. Their perspective on things really. All the information we have is rather one sided."

"Please tell me you aren't trying to create your own Spartan." Ross said. The science used to create them in the first place was extremely unethical and had been banned in most countries. Genetix had been flying under the radar with the Spartans, and Mother had broken every rule in the book. A fact Mother had been perfectly aware of and more than a little proud of. Dufort looked shocked at her suggestion. "Of course we aren't looking to make our own. Why would you think that?"

"Surely you would have enough information from Mother's notes. In talking with one, you would get a lot of information about their training and all that went into developing their skills." Ross pointed out, ignoring for the time being that Dufort had not answered her question.

"I have a team of scientists pouring over her very detailed notes. Most agree that Mother was careful to leave out a few key steps as to make the process impossible for anyone else to replicate." Dufort said. Ross stopped to think about that.

"That's not what we do. We are trained to make our work repeatable. Why would she do that? That means that only she knew how to create a Spartan."

"There is some indication that her co-creator, Father, was the actual genius behind the technology. Mother was careful to remove his name from most of the notes and replace it with her own in an attempt to keep him in the shadows. The only reason we suspected anything was because Father told us himself in interviews after everything exploded. Mother was very careful, very methodical, but there might be some truth to the fact that she didn't want other people to be able to replicate their work." Dufort shrugged, "Whether that was for charitable reasons or control issues, we may never know." Ross was finding it harder and harder to understand this Mother person. She seemed to have burst through scientific norms and done this great but terrible thing. Made sure she got all the credit for it, and also made sure that it could never be done again. Why?

"Has your tech team checked to see if any of the information on her thumb drive had been tampered with? Maybe encrypted?" Ross asked. A crease developed between Dufort's eyebrows.

"They are still working on it. Should they be looking for something?"

"Mother was obviously a scientist at the top of her game. All indications were she was going to show off what she and Genetix could do. The Ikan Hui resort was supposed to be their showpiece. I think Mother had everything on that thumb drive, down to the last detail. I bet if you look back through it, you will find she altered it soon before she died. I think Mother found her conscience at the last minute."

"You think she purposefully made it to where the Spartans couldn't be created again?" Jack asked.

"I do. If I had to guess, she made the changes right before she handed it over. Mother would have known better than anyone what they were, she hadn't created them to be out in the world. They had been created for a very specific purpose that they were then not used for. I think Mother sabotaged the records before she killed herself. I also think she wouldn't have been able to let go of her work completely. The encrypted bit may be the missing pieces." Dufort blinked hard, and then his eyes lit up.

"Part of the Spartan's demands were that she hand over all the records proving their creation. You think she destroyed evidence before she handed it over so that it would satisfy the Spartans, but make it impossible for anyone to duplicate her work?"

"I think that is exactly what she did." Ross answered.

"Why encrypt it?" Dufort asked. "Gentix was caught. There must have been no doubt in her mind that they would be shut down. That she and anyone else involved would be sent to prison, their own work used as evidence against them." Ross rolled her eyes.

"Mother and Father figured out a way to custom make humans. I don't know a lot about genetics, but I do know that everything is connected, so for her to figure out a way to take away certain things and add other things without completely destroying what was needed to create a viable human being would require absolutely no moral scruples, because there are going to be a lot of mistakes. It would have taken careful planning, methodical procedures, and an attention to detail that is almost inhuman. And they did it. They did it several times over. Not only did they create the Spartans, but they saw to their education and training. Mother and Father would have known all the pitfalls, the genetic trials and errors. It had to take years to create a high-functioning Spartan. Who funded all that work? How did they keep it secret all those years? If you spend that much time, energy and brain power working on something so impossibly complicated, and it works beyond your wildest dreams, are you going to throw it all away? Never tell anyone how you did it? Even at the threat of death? Or are you going to hide it?" Dufort blinked. Everyone had thought Mother and Father destroyed the evidence in the name of self-preservation, but now it seemed so obvious. "Excuse me, I have to go make a call."

21

"Do you really think that's what happened?" Jack asked. Fascinated at what Ross had possibly revealed. In the past twelve hours, Ross had taken down a Spartan like she had been born to do it, and now had cracked open a top secret MI6 mission. Was there nothing the woman couldn't do?

"It makes sense. Say the Spartans had been a success instead of the failure they were. Mother had every reason to think that other countries would want their own Spartans. If the Spartans had gone on to fight in America's wars, they would have eventually needed more of them. She and this Father person would have needed very precise records to be able to repeat their work. It doesn't make sense that she would leave gaps in the notes and rely on her own memory or the memory of someone else to repeat what had to be a very precise formula."

"But they were a failure, they were sent back."

"They were a failure in that the United States Government no longer wanted them. In terms of achieving what she had sent out to do, Mother succeeded. Also, the woman obviously wasn't stupid. She would have known as well as anyone that even if the U.S. military didn't want the Spartans, there were other governments who would. The Spartans were only a failure if you are looking at it from a sales point of view."

Ross's phone rang. "Shit, it's Sam."

"Ross, you didn't post those pictures of us getting on the plane?"

"I'm not stupid Jack. I did send them to Sam, though."

"What the hell for?"

"I wanted to share it with someone." Ross got up and went to the back of the plane where she was sure to get an ear full.

"Hello?"

"Those better be fake pictures, Ross. You are getting married in three days. You are supposed to be here tonight. I have five people coming to my house for a bachelorette party in two hours."

"Sam, turn on the news."

"Don't tell me what to do, Ross, you knew I was planning this thing for you. You can't even call me and tell me to cancel?"

"Just turn the news on, Sam. Please." There was muttered cussing while Sam did what she had been told.

"What exactly.......Ross? Where was your thing today?" Ross could hear the announcer in the background. "A Spartan! Ross, are you okay?" Sam's tone changed from anger to fear.

"I'm fine, babe. I'll tell you all about it when I get there. Inspector Dufort met us in New York, and right now we are on our way to parts unknown for some secret he wants to show us."

"But you're okay? Jack's alright too?" Sam needed more

assurance.

"I sent you the picture of us in front of the plane right? We are fine."

"What does Dufort want with you guys? Did you tell him you are getting married?"

"I have no idea what he wants with us. He's started some task force to help track Spartans and it has to do with that. Of course, I told him we were getting married."

"Ross, you know they have shut down all the airports? I hope Dufort has already figured out a way to get you home." Sam's voice was calm, but Ross knew not to be fooled. Ross could get away with a lot when it came to Sam. More than almost any other human being on the planet. But if Ross missed her own wedding, Sam would be first in line to kill her, and Ross's mother would dig the grave. Ross had been surprised to find out that she had apparently been making them wait a long time for the joy of her getting married. A fact that had baffled her.

"He said we have special clearance."

"What does that mean?"

"I don't know for sure, but he is working for MI6, so I'm sure it will be fine."

"Ross, if for one second I thought you had done any of this on purpose…"

"Sam, for Christ sake." Now it was Ross's turn to sound indignant. "If I didn't want to get married, I would just say so. I wouldn't arrange for a Spartan to crash an important event. I certainly wouldn't have chosen to watch it kill three people, including two of the world's top scientists. And an innocent security guard! Oh, and then call Dufort away from whatever much more important thing he was doing to whisk me away to parts unknown just so I wouldn't have to get married." Ross took a deep breath and then let out the words she had been wanting to say since she picked up the phone. "I killed someone today, Sam." Ross blurted out. "I killed the Spartan, apparently her name was Natasha, and she was created for Slovakia. And while Dufort doesn't seem worried about it, I might have caused a slight international incident there, not to mention I KILLED SOMEONE. I know we all hate Spartans, but I still ended the life of something that was living, and according to Jack, I did it rather well, which is also giving me mixed feelings." Rambled off almost as one word. Jack turned to look at her and saw her arms flying. Jack wasn't sure he had ever seen Ross so animated.

"You shot her? Ross, did you just tell me you killed someone?" Sam's voice was full of questions and concerns.

"Yes, I did. I got mad. It seems like anytime I leave anywhere, there is another fucking Spartan there. She shot the two Nobel Prize winners for advances in chemistry this year, which pissed me off. Then she shot at Jack and I lost it. I blinded her with a fire extinguisher and took the gun off the dead security guard, and I shot her twice in the legs. And then when she raised her gun again, I shot her in the head. Right between the eyes." Ross could see the Spartan looking at her now in her mind's eye.

"Wow. I mean…I've made you mad before, but damn!" Sam said, with an attempt at levity.

"It's not funny Sam. I feel terrible about it."

"Ross. She would have killed you." Sam tried to soothe her. "She would have killed Jack too. You understand that, right?"

"She was out of bullets. I didn't know that at the time, but she was out of bullets. That fact remains that there is one less heart beating on the planet, and it's because I killed it." Ross was crying. There was a pause while Sam thought of what to say.

"Ross, I need you to listen to me." It was the same voice Sam had used countless times to soothe Ross over the years. It had an immediate effect. "You may have stopped her heart from beating, but she raised a gun, honey. Because you acted the way you did, you may have saved your life and Jack's. You didn't know the gun was empty. Not to mention the people that were going to be killed by that Spartan in the future." There were big sobs coming out of Ross now. "I know you, this isn't the life you imagined for yourself, but it sounds like you handled things beautifully."

"Jack thinks I handled it a little too well."

"You know, I'm totally fine with Jack being just a little scared of you." Ross laughed while she wiped away the tears. "You really need to stop getting yourself in these situations. My heart can't take it. I'm going to have to ask your mother for one of her pills." Sam sniffed her own tears away on the other end of the phone.

"Save one for me."

"Get your ass home, and you can get it yourself. The woman is like a pharmacy. Anything you want, she's got it in her purse." Ross chuckled. "So you have no idea where you are headed?"

"Some secret place in England."

"Ross, they've shut England down. No flights. No trains. No buses. They've sent everyone home. You're only allowed out if there is an emergency. Or you have to walk your dog." Ross's heart sank.

"We'll get home, Sam. Don't worry. Somehow or some

way, we will get home."

"Don't be too long. I've waited just over six months to see you honey, I can't hold out much longer." Ross hung up with Sam. Ross took a deep breath before walking back to the guys who were doing a poor job of acting like they hadn't heard every word she had said.

"Everything okay?" Dufort asked.

"Sam says they've just closed England." It sounds ridiculous to say it like that. As if England had a huge door on its border that had now been shut and locked. She wasn't sure how else to say it. "There is no transport. People aren't allowed out unless there is an emergency.....or to walk the dog."

"I know, I have been informed." Ross leaned over the table and looked Dufort in the eyes.

"I am getting married..... in Boston..... in three days. If I am not there, I will not be responsible for my actions."

Ross didn't see Jack sit up a little straighter and smile at her when she said this. She did feel his hand on her thigh under the table.

"I will get you home, Dr. Halloway." Though he would not admit it even under torture, Dufort 'hoped' he could get them home. He was *pretty* sure he could get them home. *Fairly* sure.

22

After driving past Tower Bridge and the Tower of London just so they could say they had seen them, the trio hopped on the motorway and headed out of London. The lights of the city faded, and soon there were large dark swathes of landscape on either side of the car.

"It's seven o'clock local time. We should get there at about nine. I've called to let them know we are coming and asked if we can make use of the canteen as well." Dufort told them. Ross noticed he had been texting on his phone nearly nonstop. Not all of it had been business judging by the smile on his usually stern face. She had wanted to comment that wearing his mask hanging loose from one ear didn't actually count as wearing it, but left it for the time being. She and Jack were both wearing theirs.

"Can you tell us yet where we are going?" Ross asked. Like Jack, she was getting less amused the longer this went on.

"I thought you had already figured it out?" Dufort said, lifting an eyebrow.

"I can make a guess, but I have no way of knowing if I'm

right." Ross replied.

"You could wait and find out." Dufort suggested.

"You could tell me before I scream my head off in frustration." Ross threatened, enjoying the banter more than she would ever admit.

"We are heading to Porton Downs." Dufort confirmed. Ross elbowed Jack in the ribs with a smile.

"I knew it. I told you." Ross said, pleased with herself.

"Why?" was Jack's unimpressed answer.

"I could tell you, but to be honest, it will make more sense when we get there. I have made accommodations for you to get some rest after I show you around."

"When do we get to go home?" Jack asked.

"That very much depends." Dufort said. Jack sized the man up. Jack assumed Dufort had some defense training, and he had learned a long time ago to never fight someone smaller than him. They never fight fair, but even with that, Jack was pretty sure he could ring Dufort's bells.

"You still haven't told us what kind of help you want from Ross." Jack pointed out. The sick feeling was still in his stomach. If anything, it had gotten worse the farther away from Boston they had gotten.

"I understand your impatience. Everything will be clear soon." Dufort went back to texting on his phone, completely aware that Jack was boring a hole through the top of his head. The car fell into silence as a scenic village passed them in the dark. Medieval looking buildings went by on either side of the street before they hit the countryside again. Every once in a while, Ross could make out a sheep standing in the field. It was probably lovely in the daytime.

The darkness of the early evening mixed with the rain and the chaos of the day, Jack and Ross were soon leaning on each other, their eyes closing. Jack was nice and warm as Ross nuzzled in. She wasn't sure how long she had been asleep when she was awakened by the car coming to a stop. The guard shack immediately outside her car door informed her that they had arrived at Port Downs. Military Research Facility. The person at the gate was military and heavily armed. They were waved through after a brief conversation.

"Welcome to Porton Downs." Dufort said. "Where some of the world's leading science is being done in the name of defense."

"They are working with nerve agents here, aren't they?" Ross asked.

"Amongst other things, yes. They have been doing a lot of work to reverse the effects of Novichok." Ross knew the name immediately. It was the nerve agent that had been used to kill Dr. Lillian Petrov and her family. They looked in silence as the car pulled forward and bland red brick buildings passed by one after the other. Even without the guard shack, Ross would have known she was in a military base. The buildings were all carbon copies of one another. After a few minutes, they pulled up to a white-washed brick building that was much larger than the others. Ross smiled. "This is the lab." Ross stated.

"How did you know that?" Dufort said, since it was classified.

"Those are extra shafts for independent ventilation. Those hoses over there are yellow, green, and red because of the various chemicals they carry. In more modern buildings, you have them running on the inside, but I'm guessing from the age of the buildings around here, they are retrofitted to work." Jack and Dufort looked at her in amazement and slight annoyance.

"Leave your bags, I'll have someone come and get them." Dufort said, though he retrieved his backpack. Ross looked down at her beautiful pants suit and gave a slight grimace at how many wrinkles covered it. They were unlikely to see anyone else at this time of night, but she looked almost as tired as she felt. She undid the jacket buttons revealing the blouse she had on underneath and pulled the tie out of her fashionable side ponytail, using her fingers to gather her hair into a messy bun. Feeling slightly more like herself, Ross asked, "Is there somewhere we can get a cup of coffee? I'm starting to feel the journey."

"I'm sure we can stop along the way and get you something, it will be rather basic I'm afraid." Dufort answered, he wouldn't mind a coffee himself.

"She's been stuck on a boat with my father, Inspector. You don't get much more basic than that." Jack said, thinking of the time he saw his father chewing the leftover sludge at the bottom of the pot. They entered the building to an almost blindingly bright light. Their shoes announced their presence on the polished white floors as they walked down one white hallway after another. Ross hardly knew where she was until she smelled food. Dufort led the way to the coffee machine of the canteen where they all gained the strength to move on.

"I don't suppose we could stop for a bite?" Jack asked.

"We are pressed for time, I'm afraid, I promise to bring you back when we are finished. The lab is just upstairs."

Ross's ears perked up at the mention of a lab. They continued to walk down the white hallways, Dufort scanning his ID card every time they opened a door. He was enjoying himself a little too much. Dufort knew they were losing patience with him. He also knew the wait would be worth it. "Since defense is the main goal of Porton Downs and it already holds some of the world's best scientists, I thought it would be a great location to base my task force."

"Why do you need scientists to track down Spartans?" Ross asked.

"That is a good question, Dr. Halloway." Ross waited, but that was all Dufort said. He pushed the button for the elevator to open, but didn't answer her question. With another swipe of his card, Dufort led them into another room. This room was very different. The bright lights were gone, dimmed lights with computers along the walls. A giant screen dominating the wall in front of them. Pages of data flipping across it. Dufort went over to the two people who were working, and whatever he said, they left the room. Ross's attention was grabbed by microscopes on a few of the tables. "A Trinocular Koehler 2500. Impressive. Are you doing work on a cellular level?" Ross asked. Jack smiled. So did Dufort.

"You, once again, have gotten ahead of me Dr. Halloway. We are." He pushed a button on one of the computers. A double helix came up on screen with a bunch of other stuff Jack didn't understand.

"This is the genetic profile of the Spartan you met today. We have samples from only three other Spartans to compare it to. Do you notice something?" Dufort hit a button and lined the genetic profiles of each Spartan on the screen.

"Natasha's varies more strongly than the other two." Ross said. She wasn't a geneticist, but she could read data. "Why are you running their genetic profiles?" Ross asked. It wasn't unusual to store genetic data, but not to run their profiles. For one awful moment, Ross thought Dufort might be on the wrong side of things. What if she had been helping someone who didn't want to get rid of the Spartans, but wanted to make more of them? She stepped back until she felt Jack behind her. Jack put a protective arm around her. His gut was telling him to get the hell out of there, and he would take any excuse to do just that.

"Before I tell you, I want you to promise that this conversation goes no further. I can't make you. This is not official in any way, and therefore, has not been classified. I am going to have to trust you." Jack and Ross exchanged looks and shrugged.

"You can't create new ones." Ross blurted out. Dufort looked at her with a blank stare. "For one thing, there are the ethics. It is very clear that no good can come from it. Not to mention these cells have been manipulated. Who knows what will happen to them if you manipulate them further."

"Dr. Halloway, I have no intention of making more Spartans." Dufort said this like it was obvious.

"Then what are you doing running genetic profiles on them?"

"I had a whole speech worked out. I should have known better." Dufort said, in frustration. "I want to use their genetic profiles so that we can repurpose the remaining Spartans."

"Repurpose?"

"Yes, use them for something else." Dufort clarified.

<h1 style="text-align:center">23</h1>

"What are you on about man?" Jack said. "Repurpose them for what exactly?"

"Hear me out." Dufort said, pulling out chairs for them. Jack and Ross sat down. "Spartan's were created so that they felt no emotion, and little pain. They were raised as killers. Literally taught various ways of killing people. Specializing in different methods. Killing is all they know. But what if Spartans didn't kill?"

"Then they would just be weird emotionless people." Jack offered. "They would still feel less emotion and less pain." Ross said.

"Exactly!" Dufort said, more animated than they had ever seen him. "Fear clouds the judgment. The fear of pain and death is what holds us back in dangerous situations."

"Yes, that's why the military wanted them made that way." Ross said, wondering where exactly this was going.

"Yes! We know through Mother's records that the reasons the military was looking for something like a Spartan was because of the cost of loss. For every soldier killed, there is a family that had to be informed and supported. Likewise, if a soldier is returned home injured either physically or mentally, there is a cost to that as well. In most militaries of developed countries, continued medical support after retirement costs billions."

"Get to the point, Dufort." Jack said, completely losing patience.

"How many firefighters are there in the world? Coast guard? Think of the most daring rescues you can. Who is doing them?"

"People." Ross said, shrugging her shoulders.

"People. People who have families at home, families who will mourn their death. People who will need financial help if they get badly burned or otherwise injured in the line of duty. But what if they don't have to?"

"Inspector, there are millions of firefighters and other rescue workers throughout the world. You just said there are about a hundred Spartans. You would have to make more on an epic scale to replace them and that is incredibly illegal." Ross pointed out. "Not to mention immoral."

"You could remake them the old fashioned way." Jack said, half grinning. "You know, make it to where they can reproduce."

"We wouldn't have to make more." Dufort leaned forward, growing more animated. "I have no desire to get rid of firefighters and police. But what we could have is an elite rescue team that could be sent out to assist existing crews. Imagine how much help they could be in the fires in Australia right now. Going into the places people wouldn't because it's too dangerous."

"Because the Spartans are known for playing well with others." Jack pointed out.

"I did think about that. They were disbanded for

freaking out their fellow soldiers. I am hoping that by keeping them in their own groups and re-educating them, we can avoid problems."

"What are you going to do when they kill a person instead of rescuing them because they are too injured to be worth saving?" Ross stated. "Humans can be sentimental creatures, but we have achieved great things simply by trying rather than giving up." Dufort had thought about this problem since the idea had occurred to him. It had been one of the reasons sighted for sending the Spartans back. Several times they had shot their fellow soldier because they were too injured to survive, or their injury compromised the mission.

"Do you think adding some emotions back in would help with that?" Dufort asked, urgently.

"I have no idea, I'm not a geneticist."

"The problem is, there isn't a geneticist out there I trust." He was looking at Ross without blinking.

"Do you want me to recommend one? I can ask around." Ross asked, looking at Jack in confusion.

"You can hire whoever you want." Dufort answered, smiling. Ross's eyebrows shot into her hairline.

"What?" Jack leaned forward more. "What are you talking about, mate?"

"I want you to look over the lab that would be in charge of this project. In short, Dr. Halloway, I have asked you here to join my task force as head scientist in charge of research and development. You would have a small staff to assist you. Because of the popularity of the Spartans at the moment, I was able to get funding without even having to ask. I can offer you a considerable salary and a decent budget for whatever equipment you would need for the lab. The only detractor being that you would have to live on base and you could never tell anyone what you are doing."

"How much are we talking?" Jack asked. Ross hadn't even got that far, she was still hung up on having her own lab. Even if it was in a subject she knew little about. Dufort typed a number into his phone and slid it across to Jack.

"Jesus!" Jack said. Ross looked down at it and was amazed.

"This is more than I earned in the past four years combined." She stated.

"You would be in charge of a top secret lab, Dr. Halloway with all the rights and inconveniences that go with that. The salary reflects what we expect."

"I thought you said this didn't have a classification yet? How is it top secret?" Ross asked.

"It doesn't, but if it becomes official, I expect it will be very classified." Dufort answered, avoiding looking at Jack.

"What about Jack?"

"He would be housed here as well, as a spouse."

"And do what?" Jack said. There would certainly be no boating happening in this landlocked military base. "Salary and all that aside. What happens once the Spartans figure out what you are doing?" Jack added.

"There is no reason to think the Spartans will do anything when they find out what we are doing. The Spartans kill for money, Jack. That is all."

"Any animal will strike out if they are cornered." Jack informed him.

"You plan on getting DNA samples from all the Spartans? And then what, retraining them?" Dufort suspected Dr. Halloway might ask this question. Mother had used conditioning to train her murderers. There was not a genetic sequence she could use that would erase their ability to shoot a gun with pinpoint accuracy. Simple enough really. The military had some very effective ways of doing such things, but most people found them distasteful. Ross did not wait for his response.

"Inspector, you are talking about gathering all the Spartans together, extracting their DNA, and then holding onto them while figuring out how to change them from killers to cuddlers. This kind of work could take a lifetime. Not to mention Spartans have been trained to escape. You would have to get them to agree to stay for this project." Ross spelled it out for him.

"You don't think they could be persuaded? They were designed to follow orders. I've also thought about trying to raise funds to pay them to stay put, though I'm less optimistic about that happening." Dufort said.

"Inspector, has it occurred to anyone that the Spartans aren't looking for another master? That they prefer the life they are leading now?" Jack said, his temper was getting shorter by the minute.

"According to Mother's records, they were designed to follow orders." Dufort defended himself.

"No offense mate, but the last time I saw one for any length of time, they seemed to be making a point of destroying their creator. They have been raking in the money, apparently bumping off the enemies of the rich. I'm not sure they are going to be easily convinced to put down their arms, come lock themselves in here for however long it takes you to figure out how to make them not want to kill people. Ross says it could take a lifetime. Hell, by the time you figure it out, these guys could be too old to be of any use for what you are talking about." Jack said.

"Inspector, while what you are saying in theory is doable, the time frame we have to do it in is somewhat unrealistic." Ross said basically what Jack said, but more politely. "Jack is right. The average working life of a firefighter is thirty years, give or take. That's going from twenties to fifties. The Spartans are already into their thirties. You are expecting someone to completely reverse their purpose in a few years. Furthermore, to do what you are asking, they are going to have to figure out how to effectively and humanely do what you are asking. That alone might take years. It just isn't possible."

"MI6 isn't extremely concerned with how humanely it is done." Dufort said, with as much empathy as he could. Ross's eyes got big as she realized what he was saying.

"They have basic human rights inspector."

"Actually, I think you will find, they don't." Dufort informed her. Ross sat back deflated.

"What do you mean?"

"Spartans may look human, but according to the letter of the law, they aren't."

"Then what the hell are they?"

"The law sees them more as robots really." Ross stood up and crossed her arms over her chest.

"And so you think that gives you the right to do whatever the hell you want with them?" Now Dufort was enjoying himself more than he knew he should.

"There is a long history of science doing unsavory things to better humanity." He responded. Jack thought Ross was going to crawl over the table. She was vibrating with anger.

"And so you plan to do the same thing? Follow in the footsteps of Mengele, and say 'it doesn't matter, it's all for humanity'? Listen here, you will never benefit humanity by pretending a certain portion of it isn't human. I should warn you, Inspector Dufort, if you go ahead with your project in this way, I will take back my promise. I will not only refuse to join your task force, I will tell the world what you are trying to do and how you plan on doing it."

"It sounds like you are turning me down."

"You bet your sweet ass I am." Ross said, Jack left a breath out he didn't know he had been holding in. Dufort leaned back in his chair and crossed his legs.

"If you disprove so strongly, how would you do it Dr. Halloway?" Ross sat down as well.

"Honestly Inspector, I wouldn't. Let's put aside the fact that you are talking about inhumane scientific practices to get what you want. The logistics of it are prohibitive on their own."

"Such as?"

"Costs for one. I would imagine Mother had the entire financial backing of Genetix."

"Yes, we have found that the profits from other smaller projects were fed into the start up of the Spartan project."

"It will take millions of dollars to simply get the technology and staff to make this possible. That's millions with an 's'. Hundreds of millions. Making a human is a very delicate process, you will have to have people working around the clock. Then, even after you have successfully managed to create another Spartan, you will have to teach them and train them. This project would take decades before you saw any return, and that's if everything goes to plan. The more Spartans you make, the more money it will take. Unlike Mother, who was selling them off, you will have no return on your investment."

"And there is no other way that wouldn't cost millions?"

"You could either capture all of the Spartans and make it to where they could reproduce and convince them to let you train their children..."

"Or....?"

"Or, and this is also unethical, find the sequence of genes that Mother altered in the Spartans to remove emotions and reduce the feeling of pain and apply it to humans, voluntarily of course."

"All of those situations seem just as unlikely as the previous one." Dufort said.

"Which is why I said I wouldn't bother." Ross said, crossing her arms over her chest. Dufort let out a breath of defeat and then slapped his hands on his lap.

"You will forgive me, Dr. Halloway, Jack. The Spartans are a scientific breakthrough the world hasn't seen in my lifetime. It seems such a waste to let it be negative instead of turning it into a positive." Dufort let out another breath. Ross could see where he was coming from. The Spartans abilities could be useful if they had been conditioned another way. "I suppose things will have to stay the way they are. In the meantime, the task force will continue its work of tracing every Spartan still alive. We are still going to get DNA from those we capture. Are you sure you won't join and head up the lab?"

"I told you, the whole thing is a waste of time." Dufort shrugged.

"Then waste it. Dr. Halloway, even if we never achieve our goals in this lifetime, would it not further research for future generations? You know as well as I do the Spartans have proven that, despite science as a whole agreeing that this type of genetic manipulation is unethical, there are people out there doing it. Would it not be in the human race's best interest to make sure we have a better answer when the inevitable happens?" Ross twirled her hair. "In the meantime you would be getting paid very well. Room and board covered. Do this for a few years and you and Jack could get a boat and sail around the world without worrying about money." Ross and Jack exchanged looks. It was tempting. If Ross did have such a strong moral compass, she would do it in an instant.

"Thank you, but no." Jack nodded that she had made the right decision. Dufort shrugged his shoulders again.

"I am sorry then, it seems like this was a failed mission. I hope you will understand why I had to bring you out here though. This wasn't exactly a conversation we could have in a neighborhood coffee shop. Also, I wanted you to see the set up we have here. If you were going to make such a big decision, you should see what it's all about." They put their chairs back where they had found them. "The least I can do is get you something to eat. Follow me and we will see what the canteen has to offer. After that I will let you get some rest while I organize getting you home tomorrow."

"Inspector, I was going to be getting married regardless of whether I said yes or not. What was your plan if I had agreed?" Dufort led them out of the room and back into the glaring white hallway.

"Well, I was going to fly you home, and then after you had organized your things, I would have flown you back where you would have to lockdown with the rest of us." Nothing Dufort had just said made Ross sorry about her answer. Being locked down in this whitewashed government facility (even with its secrets and technology) seemed like a different kind of hell for Ross.

24

Dufort looked at his watch and then said, "Dr. Halloway, would you mind terribly if I introduce you to a fan of yours?"

"A fan?"

"Yes, she is a biochemist working on reverse engineering Novichok. We have struck up a bit of a friendship since I started working here on the task force, and I may have mentioned that I was going to try and get you to join our team. She asked if I could introduce you if you came here. Her lab is just down here, do you mind?"

"Of course not." Ross said, trying to smooth out the wrinkles in her clothes. Ross got a thrill when other scientists knew who she was. Ross looked at Jack and raised her eyebrows. "A fan."

"I heard." He responded.

"Wonderful." Dufort said, giving one of his grins that made Ross think he was up to something.

"Are you going to stay all night?" The technician asked Dr. Kuzlow as she passed.

"I could ask you the same thing. It's nearly eleven." Dr. Kuzlow commented.

"I just have to make sure these are put away properly and then I'm going to head out." The technician commented.

"I won't be far behind you. Inspector Dufort wanted to speak with me about something, I'm just killing time until he gets here." Dr. Kuzlow wanted to go over her findings one more time. Dufort had texted her, she knew he and her surprise were in the building. While she was intrigued that Dufort would even bother to get her a gift, much less a surprise, what she was really interested in was picking Dufort's brain about the virology work being done in the other parts of the building. She had been trying to investigate on her own, but hadn't gotten very far. The virology department was in a completely different part of the base, and security was tight. Try though she might, she could not keep the thoughts from spinning in her head. Mainly, that she was working for a lab that had created the virus killing people the world over.

Despite this, and the three cups of coffee she had consumed, her leg was hurting like hell. She was tired and she wanted to go to bed. Dufort better hurry. She looked at her watch again and promised Dufort ten more minutes and then she was going to her apartment and he and his surprise could wait until tomorrow.

The technician left, wishing her goodnight, and Dr. Kuzlow leaned against one of the desks in the almost dark lab to give her leg a rest. To kill the time, she went over the results of the recent testing again. They had been good.

They were very close to a major breakthrough. The security door buzzed again. "Did you forget something?" Dr. Kuzlow asked, not bothering to look up.

"Yes, I forgot to tell you how amazing you are." Dr. Kuzlow's head shot up to the voice of Dufort.

"Don't be ridiculous." She said, but she was smiling while she said it. "About time you showed up. I was about to hobble back to my apartment and call it a night where I would think of cutting remarks to say to you when I finally did see you."

"Sorry, I'm later than I wanted to be." Dufort stood close to her, but kept his hands in his pockets, knowing full well that there were cameras all over the lab. Cameras that thankfully could not see the way he was looking at her. Eyes that were made more obvious by the mask he was now wearing properly. Dufort was well aware of how frail she was. He had been out in the world and he would never forgive himself if he got her sick. She knew just as well as he did the cameras would pick up their every move. The way he looked at her was making her blush. Not something she was used to doing. "Are you ready for your surprise?" He asked in almost a whisper.

"Before we do that, I was wanting to ask you a few questions, actually." She said, turning serious again. It was alarming how quickly she could change her mood. "I thought about texting you, but I know you have your own things going on with the task force."

"What is it?" He could tell she was frazzled by something.

"It's ridiculous really, just this thing that kept me up all night last night."

"Nightmare?" She had nightmares when she first

arrived. Very realistic. It was the real reason he had given her his cell phone. Rarely sleeping himself, she would call him and they would talk until she fell asleep again.

" No, I haven't had one of those in a while, thankfully. I was talking to one of the lab techs in the canteen, and she said something and now I can't get the idea out of my head."

"Tell me, the suspense is killing me."

"Did Parid escape from this lab?" His eyes squinted.

"What?"

"The technician said there was a theory out there that Parid was man made. Then she insinuated that the lab here might have been the one to do it. I completely discounted it at the time, but the more I thought about it…."

"What makes you think I would know if it was created here or not?"

"I don't know. You probably don't. Nothing seems to leak out of this lab, believe me, I've been trying to poke holes in it all week."

"I am not connected to the lab working on viruses in the very least, but I will tell you what I do know. The lab is working on curing some of the world's worst diseases, not creating them. I know they actually applied for a national grant to work on coming up with a vaccine for Parid. Now, I'm sure an argument might be made that it would be a great way to cover up a mistake."

"I know, but what if in trying to cure one, they made another one by accident?" That particular thought was the one that had lodged in her head and kept her from sleep.

"Is that even possible?" Dufort asked.

"I don't know. I know as much as the next biologist about viruses, which is apparently enough to argue yourself into circles." Dufort took a step towards her, though careful to make sure nothing looked too cozy. "Listen, you work for the good guys here. Not that we don't make mistakes, but usually it's with the best of intentions. Not to mention, as you found out, nothing gets out of this place." Dr. Kuzlow let out a deep breath. "So you don't know?"

"No, and I have no way of finding out, to be perfectly honest. However, I would tell you if I thought it was a possibility, and I don't think it's a possibility." She doubted it would make the strange dreams stop, but it was something. "Now, would you like to meet some people?" Dufort changed the subject.

"It's late Louis." Kuzlow said, suddenly feeling all those missed hours of sleep.

" I know, and next door is one of the world's leading scientists. Or I wouldn't bother you. She's very eager to talk to you."

"Who is it?"

"Dr. Halloway." Dufort said, with a sly grin on his face. Her reaction was exactly what he had hoped. Dr. Kuzlow's face went still, and then her mouth opened, but no words came out.

"She's here?"

"In the next room."

"I wish you would have told me, I look a mess. I've been in the lab since nine this morning."

"I don't think she's going to care what you look like. But if it helps, she was in a shooting this morning and then thrown onto a plane to come here. So, she's not exactly the freshest daisy herself."

"A shooting? Is she alright?" Dufort was already leading

her out of the room.

"It's Dr. Halloway, of course she's alright."

"You could have warned me, Louis." Dufort let out a laugh and said, "If I had told you, it wouldn't be a surprise, would it?" Dr. Kuzlow grabbed his arm, holding him back from opening the door that separated them.

"What if this doesn't go well?" He had never seen her look so worried. Placing a hand over hers he said, "Then it will all be my fault, but it's going to be fine, you'll see."

The door opened and Dufort came through one of the secure doors. "Dr. Halloway, Jack, I would like you to meet Dr. Kozlow." Dr. Kozlow stepped through the doorway, lifting her head to meet Ross's eyes. Ross's mouth fell in shock.

"What the Hell?"

"Bloody Hell." Jack said. Ross's eyes worked very hard at convincing herself she was seeing what she was seeing while her brain argued vehemently that it was simply impossible. Dufort watched with pleasure the confusion on both of their faces. Dr. Kuzlow stood some distance away in silence, not sure what to do. Finally, Ross whispered, "Lillian, honey……. how?" Lillian smiled and stepped forward as fast as her cane would allow.

"Hello Ross. How have you been?" Ross swallowed her up in a hug.

"I thought you were dead? Oh my God. I thought you were dead." Ross cried and wrapped Lillian in her arms. Though still in shock, Ross did register that Lillian was thinner than the last time she had hugged her. Overall she seemed frail.

"I am dead in many ways." Lillian said, wiping the tears aways. She was very much enjoying seeing familiar faces.

More than she thought she would.

"I don't understand." Ross said.

"While we are in this room, it is okay to call her Lillian or Dr. Petrov. Once we leave, she is Dr. Lillian Kuzlow. It is very important that no one knows. Do you understand?" Dufort said, going very serious.

"How though? With the Novichok?" Ross looked at her cane. Lillian was leaning heavily on it. It wasn't just for show. Jack saw it too, and grabbed a chair for her to sit.

"Thank you." Lillian sat down. "What you saw on the news was true, to a point. I got a smaller dose than my father. The Novichok had been sprayed on the gate of my house, they found out later. My father held it open for me when we left that day. He got a direct hit. By the time we got to the park five minutes later, it was already taking effect. I knew what it was immediately." Ross sat on top of a table and listened. Jack leaned next to her, his hands in his pockets. "My father collapsed onto the park bench. I knew what it was, but I didn't even think. I touched him to get his pulse. As you know, you only have minutes. I knew there was nothing I could do."

"You got a lesser dose when you touched him." Ross said, Lillian nodded.

"Your mother?" Ross asked.

"My mother also got it from the gate. After we left, she saw a neighbor walk by. She touched it when she opened it to give them some soup. I was told she collapsed just inside the door." Lillian's face contorted in the way it does when you are trying not to cry. "My biggest regret is that she died alone and so far from home." There was a pause while Lillian regained control, then she continued. "I was weakened by my dose. I probably would have died if it hadn't been for the quick response of the medical team. Inspector Dufort found me in the hospital a few days later. I was weak as a kitten, not sure if I was going to live and not really caring. He suggested that if the Russian government wanted me dead so badly, why disappoint them? For a moment, I thought he was going to put a pillow over my head." Lillian smiled slightly. "What he offered instead was to let them think I had died. The hospital reported me dead. A death certificate was issued. Considering I had already lost everything, it seemed silly not to take him up on the offer. As soon as I left the hospital, I was Dr. Lillian Kuzlow. A new background was created for me and Louis brought me here. I have been working on Novichok ever since."

"That's amazing Lillian. That is right in your line of work, what a way to fight back. " Ross said.

"For the most part, I think my cells have helped more than my mind, but it has been good to be a part of the research."

"You are studying your own cells as part of your research?" Ross asked. "Brilliant."

"Most of the information we have as to how Novichok works is from smuggled out information originating at the lab where it was created. For obvious reasons, samples of cells after they have been exposed to Novichok are rather thin on the ground. We have been able to gain a lot of information about lasting effects on the cells after Novichok has been used from my cells."

"With the Russian President dead, do you still need to be in hiding?" Jack asked. Lillian hadn't looked that great the last time he had seen her. Having recently been shot in the stomach. She didn't look much better now. Jack had no idea how old Lillian was, she might be around Ross's age, but she looked at least a decade older at the moment. The woman's wrists looked like they would snap like a twig.

"The truth of the matter is, we don't know if the new president intends on continuing in the same vein as the previous administration. There are still people who were loyal to the previous president who are more than willing to carry out his vendetta. Until we are sure, it is best to lay low." Dufort answered. "There may be a day when Dr. Lillian Patrov can walk the earth again, but not right now."

"Part of me rather likes the fact that I am someone else. It's a new start. I can finally leave my past behind me." They sat in silence for a moment before Lillian said, "You two must be starving. Let's go get something to eat." With an effort, Lillian got up and she led the way out of the room and back into the overlit hallway. Ross was glad to see that the iron core that had been a huge part of Lillian's personality was still very much intact.

<h1 style="text-align:center">25</h1>

Lillian was feeling the late hour of the day. Jack offered her his arm, leaving Dufort and Ross to walk ahead down one of the endless corridors back to the canteen.

"Please forgive me, for before. I didn't mean to offend you. It just seems a waste to let the Spartans go to waste. I genuinely feel like we could use their skills for the betterment of humanity." Dufort said.

"I understand, but I feel like science should be used to propel us forward. I don't see using questionable methods to reconfigure how a Spartan thinks as doing that." Dufort waved his card and held it open for her to go through.

"I wouldn't have thought of it at all except there is a strong consensus amongst the military brass that we should simply hunt down the Spartans and kill them. Not that there is much chance of that really happening. We have been looking for them since we've known about them and haven't found one."

"Maybe you should use me as bait. They seem to follow me wherever I go." Ross said, jokingly. Dufort smiled. "That suggestion was also made." Ross looked at him in horror. "Don't worry, it didn't go very far. None of it went very far really, but it did get me thinking that the world as a whole might be able to use the Spartans in some way."

"Your thoughts are admirable. I'm afraid that there is not an ethical way of accomplishing what you want."

"Dr. Halloway, either we find a way of using the Spartans for good, or they go on killing. While the powers that be haven't figured out how to kill them just yet, I don't see the idea going away. Maybe now you understand why I was willing to bend the ethical playbook to make it work. The fact of the matter is the Spartans have made themselves very useful in areas of the world where killing your opponent is a legitimate way of running a campaign. While Natasha did a lot of good by killing the president of Russia, it also terrified a lot of elected officials. As you can imagine. Not to mention the countless other people she has killed. Though it was never my intention to handle such things as part of the task force, I have been charged with figuring out what to do with the Spartans once and for all."

"While I can sympathize with being given a job for which you have no qualifications, I really don't see how I can help in this?" They continued on in silence for a while.

"Is Lillian okay?" Ross said. She had looked back, Jack and Lillian were some distance away. Lillian was talking and laughing, but also looked very pale. Dufort looked back as well.

"She's okay....for the most part. Some days are better than others. The nerve agent permanently affected the right side of her body. She still suffers from extreme weakness. The doctors here are working with her and there has been some improvement." Ross smiled to herself. It was clear that whatever was going on with Lillian, Dufort was more involved in her life than just work colleagues.

"I'm glad she finally found some place where she could be herself. She looks happy." Dufort nodded.

"How about you Dr. Halloway? How are you? You certainly look better than the last time I saw you. It looks like living on the sea agrees with you."

"I'm good. You're right, living on the sea did agree with me. A lot more than I thought it would actually. I still get stiffness in my neck and shoulder. It's a bit of a shock still when I look in the mirror and there is the scar, but I'm fully recovered."

"I was worried when I left you last that I had made the wrong decision."

"What? Letting Jack take me out on the boat?" Dufort nodded.

"But as usual, I was right. It all turned out for the best. Not only did the Russians or the Spartans not find you, you are going to be married." Ross looked over her shoulder. Jack was leaning over listening to what Lillian had to say. Still holding her arm.

"He might be wondering who in the hell he's marrying at this point." Ross said. She hadn't meant to say it out loud. Something in her tone caught Dufort's ear.

"You have been living together on a boat. I would think he knew you as well as anyone could know another person." Dufort said, a twinkle in his eye. Ross said nothing. "Oh, you mean because of the incident with the Spartan. You think he might be put off by how well you handled yourself?" Ross thought about ignoring him. Her mind flying through other things to talk about, all more ridiculous than the first.

Did you know whales have a floating pelvis proving they once walked on land? A dodecagon has twelve sides.

Instead, she went with uncomfortable honesty. "Inspector I don't even know who that woman was. The one who shot someone today. I have never shot at another living thing in my life. My Dad taught me how to shoot a gun when he gave me one before going off to college. I've shot targets. Nothing more. So how in the hell did I know to do all that? How was I not panicking? Why didn't I run out of there like Jack wanted me to?"

"Well, why didn't you?" Dufort still had that twinkle in his eye and it was throwing her off. She shrugged her shoulders. They had stopped at the next door waiting for Jack and Lillian to catch up.

"Because I was mad as hell. I wanted it to stop. I wanted to stop being afraid, I wanted the Spartans to stop interrupting my life every time I got it back together. I wanted her to not have killed two of the leading minds in the world. Then she looked at Jack." Ross shrugged. "I was fucking mad."

"Dr. Halloway, I want you to know something. You are an extraordinary woman." Ross looked at him, confused. Dufort held up his hand. "I mean that with complete honesty. I have never in my life met a woman who can do what you have done. Which is why it surprises me that you don't know how extraordinary you are. Usually people have some idea.

"This is not the first time you have found yourself in a life or death situation. In each previous instance, you have not panicked, you have taken appropriate steps to save yourself and others. Now, you have never killed anyone in defense, that is true. Having been taught how to use a gun, and being a reasonable person, I see no reason why you should think that you couldn't effectively defend yourself if you needed to."

"I was scared shitless." Ross started to tear up thinking of the previous year when she had been hunted down by a Spartan on a boat in the middle of the icy ocean. She and Lillian hid. All they could do was wait. "I thought I was going to die. I almost did." Dufort looked her in the eye, his voice was calm when he spoke to her.

"Of course you were. You are a human Dr. Halloway. Being fearful is what has kept us alive. Spartans don't have fear and they die young. The point is, Dr. Halloway, that despite you heart rate increasing, the adrenaline running through your body, you have the ability to stay smart. You are able to make good decisions. That is extraordinary."

"That's not who I am though. I really am a quiet chemist who loves neat formulas and early nights." Dufort nodded his head like he was thinking.

"Well, there are two possibilities. Either this is who you are, you just never knew you had it in you because you had never been tested in that way, or this is who you are now, and the quiet chemist is a thing of the past. Though there might be a third possibility." Dufort's smile was really starting to freak her out now.

"What's the third option?"

"You have never had something you were willing to kill for." Dufort slowly turned his head to Jack and Lillian. "When we are looking for recruits, orphans often make the best agents. No connections. I used to think it was because the people agents left behind, girlfriends, wives, children, were liabilities, and I guess there is some truth to that. The other side of that coin is that emotions make you do things you wouldn't normally. Strong emotions, like.....love. They can make you do things you never imagined." Jack and Lillian came up behind them, Jack took the door and Dufort and Ross walked on. "What we do know is that you are here now, you have survived three Spartan attacks, and done something very few humans have done. Kill a Spartan face to face." Dufort said, an eyebrow arching.

Ross was still thinking about what Dufort said when they reached the canteen. The canteen was completely empty, though the fluorescent lights were still buzzing brightly. Dufort pulled out a chair for her and she sat down without thinking. His words interrupted her thoughts. "We are starting to think that the Spartans have an oath against being caught." Dufort said, to no one in particular.

"Why's that?" Jack said absently, looking around for food.

"There have been signs here and there. We have found nothing official stating such a thing. One was found with cyanide in their system after they had been captured in Afghanistan. Another was found having shot himself. It is unclear whether Spartans are capable of depression. It was ruled a homicide, but after today's case, I think a decent argument could be made for them killing themselves to avoid capture." Ross and Jack were now paying close attention.

"What are you going on about man? It's late, can we stop talking about bloody Spartans now?" Jack asked, grabbing two sandwiches.

"I've been following your work on PAUL Dr. Halloway. Congratulations." Lillian says.

"Stop calling me Dr. Halloway. It's Ross. Regardless of who you are." Lillian smiled.

"I admire the fact that you have contributed so much to

humanity." Lillian finished. Ross looked at her.

"You are donating your own cells to find a cure for Novichok. I created a safe way to dispose of PAUL's waste. I wouldn't get too excited." Jack smiled. Dufort came back with a tray filled with crappy but tasty food.

"I'm afraid I haven't been able to convince Dr. Halloway to come join my task force." Dufort said, unwrapping Lillian's sandwich before placing it on her plate. "Don't forget your tablets." He said to her casually. Lillian nodded and pulled out a small container from her lab coat pocket. Ross took a bite of her food and closed her eyes. It was the best ham sandwich she had ever tasted. Dufort's phone rang and he spun away to answer it.

"Bit late for phone calls. I hope everything is alright." Jack said.

"Rarely." Lillian said, handing out bags of chips. "It has always been my experience that nothing good happens after midnight." As if to prove her point, Dufort came back into the room with a scowl on his face.

"Dr. Halloway, I'm afraid there is another problem that I would like your help with."

"You have got to be fucking kidding me?" Jack said, around a large bite of roast beef.

26

"I'm terribly sorry, but a situation has just come up." Jack growled around his food. Ross rolled her eyes. It was too late to be doing all this spy shit.

"Inspector, it's just us. Whatever you have to share can surely be shared with all of us." Dufort rolled his eyes. "Inspector, let me put it to you this way. I'm exhausted. If you want my help you better start talking. Otherwise, I'm going to bed." Ross was in fact telling him the physical truth. Now that she had eaten, her head was getting heavy and her eyes wanted to close.

"Louis, there is no one here. Surely you can bend the rules a little." Lillian said. Dufort took a deep breath and leaned against one of the tables. He ran his hands down his face. He too was exhausted and yet things kept on happening that needed his immediate attention.

"One of our agents has reached out from China. A team was sent there to figure out what happened with this Parid thing."

"Did they find the origin?" Ross asked with genuine curiosity.

"Was it a lab?" Lillian asked.

"No, well, they don't know. They are still investigating." Dufort's head was starting to hurt. "They found something else though equally concerning."

"It will have something to do with Spartans." Jack said. "It's always Spartans. Go on, what have the bastards been up to now?" Jack threw a chip into his mouth.

"Well, if the bastards you are referring to are the Chinese, it turns out they have been making Spartans." Dufort said. Ross replayed what he had said in her head, convinced she had heard him wrong.

"You're joking." Jack said. He had stopped chewing. They all sat there looking at Dufort with shock.

"I very much wish I were." Dufort said. Ross had never seen him look so tired.

"How? I mean they are literal Spartans?" Ross asked.

"The information is still new, but what we know so far is that they have a lab where they are making genetically altered humans. I think it's safe to say if they aren't exact Spartans, they are meant to be close to it."

"But how?" Ross was running the timeline in her head, and while it wasn't outside the realm of possibilities that someone had figured out how to make Spartans in the time between Spartans being discovered and now, it would mean whoever they were had a lot of money and really good luck. Dufort walked around the room for a while, his hands in his pockets. He took so long in answering, Ross wasn't sure he had heard her.

"To answer that, I think I am going to have to go back to the beginning. Right after we found out there were Spartans. You have to understand, Gentix knew what the Spartans were up to before we did. As soon as it hit the news that the Spartans had taken over the resort, we know for a fact the higher ups at Genetix started destroying evidence. It never fails to amaze me that even when people are caught red handed, they still feel the need to try and cover their crime. Mother didn't of course, but then she didn't stick around to deal with the aftermath either." Dufort took a long breath and remembered the scene when they had walked into Gentix headquarters. Papers all over the floor, hell, one secretary was still in a closet shredding away when they slapped the cuffs on her. "It became clear quickly that there was a leak."

"How did you discover the leak and do you have any idea what they leaked?" Ross asked, thinking she already knew the answer.

"Not exactly, no. But there was indication that what was being leaked was connected to the Spartans project. Our fear at the time was that someone working on the project had figured out how much people would pay and was selling off information to other countries." Ross almost felt sorry for Dufort. He looked so worn out.

"It would have to be someone who knew what they were looking at." Lillian added. "You are looking for one of the geneticists or someone who worked closely with them."

"You said it would take millions of dollars and years to make a Spartan." Jack said to Ross.

"It would. Not to mention with incomplete directions, whoever used them would have to be able to fill in the gaps. The Chinese have been working with CRISPR technology for years. Getting the money would be no problem if it was a government operation. It's possible. So they have successfully managed to make Spartans? Spartans who are walking around?"

Dufort nodded. "According to our sources, they have just put their first generation into training."

"Any idea how many are in this first generation?" Jack asked.

"Just shy of two hundred." They stood there in silence while they all digested this.

"What do you want Ross to help you with?" Jack asked.

"We can't allow it. The Chinese are friendly with just about every nation that moves against democracy. If they have managed to accomplish making Spartans, then one or two scenarios will play out. Either China will sell their complete plans to the other countries, or they will sell their complete Spartans to the other countries. Either way, there is real concern that in the future, the only countries who don't have Spartans to fight their battles for them are the democratic ones."

"You still haven't told us what you want from Ross." Jack pointed out.

"Honestly Dufort, while I can appreciate how bad this is, I have no idea what you want me to do about it."

"As a member of the Spartans Task Force and as the team's leading expert on Spartans, the generals have asked Ross and her team to come up with a solution to this new problem." Dufort said, staring Ross in the eyes.

"When did I join this taskforce?" Ross asked, hands on hips.

"Right before you got on the plane to come here. You and Jack both did. It was how I got clearance for you to fly here. I listed you as experts for the task force. It wasn't a stretch, you are in fact my leading Spartan experts." Jack stood up. Ross pinched the bridge of her nose.

"She told you she didn't want to join your damned task

force. You heard her." Jack was coming around the table in a rather threatening way. Dufort didn't back down, but stood up.

"In fairness, she said she wouldn't join my taskforce after we got here. You were going to be dismissed as soon as you left on your task force flight to Boston. I can't help that a Spartan crisis occurred in the limited amount of time she was employed by us." Jack threatened to pounce. Dufort put his hand up. "Staying employed with the task force is the only way you are going to get back to Boston."

"Stand down boys. Beating the crap out of each other isn't going to solve any problems." Ross said.

"It will make me feel better." Jack said, not looking away from Dufort.

"Listen, Dufort, I am far too tired tonight to think about it if I'm perfectly honest. I will be happy to brainstorm with you tomorrow. Even though I'm not sure what a chemist who has no training in the field of genetics, or global affairs for that matter, can do to help you. Right now I think I need to go to bed." Ross looked at Jack who hadn't stopped glaring at Dufort.

"I fear I must agree with Ross." Lillian said, slowly getting up from her own seat. "Only bad ideas can come from trying to sort it out in this state. Meet you both in my room tomorrow morning and we will see if we can't come up with something. I'll have Dufort get us some breakfast and plenty of strong coffee." Lillian smiled at Dufort who nodded his head in agreement.

27

Jack came out of the bathroom feeling better for having had a shower to find Ross standing next to the window. He thought about making a move, but something about the way she was standing stopped him. She was leaning with her head resting on the glass. A blank stare on her face and twirling her hair slowly.

"Ross, you okay?" Ross's appearance didn't change. She was a million miles away. Jack crossed the room slowly. Ross showed no sign that she heard him. "Ross?"

"Hmmm?" She said, absently.

"You okay?" Ross blinked and looked at him. Taking a deep breath she said, "Yeah."

"What's bothering you, Love?" Jack was a little concerned. It had been a hard day. Ross seemed to be swinging between being fine and mortified.

"Today has me thinking a lot about the resort. What happened two years ago. I haven't really thought about it. Not in a while. I've tried very hard to leave it behind." Jack wrapped his arms around her and Ross leaned her head on his chest, but continued looking out the window at the single street lamp illuminated beneath them.

"Me too. Mind you, a lot has happened in those two years to take my mind off of it." Ross absentmindedly touched the scar on her neck. "I have dreams about it though, sometimes." Jack had never told anyone. Ross turned to look at him.

"You have dreams about it? Me too. What happens in your dream?" Ross sat on the end of the bed, but kept Jack's hand in hers. Jack didn't look her in the eyes.

"Mostly what happened in real life. Usually worse actually. I find you floating face down in the water. I'm there too late to save you. The Spartans shoot you and Sam when we get to the tower. That sort of thing. Usually whatever it is I am trying to prevent, I am just too late." He left out the part where he lifts Ross's limp body, struggling to get it into the boat. Or, in the tower, he holds her to him. The dream is so real he can still feel her blood on his arm after he wakes. "What about you?" Ross sighed.

"Sam's face as the Spartan is pulling her away, up to the tower. I don't think I will ever forget that look. She was terrified. Or we are in the water. I can feel the blast behind me all over again. I usually wake up with that one. Or the Spartans don't shoot you in the leg, but straight between the eyes and you are dead before you hit the ground." There were tears in Ross's eyes. "Sometimes when I wake up, I can still smell the salt water and feel the weight of it on my clothes." There were tears in Jack's eyes as he kneeled before her, pulling her in for a hug.

"We were extremely lucky to get out of there when you think about it." Jack said, into her hair.

"When you think about it, we should have died. Sam had never scuba dived before."

"You know what the scariest part for me was?" Jack asked. He held on tight to her, needed to feel the weight of her and not wanting her to see his face.

"What?"

"I was by myself in the water. For a while. I couldn't find you. I couldn't find Si or Sam. It was just me. Through all of that, I hadn't been alone. What wakes me up at night is that feeling."

"I thought you were with Si?" Sitting up to look at him.

"It wasn't for long. I saw him sinking into the blackness of the water and a whole new fear hit me. Then we got to the surface with the boat and I couldn't find you or Sam and another fear hit me. It still shocks the hell out of me it all happened in an afternoon. Right after lunch. We were in the hospital on land by tea time." Ross thought about telling Jack that Si hadn't wanted to be recovered. He was having a wonderful conversation with his beloved yet dead wife and was very happy to stay there. But, that wasn't really her story to tell. Si might not even remember telling Ross. They had all been in their own kind of shock afterwards. Si had seemed alright, but maybe not. Si had been the closest to the bomb blast after all. He had made slipping away into the sea sound like a comforting thing, instead of terrifying.

Without saying anything, Jack lay down on the bed and motioned for her to come to him and Ross slid next to him in the bed. Ross nuzzled up on his shoulder and breathed him in. Jack wrapped his arm around her and they lay there in silence for a while thinking of the past they shared, but avoided.

"I didn't know you before Ikan Hui. Well, I did, but only for like a few hours. Do you think you were a different person?" Ross asked.

"Do you think you are a different person?"

"I might be. Not completely. I feel more confident now, but also I'm more afraid at the same time."

"I know what you mean. You feel more confident that you can handle yourself, but now that you have seen what is out there, you never want to go out in the world again."

"I wish I could say enough time has passed to change my mind, but if anything, I have every right to become a hermit at this point."

"There is one thing about those few days I do think about."

"The amazing food?"

"No. Us. As bad as Ikan Hui was, I don't think there would be an us without all of that happening." Ross sat up a little and looked down at him.

"But we met the night before."

"And if you remember, by lunch time the next day, we had talked ourselves out of seeing each other. It's a very real possibility that we would have simply gone our separate ways." Ross thought about it. It was easy to forget those moments leading up to the explosion. Ross had a vague memory of the morning, but what she did remember was Sam hounding her to chase down Jack while they were there and Ross refusing.

"You are probably right, but I hate that our relationship started off in such a way."

"I don't see why. Somehow violence and danger seem to have made up most of our relationship."

"It will be nice when everything goes back to normal and I am in the lab mixing chemicals and you are running your shark diving business." It was the lack of sleep, but Jack laughed. Then Ross laughed. Then neither one of them could stop laughing.

Jack sat straight up. Ross was mumbling expletives from the bed next to him. The banging on the door paused for a moment only to be started again. Louder. "Hang on!" Jack yelled.

"It's six in the morning. Who the hell is that?" Ross asked. She had fallen asleep on his shoulder and wiped the drool away from her chin before he could see it. She was still wearing her clothes and Jack was still wearing nothing but a towel.

"We didn't get to bed until two. If he is here to tell us anything other than when to be on the plane home, I'm not responsible for my actions."   Jack went to the door and opened it. Lillian was standing there, leaning on her cane, Dufort looking grumpy behind her.

"Lillian, is everything okay?" Ross asked, from behind Jack's shoulder. If she had been more awake, Ross would have noticed Lillian looking Jack up and down in his towel, giving an approving smile. "Yes......... and no. Louis has some bad news and he's too chicken to deliver it himself." Ross started twirling her hair.

"How bad?" Jack asked, his voice low and gravely. Lillian stepped back so Dufort could step forward, past the two of them and into their room without a word. Picking up the remote, he turned on the TV.

"The Prime Minister announced late this evening that
England would be in lockdown until further notice.
Parid-21 cases in the country have doubled in the

196

past few days and there is real fear of overwhelming the NHS. "This is a measure we take with only the well being of the country in mind. While this will affect everyone and cause a certain amount of hardship, I feel certain that we will band together as we always do in tough situations and get through this with our British spirit intact." The Prime Minister said in a speech at Westminster yesterday adding, "The future of our nation is in the hands of the NHS..."

Dufort turned the TV back off and turned to look at them. Ross looked at the TV and then at Dufort. Jack did much the same thing.

"To save you from having to look them up, the new lockdown regulations mean they aren't giving clearance to any aircraft. I brought you here classified as persons essential for operations. Meaning that you were not part of our organization, but you were here in a consulting capacity. While you have been here, that is no longer seen as essential." Ross's heart sank. She did not want to live here.

"In English?" Jack said, with way more calmness than the situation warranted.

"I can't get you a flight home." Dufort said, avoiding eye contact with anyone.

"You promised you would get us home." Ross said, in a voice that was very much not calm. "You promised, that is the only reason we agreed to come with you. We are getting married the day after tomorrow!" Ross's voice got louder the longer she spoke.

"I never dreamed they would clamp down so hard." Dufort said, and it was true. Never had he ever seen the borders shut so tightly. "I can think of only a few times when they have closed before, but even then we were able to get our people through. I'm sorry." The last words seemed to cause him physical pain.

"There has to be a way. They can't just trap us here."

"The airports are full of people caught in the same mess. The rules are changing almost minute to minute. I have called in every favor I know. I'm sorry guys. I haven't stopped trying, but it isn't looking good. At least not in the time frame we need it to."

"You need to fix this. Do you understand me?" Ross had drawn herself up to her full height, she was standing closer to Dufort than she should, especially with a pandemic out there. "You got us here, you get us home. I haven't been home in over six months…..almost seven months. I want to go home! I want to see my cat, my mom, Sam. I want to get married. I do not want to spend another day in this place. Do I make myself clear? There has to be a way, go find it." Dufort nodded and then left the room. Turning back he said, "I am afraid I am going to have to postpone our meeting this morning. We will discuss the matter once I have dealt with this." As soon as he was gone, Ross clamped her hands over her mouth in absolute shock.

"I am so sorry. That was so rude." Ross said. Jack and Lillian smiled.

"He'll get over it." Lillian assured her.

"I was about to hit him." Jack said.

"Since you are going to be here with us longer than we thought, and since you were planning on getting married, I've had an idea." Lillian said, a wry smile on her face.

"What?" Ross said.

"We have a little chapel here. A few chaplains who could do the ceremony and a base full of witnesses." Lillian was still smiling.

"Are you saying that because you think there is no way Dufort is going to get us out of here in time?" Jack asked.

"I am actually fairly confident that Louis can twist enough arms to make it work. According to him, half the crowned heads of Europe owe him a favor. He hasn't been able to get a hold of half of them. Give him some more time. In the meantime, I would just love to see a wedding." Jack and Ross stood there silent for a moment. Ross had already been buzzing, so it was hard to say whether it was because of what Lillian had mentioned or generally what was going on. Ross looked at Jack who had a sly grin on his face, but he was saying nothing. A thought occurred to Ross, and before she could talk herself out of it, she said, "Jack, will you marry me?" She didn't bend down on one knee. But the fact that she asked at all was enough to make Jack's eyebrows shoot up into his hairline.

"What?"

"Will you marry me? Here."

"Ross, I love ya darling, I'll marry you wherever in the world you want. But what about your family?" Jack said, blushing for possibly the first time in their relationship. "What about your mother? The wedding dress?"

"We can still get married there. This one, this one would be just for us. Just you and me." Jack was speechless. Considering Ross had nearly run off the boat when he proposed and had several panic attacks since then at the thought of a wedding, this was the last thing he expected. At the same time, perfect.

"Yes. I'd love to." He finally said. Lillian clapped her hands.

"Fantastic! Because I have already arranged everything." Lillian said. "I'll send someone to collect you around ten.

The canteen has arranged a small lunch for afterwards." Filled with renewed energy, Lillian took off down the hallway, leaving Jack and Ross alone. Again, Ross felt drunk. She wasn't sure at this point if it was the lack of sleep or the fact that she had agreed to marry Jack twice. Ross's hands were sweaty and the rest of her was starting to feel cold.

"You can't freak out on me now." Jack took a step closer to her, turning her to look at him. "There will be no getting rid of me now. Married in two countries." Jack tucked her hair behind her ears.

"I'm going to make it as hard as I can for Ivy." Ross said, still feeling buzzy. "Sam will kill me if she ever finds out, and if my mother finds out....I don't want to think about it."

"Why does it seem very 'us' to have a secret wedding?" Jack asked.

"It does seem more like 'us' than a church wedding, doesn't it?" Jack kissed her gently. "Come one, if we are lucky the bed is still warm." Jack said. They were asleep again almost instantly.

28

Ross woke up to Jack making a powerful suggestion.

"What time is it?" Ross said, who wasn't adverse to his suggestion, but also wouldn't have minded a few more hours of sleep.

"I haven't got a clue. The sun is up."

"That's not the only thing. How can you possibly be in the mood? I feel half dead." Ross said, still struggling with whether to give in to Jack or try for more sleep.

"Come on, it's our wedding day." Not able to argue with that, Ross gave in. She could sleep later.

"*Shit!*" Ross said, afterwards. "It's nine-thirty. We have half an hour to get ready for our wedding." Jack, seemingly not phased, propped himself up on his pillows and turned on the TV while Ross got out of bed and ran into the shower.

Ross thought Sam would have been proud that she had managed to make herself look reasonable with very few resources. Despite washing and blow drying her hair, Ross still couldn't make it do what she wanted, so she put her hair up. The dress she found was far too casual, but the nice outfit she had been wearing the day before was wrinkled crepe paper. The thought occurred to Ross that it might not be the best idea to get married in the same outfit you killed a person in. So she went with the casual dress.

Jack, of course, rolled out of bed, put on the same pants from the day before, pulled a clean shirt from his luggage. He ran his hands through his hair with a little gel, added a blazer and he was ready to go.

"I wonder if Dufort will forget he wanted me to brainstorm on what to do with the Chinese Spartans." Ross mused while putting on her incredibly uncomfortable heels.

"I don't think we will be that lucky, even though he looks so worn out I almost feel sorry for him. Almost."

"It does seem like since Parid hit, the world has been falling apart. I suspect that if anything good comes out of this pandemic, it will be that we learn what is truly important." Ross said, feeling oddly sentimental. "That a lot of the things we thought were important don't really matter that much anymore. That time means more. Time doing what we love." Ross took a step closer to Jack, "With the ones we love will mean more than it ever did." Jack stood up and there was now no space between them. Jack cupped Ross's face in his hands and ran his thumbs across her cheeks.

"I seriously hope that one day you know just how much I love you." Jack said, also feeling sentimental. Whether it was where they were or what was going on, it seemed more important than ever that Ross knew exactly how he felt about her.

"Ditto." Ross said, and with a half grin on his face, Jack

gave her one of his best kisses. "I'm starving. You want anything from the canteen?" Jack asked while Ross was still bringing herself back down to Earth. If Ross hadn't already done her hair, she would have thrown him down on the bed and satisfied her own hunger, but there was no chance she would get her hair looking that good again before they had to leave. Ross bit her lip and kissed him back with everything she had.

"Jesus woman." Jack said, beginning to think breakfast could wait.

"I want coffee. Hot, strong, coffee. With cream and four sugars. If they have anything that looks like an egg and sausage biscuit, I'll have that as well." Jack was now confused because her mouth said she wanted food, but every other part of her said she wanted to devour him and he was willing. He was extremely willing.

"Ross, I'm confused. Do you really want food?" Jack said, ready to act regardless of the answer. Ross immediately broke the sultry act and said, "Yes, I'm really hungry."

"What about the other thing?" Jack said, slightly disappointed.

"Jack, there is a very good chance we are going to be locked down for the foreseeable future. There will be plenty of time for 'the other thing'." Jack let out a sigh and got up to go to the canteen.

Thankfully, the canteen seemed to model their breakfast options after fast food chains, and Ross got almost exactly what she wanted. Never had food tasted so good.

"What is it about traveling that makes food taste better? Oh no, you have a yellow stain on the back of your shirt." Ross said.

"I know." There was something in the way he said it that made her stop and think.

"It's not. Is it?"

"It is."

"You kept the shirt you were wearing when I ran into you with the crab legs and butter?" Ross asked.

"It's my lucky shirt. I was wearing it when I met my wife. And thanks to her spilling butter on it, I had to leave it at the cleaners at the resort. With everything that happened, I had completely forgotten about it. They handed it back to me as I was flying out. The stain was still there. The only scrap of clothing I had left in the world, and it was this shirt."

There was a knock at the door, sharp and determined. Jack gave Ross a look and smiled. "Here we go." Jack opened the door to two tall marines in formal dress uniforms. Ross jumped when they snapped their heels in attention.

"If you please, we have come to escort you to the chapel." Jack grabbed his blazer and put it on.

"Shall we?" Ross went out into the hallway where the marine offered his arm. Ross awkwardly accepted. It seemed strange to take the arm of a handsome marine when your fiance was standing right there. They walked out of the building and along the street. Ross was glad to see the sun was shining, and she wondered to herself what day it was. Ross had expected today's wedding would be in a rather small room that they had done their best to make look like a chapel, but could be converted to a meeting room with little trouble. She was very wrong.

"That's an actual chapel."

"Yes madam. Porton chapel was built in 1655 for the use

of the servicemen stationed here at Porton Downs." The stone structure looked weathered but strong, and Ross loved it on sight. Its slate roof, heavy wooden doors, and gray stone walls looked like something out of a storybook.

"1655, my country wasn't even on the map." There was white bunting on the doors, and Ross assumed it was for them. The marine opened the door and there stood Dufort looking incredibly awkward in a tuxedo. "It would be an honor if you would allow me to walk you down the aisle." Dufort said, offering his arm.

"Of Course." Ross said, looking back at Jack who was glaring at Dufort. The marine opened the doors to the main chapel and warm light greeted them. Lillian was standing off to the side with a small bouquet and a smile on her face near one of the doors.

"You look lovely, Ross. I managed to gather these this morning and thought they would make a good bouquet. I hope you don't mind."

"I can't believe you arranged all this in the middle of the night." Ross said.

"With everything being so strange at the moment, people seemed eager to help with a joyous occasion." Lillian said. Organ music started. A smile had pasted itself on Ross's face that she didn't seem to be able to get rid of. A loud humming filled her head, and she struggled to concentrate on what anyone was saying. She felt flushed. Dufort came up next to Jack and indicated that he should go towards the altar. Jack straightened his jacket, gave Ross a wink, and went to go wait for her at the altar. Ross got short of breath. It was all looking very much like a wedding.

"I have to pee."

"I'm sorry?" Dufort said.

"I have to go to the restroom. Be right back." Ross made the 'one minute' sign to Jack and disappeared.

"Where the hell is she going?" Jack said.

"Don't worry, she can't get off base without clearance." The vicar said with a smile. Lillian ran behind Ross to the tiny restroom.

"I'm so sorry, I should have gone before we left."

"Don't worry Ross, they aren't going to start without you. Actually, while you are here and can't really go anywhere, there is something I've been wanting to tell you." Ross froze.

"Lillian, before you continue with that thought, I think it's important to remember that as soon as I leave this stall I am going to get married. Something that tends to stick in the memory of those involved. So, is this going to be something that will lessen my otherwise pleasant memory of today? If so, can it wait?" Lillian bit her lip.

"Most likely it isn't going to make it better." Ross pulled her pants up and tried to straighten herself up.

"As curious as I am to hear it then, can it wait until later?" Ross opened the stall door and looked Lillian in the eyes.

"It is something that should be said without others around."

"Deal."

"Well, let's get you married then." Lillian smiled and handed Ross her small bouquet.

"Why the hell didn't she go to the bathroom before we left the room?" Jack said, the sweat running down his back. This had been in part Ross's idea, but the thought was still there that she would scare at the last minute and run. Dufort was standing next to him, his hands tucked into his pockets. "I had no idea your family had worked with the agency before. Your father is a bit of a legend I have gathered. You never said." It took a minute for the words to register in Jack's mind.

"What the hell are you talking about?" Jack asked. Duffort's face revealed nothing.

"Si apparently did some work for us back in the eighties and nineties. I can't reveal much of his record since most of it is still classified, but he worked for us for about a decade. Did some fine work apparently."

"Si?" Dufort nodded his head.

"I guess I should have assumed you didn't know anything about it. He would have had to sign a declaration stating he would not discuss any of his missions. Most people ignore them to a certain extent. They can't help telling their family they are agents. Especially after a certain amount of time." Jack was standing in stunned silence.

"What the hell would Si be doing working for your lot?"

"As I said, those files are still marked 'classified'."

"Classified?"

"Ah, here we go." Dufort left Jack standing there in stunned silence as he hustled back down to where Ross and Lillian had once again appeared. Jack's mind was still reeling from what Duffort had told him when he locked eyes with Ross. Ross smiled at him. Classical music came on. Every muscle in Ross's body seemed to tighten when the music started. Ross maintained eye contact with Jack and somehow, putting one foot in front of the other, she was soon standing in front of Jack. "You made it." He whispered to her.

"It would appear so." Ross said back. They were interrupted by the clergymen saying some words. A strange humming started in Ross's head that made it hard to hear what was going on around her. She heard the words, "I do." Leave her mouth. Jack said the same. Some more words were said and then Jack kissed her. As suddenly as it had come on, the humming in her head left, and she was once again able to understand what people were telling her.

"That's it, babe." Jack said, smiling from ear to ear.

"That's it?" Jack nodded. Ross's smile was just as broad as Jack's. "That wasn't bad." Not for the first time, Jack wondered what the hell Ross thought happened during weddings. The marines showed them to a small room off in the wings of the chapel where the clergyman explained where they should sign. Ross and Jack did what they were told. They left the church a mere half an hour after entering it. The sun was shining and there were smiles on everyone's face. Dufort kissed her on the cheek through his mask and shook Jack's hand. Lillian kissed them both on the cheek through her mask.

"That's it!" Ross said, to the group.

"The canteen has a small lunch for us." Lillian said. Ross thanked the clergymen a little more than was necessary. The small party left the chapel.

"We can't forget the photos." Ross said, pulling her phone out of her pocket.

"I thought this was a secret wedding?" Jack said. If he was honest, he was glad to be married, but he was even more thrilled that Ross hadn't made a run for it. If she married him once, there was a very good chance she would marry him again when they got to Boston.

"Just for us. To look at in secret." Dufort took her phone and took pictures of the small party. A passing woman managed to get one of the group. "Our little secret." Ross said, looking at the picture quickly before putting her phone back. The group walked to the canteen in good spirits. Lillian held onto Ross's arm and Ross found that they were falling far behind the boys.

"There was something you wanted to tell me?" Ross said, seeing what Lillian was doing.

"Louis would not be pleased if he knew I was talking to you about this, but it has to do with the task force."

"What about it?"

"Louis is the director, but there are people above him. These are powerful people Ross. People who aren't used to being told no."

"Lillian, it's my wedding day, I really don't want to talk about the task force."

"Louis asked you to be a part of it."

"Yes, and I said no." They were getting close to the main building and Jack had turned around a few times to see where she was.

"It might not be that simple. It is widely known Ross that you have a rare talent for both surviving the Spartans and finding yourself in the same room with them. Louis was sent to come and get you to join the task force, he phrased it as a question because he knows and respects you."

"You're saying Louis wasn't the one who wanted me. It was the higher ups?"

"Exactly. Louis informed them of your answer and they weren't pleased. Like I said, they are used to hearing the word 'no'. Louis is stuck between a rock and a hard place because he knows this is not the life you chose. You want to go back to the way things were."

"But?"

"But the higher ups are insisting." Ross stopped walking.

"They are going to keep us here against our will? I won't do it. I'll refuse to work." Lillian held up a hand and looked around.

"That is not going to happen. Not that it hasn't been floated, but Louis works for the good guys, and while they think you are Spartan bait, they apparently don't think you are worth holding against your will." Lillian said, perfectly aware of Jack looking back at them.

"Then what?" Ross almost yelled.

"It is very likely that you will find yourself being monitored for a while."

"Monitored? By who?" Lillian gave her a knowing look. "Are you serious? Why would they want to watch me?"

"Because you seem to attract Spartans, Ross, and if you are trying to find a Spartans, then it would make sense to monitor the person they seem to find the most."

"Why are you telling me this?" Ross said, thinking she could have lived in blissful ignorance without this conversation. Lillian stopped walking, putting her hand on Ross's arm.

"Because I know what it's like to want to lead a life differently from the way other people think you should. You deserve to know."

"Ross, you coming?" Jack yelled, holding the door to the main building open.

"Yeah, be right there." Ross didn't say anything, but

nodded at Lillian who gave her a sympathetic smile and walked ahead. Leaving Ross with the knowledge that, try as hard as she might, a normal life might be nothing more than an illusion.

29

"When can we start the next generation?" The soldier asked briskly. Everything they asked him was brisk. No one seemed to enjoy casual conversation around here.

"Listen mate, I told you. We have to recalibrate all the machines. They just hatched grown humans, you can't turn around and immediately expect them to support an embryo now can you?" Riley was in the lab office. It was always dark. Some of the chemicals used to keep the pods at the right temperature didn't do well in the light. Riley looked out the large window that allowed him to see all the pods stretched out through a warehouse. They were all empty at the moment. Being cleaned by the silent team of determined workers that seemed to always be around.

"How long?"

"A few weeks." Riley was not a project manager. Never had been. Until now. Riley had been a sort of mechanic at Genetix. There was hardly a thing out there he didn't know how to fix, and these damned pods were so delicate, there was always something going wrong. Dufort thought he was looking for a leak. In truth, he was looking for a group of leaks. There were four of them in total. They had all had different jobs at Genetix. All working closely on the Spartans project. They knew what Mother and Father were doing. They knew how important it was. It wasn't hard to figure out that there would be people out there willing to pay major money for it. More money than Mother and the corporate heads were ever going to pay. They had written down what they had seen, which was considerable. Other than Riley, there was Dr. Fuqin and Jean. Between the three of them, and the army of labor provided, they had already created two batches.

"Not good enough. The Emperor wants a new generation started immediately." The general stomped his foot. Riley wondered, not for the first time, if the money was worth the near constant irritation. The group already had the Chinese lined up as buyers. They had been worried how they were going to get the missing notes to complete the instructions when the Spartans gave them the opportunity they had needed. Riley could still remember the chaos of that day. Everyone had been so worried about destroying evidence, no one questioned when Dr. Fuqin had emptied all the stored files from the main computer in the lab to a separate hard drive.   "Then tell the Emperor that he needs to send over another billion for the pods and the staff to maintain them. This is as fast as we go, and if I'm honest, we are doing pretty damned well. We only had to discard five from the last batch. Give me a few weeks, and I will have another batch up and running in no time."

"The Emperor will not be pleased."

"I would remind the Emperor that we are doing something extremely complex here. Our success ratio is higher than normal. " Riley could tell that this was not the answer that the general wanted, but there was very little he could do about it. "Now, while I have you. I have gotten your lab up and running. I have successfully shown that it will, in fact, produce viable specimens. The training is up to you, and I have worked with your team to make sure that they can run things as well as I can. I would like to go home now." The General nodded.

"I will see if there has been a discussion on that." The general curtly nodded and went to walk away.

"Maybe remind them that if I am to be a prisoner, my work may get less reliable." The General turned to look at Riley and said, "Since you have trained our team so well, it appears we may not need you for too much longer, one way or the other."

"Listen! I came here because you paid me to set your lab up and get it running. This wasn't part of the deal."

"You can let him go, General Bo. He has done as much for you as he can. He's a mechanic. You have what you need to expand the operation if you need to. I will warn you, though, the larger the operation, the harder it is to control it." Said Dr. Fuqin, entering the room. Riley's shoulders relaxed. Dr. Fuqin seemed to get better responses from these people than he did. Maybe it was because he was half Chinese himself. Even though he was approaching sixty and an eye patch covering his bad eye, Dr. Fuqin still cut an imposing figure. One that demanded the attention of those around him.

"We do not feel like our team is fully equipped to carry on the work without guidance. Until then, we will keep you and Mr. Riley here to assist us." Riley looked at Dr. Fuqin with something like panic.

"The price you were charged included all our information including suppliers and three months of assistance in setting up. Now, Riley and myself have already been here four months longer than that, with no additional pay. We have taken a great risk in accelerating the growth time. In short, we have fulfilled our end of the contract. If you are going to continue to neglect your end, we will have no choice but to charge you accordingly." General Bo squared to face him, bringing himself up to his full height.

"You are illegally selling plans to illegally create artificial humans. Exactly how do you plan on making us pay?" Dr. Fuqin took a step closer and glared at General Bo with his remarkably blue eye, and smiled.

"You may have missed the part in my file where it said I trained some of the Spartans. Bomb making, mainly. Things that were mostly chemical based. I'm a biochemist you see. A very good one. Most of the people in the lab, they made the mistake of treating the Spartans as lesser than, you know, because they weren't really human. I never thought that was a good idea. We were training them to be killers after all. Very efficient ones." Dr. Fuqin took another step towards General Bo. "You wouldn't think a creature designed to feel hardly anything would remember small kindnesses. But you'd be surprised. Now, I haven't spoken to the Spartans in a few years now, but I have no reason to think that if I called, they wouldn't answer. Because you see General, they have always answered before....when I called." The General stomped off without a word.

When the General had left the room, Riley asked, "Would you really call the Spartans?"

"No. I wouldn't have to. I can blow this place apart all on my own." Dr. Fuqin said, he then turned and left the lab.

30

The lunch was canceled.

When the foursome returned to the main building, there were Marines waiting for them. "What's going on?" Dufort stepped forward and demanded, tugging at the tie of his tux.

"We have been instructed to escort you and your companions to the situation room." Lillian had never seen Louis look flustered. It only lasted an instant, but for a second he looked nervous.

"Can you tell me why?"

"Sorry sir. My orders came from the generals." With those words, Jack and Ross's blood froze in their veins. Without another word, they all followed the marines through the dizzying maze of white hallways. At some point, Ross realized they were walking downhill. The walls were made of thick concrete here instead of cheap sheet rock. She exchanged a knowing look with Jack who had also noticed the change. A marine opened the doors, and they were in a dark room with floor lights. A large screen was at the head of the room, and though Ross had never been in the military, it didn't take a genius to figure out the people seated at the tables around her were extremely high ranking in every branch of the military. She silently wondered how heavy their medal- covered jackets must weigh. The marine said nothing, but stepped to the side of the room and stood next to the door. Ross couldn't help but think it was to keep them from escaping. A woman at the far end of the table stood up. Her hair was pulled back so tight Ross thought it probably gave her headaches, which might explain why she looked like she hadn't smiled in years.

"Inspector." She said curtly. Dufort walked to the middle of the room and said, "General Raymond. Has something happened?" Ross stood there frozen to the spot. *We aren't flying home. They are going to make us stay. I live here now in this concrete maze.* She thought to herself.

"We hadn't heard a response from you or Dr. Halloway, so we thought we would speak with her ourselves." Dufort went to argue, but General Raymond cut him off, "We also have some additional information we thought we would share with you while you were all together." Turning her attention to Ross, "I understand Inspector Dufort has explained to you that we fear there was a leak in Genetix's lab."

"Yes."

"With this information, it is feared that another agency would be able to replicate Mother's work and therefore create their own Spartans."

"Yes."

"Did he explain to you what the possible implications would be if this information was to find its way into the hands of undesirable countries?"

"He did."

"And yet I understand that you have refused to stay and help with the main mission of the task force."

"As the Inspector is well aware, I am not a biologist or a geneticist. I am a chemist, and therefore would have limited knowledge to help him achieve his goals with the taskforce." Jack nodded. Ross was doing a very good job of professionally telling them to bugger off.

"But you are two of the only people who have ever survived a Spartans attack, and just a few days ago managed to kill one. I will admit, Dr. Halloway, based on that knowledge alone, I would have reason to doubt that you were *just* a chemist as you claimed. Though I can find no record of you ever working for other agencies." Ross looked around in confusion.

"Are you asking me if I am an agent for another country?"

"No, since an agent wouldn't tell me." Ross's mouth opened and closed several times. "If you are, it will become clear in time, besides, that is not why we have brought you here today."

"Then why have you? We are trying to get home. Flights are rather hard to come by, as you know." Jack said. Another military person to the woman's right spoke up, but remained seated.

"I take it you have been made aware of our predicament with the Chinese?"

"Yes." Jack could not believe how calm Ross was remaining while these Generals stared her down. Little did he know this was very similar to when she defended her dissertation.

"Spartans, Dr. Halloway. The Chinese are making their

own Spartans. It seems that whatever the leak got away with, they were almost intact plans. They sold them to the Chinese for what we are sure was an incredibly high price. The first generation has just started training. The second generation is in no doubt in the works." Ross stood in silence at the news.

"You are looking for someone who would know what they are looking at with regards to the notes." Ross said.

"What do you mean?" The general asked.

"This isn't a janitor who got lucky and found the notes in the chaos after Mother died. They wouldn't know what they had. You are looking for someone who worked closely with either Mother or Father. Someone who knows what this information is and what can be done with it." The woman with the tight hair rolled her eyes.

"You have not been brought here to tell us who our leak is Dr. Halloway."

"Then why?" Ross said, letting a little attitude flash.

"We would like your help in figuring out what to do about the Chinese Spartans." Ross's mouth fell open.

"How many times do I have to tell you people? I'm a chemist. I'm not a Spartan hunter, or whatever it is you think I am. I'm a chemist, and I would like to go home and be the boring person I once was. Please."

"Your actions speak otherwise, Dr. Halloway. Regardless of what you would like to do, you and you alone have had more contact time with Spartans than any other person. In every encounter you have had, you have exchanged words with them."

"Very few words. Most of the conversation was centered around asking them not to kill me." Ross pointed out.

"Nevertheless, we would like your input into how to

solve this problem." Ross put her hands on her hips.

"Enough with the coded crap. What exactly are you wanting me to do?" A third general, thin, bald, mustache turned to look at her with a smile on his face.

"We want you to tell us how to kill these Chinese Spartans without making it look like we were the ones who did it." The female general grunted. "How do you expect her to give us the information we need without giving her all the details?" An idea flashed in Ross's head, but she couldn't grasp it firmly.

"I still think we should keep this an internal matter." Another general, who had been glaring at Ross the entire time said.

"Why would we not utilize specialized help when it is in our backyard?" The thin general said. Ross was trying to go back to the idea that had flashed in her head. To get a firm grip on it.

"Ross, we don't have to do this. We can tell them to do it themselves." Jack was saying to her. Ross put her hand up and closed her eyes. Where had it gone?

"She's a civilian for one. How do we know she won't sell this story to the highest bidder?" The old angry general asked.

"There is a global pandemic going on. The US is planning on confirming there are UFO's to take people's minds off of it. If she goes to the press, it will be buried at the bottom of the news cycle." Thin general answered.

"Wait." Ross said. They all stopped talking.

"Yes, Dr. Halloway." The female general asked.

"How many Spartans are there?"

"Chinese or American?"

"American."

"Around a hundred, give or take." She answered.

"Any idea how many Chinese Spartans are in training?" The generals checked the paperwork they had sitting in front of them.

"Out of a thousand eggs fertilized, only a hundred and twenty-three made it to maturity. With Genetix, some of the weaker specimens were worked out in training. Since they appear to be following their model, it is safe to assume the same here." Thin general said.

"Killed. They were killed." Ross clarified for him. "So if they have only started training, we can assume there are still a hundred and twenty-three. Do we have the layout of the facility?" The older general was glaring at her again.

"We have rough ideas from our agent and also satellite images, but we don't know exactly where in the complex the various stages are located."

"You could bomb the whole damn thing and call it a day." Jack suggested.

"We considered bombing them with Russian missiles, but we aren't dealing with people known for their measured responses, so it was decided to be too risky. That is part of the problem. Relations with the Chinese have been strained of late. We do not wish to upset this anymore, but also can not allow them to create Spartans." Thin general stated. Jack's eyebrows went into his hairline.

"How much money are you willing to spend on this mission?" Ross asked.

"Why do you ask?" Old General asked her.

"Because I can think of only one way to get rid of the Chinese Spartans and no one knows it's you. Hire the people who specialize in killing other people and making sure the blame doesn't fall on those who hired them. Get the Spartans." Ross said.

"You are suggesting we hire the Spartans to kill the Chinese Spartans?" The female general clarified.

"Yes. While you are at it, maybe you can scan their microchips and complete your catalog of them. Lord knows how much it would cost. I would imagine it's going to make a decent dent. Now, I know nothing about any of this, but it seems to me the best way to fight highly trained killers who were designed only to kill, is to get other highly trained killers to do it for you. Dufort said you wanted to kill off the Spartans anyway. You might get lucky and hit two birds with one stone."

"Call them." The General snapped her fingers, and a marine produced a phone from one of the dark corners.

"What do you mean,'call them'. I don't know how to get a hold of them." Ross protested.

"Thankfully, our intel does. This was pulled off the body of one of the Spartan victims. It was thought that the two parties were in fact going to hire the Spartans to kill the other."

"What exactly am I supposed to say to them?" Ross's voice was starting to get squeaky.

"Calm down, Dr. Halloway. You call and leave a message with a description of the job you want done. If they are interested, they call you back." Ross looked at Jack, who shrugged his shoulders. While he wanted nothing to do with any of this, he didn't feel he was in a position to get them out of it either. Ross took the phone and the number that had been given to her. Sure enough, she left a message.

"There. I did it." Ross said, more to convince herself than anyone.

"You will remain here on base until they call back."

"You can't do that! Our wedding is tomorrow!" Jack piped up.

"I am an American citizen. You can not hold me here against my will. You have no jurisdiction." Ross tried to sound like she knew what she was talking about. "We have rights." She said, louder, taking Jack's hand in hers. Surely he was covered too now that they were married. Hopefully, it wasn't dependent on how long you had been married.

Thankfully, they didn't have to wait very long. The phone rang in front of Ross. They all stared at it for a moment. It rang again.

"Answer it, Dr. Halloway." The female general ordered.

"Hello?"

"Is this Dr. Ross Halloway?"

"Yes." Ross said, twirling her hair. Jack ran his hands through his hair and cupped his hands behind his head to keep them from ripping that phone out of her hands.

"Dr. Ross Halloway, did you leave a message at Oliver House earlier today?" This was the code their voice message had warned her would signal that she was talking with the Spartans.

"Yes, yes I did."

"Is this *the* Dr. Halloway that has survived multiple attacks by the Spartans? Who recently killed a Spartan called Natasha in New York?" Ross bit her lip. "It is."

"This is a big job you are asking for us to do. Who are you working with?"

"Interpol mostly. Along with a few other intelligence agencies representing a few different countries who think the existence of these Chinese Spartans are an international threat." Ross let out a breath, hoping she sounded confident. Jack gave her a thumbs up.

"Shi. They are called Shi. We are aware of their existence. While we agree that there is no one better suited to take care of them, this will take all the resources the Spartans have and will not come cheap."

"Before we discuss your fee, we feel that as skilled as the Spartans are, this might be too big even for them. Would you be willing to work with the military? The Spartans would be in charge of course, they would follow your orders."

"It's ten million up front. That will cover the costs of intelligence gathering. Our team will then evaluate the information and come up with a plan based on our individual skills. If we feel assistance is needed, we will reach back out to you. Another ten million will be due once the mission is complete. As always, we guarantee our work. If there are any loose ends, we will take care of them at no additional cost." Ross looked up at the table of generals to see their reaction to this figure. They looked at each other and then nodded. "Yes. That sounds fine."

"An account number will be sent to your email. Once the ten million has cleared, we will start working. I should warn you, Dr. Halloway, if at any time we discover this was an elaborate plan to bring us out in the open, we will kill you." The words sent a breathtaking chill right through Ross. There was a moment of silence while Ross repeatedly tried to get her breath back enough to talk.

"Understood."

"We will call you back in a few weeks."

"I didn't give you my email."

"We already have it." The line went dead. Ross must have blacked out because the next moment she remembered was sitting at the canteen, a piece of wedding cake in front of her. It was a rather sad looking party at this point. Lillian was still smiling, trying to bring the mood back up. Dufort was ranting in a foreign language to his phone, pacing back and forth. His tie was hanging loose around his neck. Jack was slouched in his chair, picking at the cake in front of him. His tie, too, was completely undone. Dufort let out one more expletive and shoved his phone back into his pocket.

"This is bullshit." Ross said more loudly than she should have. All heads turned to look at her. "I have absolutely no business doing this. I know nothing about international peacekeeping. I should not be negotiating between the Spartans and the military of any country in regards to an international situation. Surely to god they know that." Ross looked at Dufort pleadingly. Dufort ran his hand through his hair and let out a deep breath. The man looked like he could melt into the ground right there.

"You are right. You are completely unqualified for this mission. However, you still managed to execute it brilliantly. Dr. Halloway, if you really want to stop being involved in international situations of this caliber, I suggest you fuck it up next time." Dufort's phone rang and he walked out of the room with pissed off resignation. Jack looked at her and said, "The man has a point."

31

When Dufort came back in, he was carrying a manilla envelope. A stern look on his face. He pulled the contents out and looked at them. Whatever it was didn't change his expression.

"What is that?" Lillian asked, coming up to stand behind Dufort. He did nothing to keep the contents of the file away from her.

"Intel from the Spartan lab in China. Satellite pictures and a few images our agent was able to grab for us." Dufort flipped through them. They were out of order, he would have to sit down with them and the report.

"Wait. Go back." Lillian said. Dufort flipped back a picture. "I know him." Dufort froze.

"What do you mean?" Lillian took the picture from Dufort and studied it carefully. He could tell from the look on her face that she wasn't joking. "Let's get out of here." Lillian said, looking around them. There was no one else around but them and the canteen workers. Without a word between them, Dufort led them through the hallways to the task force room. Dufort took the picture and scanned it.

The image appeared on the large screen at the front of the room.

"There, you know him? Who is he?" Dufort said, looking from Lillian to the report he had been given. Lillian had looked shocked in the canteen, but now she looked her normal calm, confident self.

"His name is Dr. Fuqin. I'm sure I used to know his first name, Phillip maybe. It was right after I arrived in England. I remember he was a young man, but he already had gray hair. Speaking at Cambridge, I went to go see him. He was a professor in biochemistry for a few years. He left shortly after I arrived. His mother was English and his father Chinese."

"What was the topic of the speech?" Ross asked.

"What the hell does it matter what the topic was?" Jack asked.

"The Benefits of Genetic Modifications in Select Animal and Plant Species. Focusing on Hydration and Growth Times."

"Sounds fascinating." Jack snorted.

"Jack, it's science for trying to select animal and plant species with less water and faster growing times. To help combat food shortages in countries with little water." Ross informed him. Jack felt like an ass and decided to keep his mouth shut for a while.

"Do you know where he went after he left Cambridge?" Ross asked.

"No, but in a way it's not surprising that he is working with the Chinese."

"Why's that?" Dufort asked.

"Well, as I said, his father was Chinese. He was censured for speaking in favor of communist ideals." A smile came to her face, as she remembered, "I actually confronted him about it. Told him it was all well and good for him to sit in a democratic country, with all his liberties and human rights intact. He would find it very different being a scientist in one of his communist countries."

"What did he say?" Jack asked. Lillian shrugged.

"He explained that the practice of communism was flawed and that the same could be said for democracy as well as any other form of government. He had merely stated that communism advocated for making all people equal in the eyes of the law whereas others acknowledged from the beginning that there would be people who had power and money and those who didn't. Dr. Fuqin liked the idea of everyone being equal."

"Sounds like a right prick if you ask me." Jack said. Lillian looked Dufort in the eye. Ross had seen the look before, when they had been on the research trip together. That sharp glint she got in her eye.

"I have absolutely no doubt that Dr. Fuqin is your leak, Louis."

"I'll have to look through the documents again, but I can't remember a Dr. Fuqin being on the Spartan project at Genetix."

"Maybe he worked in another department." Ross suggested. "Ikan Hui was supposed to be the display case for Genetix to show all that genetic manipulation could do. How it could benefit humanity. Everything from the sharks to the salad greens were genetically altered. Maybe he had something to do with that. If he managed to find Mother's notes in the chaos, he would certainly know what he had." Lillian shook her head.

"No, he was directly involved with the Spartan project.

Fairly high up." Dufort looked Lillian in the eye.

"Lillian, how do you know this?"

"Because Fuqin is one of the Chinese words for 'father'. I think you will find that Dr. Fuqin is Father." There was a long pause while they all took that in.

"There is no record of a Dr. Phillip Fuqin in the records." Dufort didn't need to look; he had spent the better part of two years going over everything that had been pulled out of Genetix.

"Look again." Lillian said, not backing down. "He's your man Louis." Dufort ran through it all in his head. There was no indication that Dr. Fuqin worked there, but Dr. P. Father's name was all over everything. To add to it the circumstances around Father's disappearance had always left Dufort uneasy. Dufort stood up and called Rand.

"It's three O'clock in the morning here, Dufort." Rand answered.

"Send me over the file on Father. As soon as you can."

"Sure. Everything okay?" Rand didn't like how he sounded.

"I'll tell you later." Dufort hung up. He looked at all of them and then said, "With Mother dead, Father was going to take the brunt of the blame for the Spartans. He started off cooperating. He seemed to understand that there was nothing else he could do but help us in our investigation. Like a man who had accepted his fate.So much so that he was released on house arrest. There was a team monitoring his movements twenty-four hours a day." Dufort was turning an unhealthy red color, and his Belgian accent was coming out more the more agitated he became. "Then, a few months into the investigation, he was found dead in his house. Single gunshot to the head. It was deemed a suicide even though no gun was found in the house. The only clue was a large amount of money that had been moved from his bank account the same evening. Nothing could be proved, but it was generally accepted that the Spartans killed him. Now, you are telling me he isn't dead. He is making Spartans in China? If I go and say that Father is alive and well, I will be calling into question my colleagues who investigated his death and putting my neck way out on the line. Mon Amour, you have to be sure." Lillian was still calm, made more calm by how agitated Dufort had become.

"When I saw him, he wasn't wearing an eye patch. But that is him. Same piercingly blue eyes and fantastic gray hair. I would swear to it."

"Wait, if there was a body, how is it possible that he is alive?' Jack asked. Dufort did not take his eyes off of Lillian but answered Jack.

"Father was found in his apartment like I said. A single gunshot to the head. From behind. With a high power rifle. A considerable portion of his face was missing. He was identified with fingerprints." There was a pause while everyone absorbed this new information.

"It sounds like instead of the Spartans being the ones that killed Father, they used their talents to help him fake his own death. They couldn't use dental records?" Ross offered.

"Only fragments were found." Dufort answered.

"Damn." Jack stated. "I always thought it was a bit strange having two people making Spartans. One named Mother and the other Father." Jack said. Dufort turned to both of them. "Don't you recognize him?" Jack asked. "You were investigating."

"The interviews with Genetix were not handled by me. I was assigned to dealing with the Spartans. The car will be here in half an hour to pick you up and take you to your plane." Dufort said, changing the subject.

"You are still letting us leave?" Ross said, before she could stop herself.

"Get out of here while you still can. I will sit on this until I have word that you are in the air. I can not promise they will not try and turn your plane around, but their hands may be tied with the pandemic. Safe journey." Dufort kissed Ross's hand and said, "Thank you for letting me be a part of your day and may your actual wedding day be just as magnificent." Dufort then turned to Jack and said, "Good luck." Shook his hand.

"Goodbye Ross. Good luck with everything." Lillian gave Ross a hug. "Enjoy every minute of your boring life." She whispered into Ross's ear.

"There is no reason we can't stay in touch now. Keep me posted on your research. And everything else." Ross shot her eyes toward Dufort.

"Jack, it was good to see you in happier circumstances." Lillian took his hand.

"Take care of yourself, mon amie." Dufort took Lillian's arm, leaving the task force room. Ross watched them leave and couldn't help but be a little sad she wouldn't be able to figure out how all of this ended. Jack took her arm and said, "I suggest we take his advice and get our things. If we are lucky, the car will be here early." Ross and Jack packed their things like they were fleeing a crime scene. They reached the outside of the building just as the car was pulling up.

"Heathrow airport, fast as you can please." Jack said, the

knot in his stomach finally starting to ease.

32

True to his word, Dufort gave Ross and Jack a decent head start. While he would claim with his last breath that it was to give them a chance of getting home without being called back, in truth, he was stalling.

"It can't be that bad." Lillian assured him. They were in Lillian's apartment agreeing that he would be harder to find there. Dufort had been pacing the room since they got there. A cigarette rolling between his fingers unlit.

"Lillian, I am about to go in there and tell some very humorless people that Father is not dead even though a team of agents signed off saying he was. That will be bad enough, but to then suggest that all our current problems are because of him is just going to be fantastic. We had him. We interviewed him no less than five times after Ikan Hui. I had Rand send over the report. The smug bastard sat there and played us like fools."

"There was a lot going on after the Spartans announced themselves. Mistakes were bound to be made. Anyway, it wasn't you who made them. You were a part of another investigation." Dufort took a deep breath.

"Ah, yes. But I will be revealing the mistakes of my colleagues. Something that is never pleasant." A short silence fell between them.

"Why do you do it Louis?" She put a hand on his arm as he passed her. "You look so tired these days. Like you haven't slept in days. It isn't good for you." Louis covered her hand with his own. Dufort was aware of his temper. It had solved as many problems for him as it had created. Never had he known something like her hand on his arm to calm him so completely. Like a rush, he could feel the exhaustion roll over him. He lifted her hand and placed it gently between both of his and brought it up to his lips. It must have been the exhaustion that allowed him to say, "You are right, mon amour. This job is beginning to take its toll. I have recently been thinking it might be time to retire." He shocked himself as the words left his mouth. "There was a time when I could not imagine doing anything but this. Still, sitting at a desk drives me insane, but running around the world like this, chasing this and that isn't much better."

"I thought you would be one of the ones to die on the job." He still hadn't let go of her hand. Dufort smiled.

"I thought so too. Go out in a blaze of glory, obviously. That's why I never worried about smoking."

"So, what's changed?" Dufort looked up and locked eyes with Lillian. With a shock, she realized what he was telling her. As if there was any doubt, he then said, "This job has already ruined one love of mine. I would be a fool to let it happen again."

"What will the world do without you Louis?"

"Continue to spin, I expect." Dufort leaned in and kissed Lillian with an urgency he had never had before. Picking her up from the chair where she sat, he carried her into the bedroom. She was snuggling into his neck in a very lovely way when his phone rang. Laying her down on the bed, Dufort answered his phone. Lillian could tell from how he was standing that it was serious. He hung the phone up without saying a word.

"I have to go." He said, leaning over her to kiss her again.

"Is it serious? Are Jack and Ross okay?" A smile crossed Dufort's face.

"They are fine, they should be landing in about an hour."

"Then what happened?"

"The generals found out without me telling them that they were allowed to leave." Lillian smiled.

"Are you in a lot of trouble?"

"Maybe, but the tip you gave me about Father will go a long way in distracting them."

"They are going to send you after Ross and Jack aren't they?"

"Possibly, but they will have gotten married by the time I get there and that's the important thing."

"Poor Ross. All she wants is to go back to the life she had before."

"Don't you worry about Dr. Halloway. I'll be the first to admit that this life isn't for everyone, but I have rarely seen a person more capable than she is. You should have seen her against the generals. May I have as much courage. I really do wish Jack all the luck. He is going to need it. I doubt life with Dr. Halloway will ever be boring." Dufort stood up and tried to smooth out the wrinkles in his shirt as best he could with only his hand. "I'll call you whenever this is over."

"I'll be here." Dufort rushed in for one more kiss before he hustled out of her apartment.

33

Jack left out a huge sigh of relief when the plane left the ground. He looked at his watch. They had another twenty minutes before Dufort said he would share what they had learned. The farther they got, the less the chance they would be called back by the generals.

"Hello husband."

"Hello wife." Jack gave one of his best smiles.

"You have to admit, that has to be the strangest wedding you have ever been to." Jack laughed.

"Hopefully, the next one will be closer to normal."

"Oh it will. Belinda will see to it. Just a global pandemic going on in the background." Ross said, waving her hand. "Do you think we are far enough away that I can call and let someone know we are on our way?" Jack looked out the window. "We are over international waters. I would think we are far enough away that the crew won't want to turn back.

"You are calling to tell me you live in England now because you can't get back and I am going to be forced to continue to live without you until this damned virus moves on. Dammit Ross! You never should have left the country." Sam shouted down the phone as a way of greeting. Ross smiled.

" What are you doing awake? It's like five in the morning over there isn't it?"

"I have a two year old Ross. I'm up, we've had cereal and are watching Mickey Mouse Clubhouse right now, and she's told me to stop telling her which mouse-sca- tool it is Mickey needs because she wants to figure it out on her own. Why are you calling me at five in the morning?" Sam sounded tired.

"We are on the plane home. Do you think you can pick us up? We should be landing in three hours." There was a long pause on the phone.

"So you are coming home? Don't mess with me Ross. You did this already and then you hopped a private plane to some part of England you can't tell me about."

"We are actually coming home. We are on our way now."

"How in the hell have you managed that? They have shut down all the airports? I have literally spent an entire twenty-four hours being angry at you because I was sure you weren't going to get back for your own wedding, much less in the next year." It was on the end of Ross's tongue to tell her *that's why Jack and I got married*. Thankfully she managed to hold it in. It was going to be harder than she thought to keep that a secret.

"You wouldn't believe what we had to do to get out."

"Sleep with the prime minister?"

"Ew."

"Sleep with Dufort? Don't worry, I won't tell Jack. A girls gotta do…"

"Shut up! No, I had to join the Spartan Task Force."

"What does that mean? Are you not a chemist anymore? It sounds dangerous. I don't like it." Sam was speaking very quickly for that early in the morning.

"Are you okay? You are talking like you're on speed."

"I've had two cups of coffee already. I chugged the last one."

"It means I advise the task force when it comes to Spartans. Yes, I'm still a chemist because this isn't a real job. It might be dangerous, but I won't know because we are only doing it to get the hell out of the country." Ross hoped her words were true. What Lillian had told her kept playing on repeat in her head.

"I don't believe that, he is going to use it to get you to do something." Sam said, still talking like a hyperactive jack rabbit.

"Like what, there is a pandemic happening? Lillian said all the agents are being sent home."

"Who's Lillian?"

"I'll tell you everything when I get home."

"Damn right you will. I can't believe you are actually coming home this time. Of course I'll meet you at the airport. I'll call around and rally the troops."

"I'm sorry I missed the bachelorette party, Sam. I'm sure it would have been great." Ross said, suddenly filled with love for Sam, who gave her so much.

"Oh I had a bachelorette party."

"What?" Ross said, suspiciously.

"I may have been a little upset that we weren't having a bachelorette party, so I may not have canceled it."

"You had my co-workers and everyone over without me?"

"Plus Si and your mother. I'm pretty sure they thought I

was on the verge of a nervous breakdown."

"Sam?"

"I was a little upset. I really had been planning this night since you planned mine. It was going to be perfect." Ross suddenly felt guilty for agreeing to get on the plane in New York. What had she been thinking? "I mean I had all that food and drink, not to mention the pole in the living room. It turned out to be a really good night actually, we had a lot of fun. Your mom was like the highlight of the evening." Sam said, with a laugh in her voice.

"Please tell me my Mom didn't get on a pole."

"Fine, I won't tell you if you don't want me to. I also won't show you the video."

"She didn't!"

"I mean, she was quite drunk. Belinda and Si got into a dance off. Can you call it a dance off when they are on stripper poles? Anyway, I tell you what, for an old man in overalls, Si can move. I don't think any of us was surprised he knew what a stripper pole was for. We were surprised he did a headstand on the pole. And then did the splits. He had to be helped down afterwards. Belinda, now I was surprised by her. Miss 'sit up straight' and 'say please and thank you' certainly knew how to wrap her leg around a pole and swing. It was impressive."

"I don't believe a word you are saying."

"I have video to prove every word."

" Where was my father while all this was going on?" Ross said, wishing she was having a harder time imagining what Sam was describing. Unfortunately, the picture was coming in very clear.

"Oh your Dad was there, cheering her on. He even brought ones. Thankfully, he just threw them, I wouldn't be able to look him in the eye if he, you know, tucked them anywhere."

"I can't talk about this anymore." Ross said, keeping her mind from wondering where her mother learned to do such things.

"Si stayed here last night, and if your folks are in the same shape he is, it's going to be a quiet day. I've really seen another side of Si this week. He really is an old softy." Ross thought about telling Sam she had found out a few things about Si recently too, but she wasn't sure who all was supposed to know, so she didn't mention it. "He was supposed to stay here with us the whole trip, and he did until we found out you guys had left the country. He went over for dinner with your mom and dad and saw how hard Belinda is having to work to take care of Frank, and the next thing I know, he's moved over there."

"What? He said it was because Ruby was getting up so early." Ross knew things hadn't been easy for her mother. Her father had lost a lot of mobility and almost all of his speech when he had the stroke. He had made great strides with therapy and medications, but he was far from back to normal. Every time she had asked her mother about it though, Belinda had informed her that things were *'fine'*.

"He said the same thing to us. It's fairly obvious now why he moved though. According to your mother, he's been a ton of help. Lifting Frank up, helping feed him. Belinda said she got the best night's sleep she's had in months while Si has been there. Frank has been in a better mood as well. Si even cooked them dinner the other night."

"I've always suspected it." Ross said. She had always felt like the grumpy old sea dog had a soft center.

"You might want to tell Jack, they announced today that Australia has shut its borders to all travelers. Even if you are a national, you have to be quarantined for two weeks before you can properly enter the country." Ross didn't say anything. Not that Jack or Si had mentioned going home immediately after the wedding, it looked like that was going to be harder to do now. "We are going to be so glad to have you back babe." Ross found herself tearing up and she wasn't entirely sure why.

"We'll see you later. Love you babe."

"Love you too."

34

When they landed in Boston, they were met with an equally stark site as they had seen in London. It looked like they had flown into a sci-fi movie set instead of one of the major hubs. All the planes were parked, and where there was usually a hive of activity on the ground, there were only a few tired looking souls.

"Come on, I'd like to get a shower before the wedding." Jack said, taking her elbow. Ross would like to sleep for about fourteen hours, but that wasn't going to happen. They were led into the airport where their temperatures were taken. After showing normal temps, they were driven in one of those little carts to the security area where they dragged their luggage through customs. Ross had no sooner cleared the security zone before she was hit with something and thrown backwards onto the floor. Hands gripped her face, and she was nose to nose with someone so close she couldn't' focus on them properly. The fabric of their mask tickled her nose.

"You finally fucking made it!" Sam said, sitting on Ross's chest. Sam leaned over and gave Ross a mask to mask kiss.

Jack had been surprised by the attack and had realized who it was just in time to keep himself from punching Sam. Security was a little nervous as well. Jack saw the nearest guard put his hand on his gun and take a step towards them.

"It's alright. They are……friends." Jack tried to explain as Sam was kissing his wife. "They haven't seen each other in a while." The guard stepped back and said, "Young love, eh?" Jack just nodded. It would take too long to explain.

"I can't believe it, you are actually here. We have never been apart this long Ross. And we never will be again. You hear me?" Sam said, with her new 'mom' voice that made it sound more like a threat.

"Sam."

"Yes?"

"I can't breathe." Between Sam and the mask, Ross was about to lose it. Sam kissed her again and then got to her feet, holding out a hand for Ross. "Jack, don't get jealous. Come here." And with similar enthusiasm, Sam grabbed Jack's face in both hands and gave him a proper mask to mask kiss.

"I didn't think you could look any better, but you might be hotter in a mask. I can't believe Ross lets you walk around like that." Thankfully his mask hid Jack's blushing.

"Good to see you again Sam." Jack said.

"I have to say, you are very awake at this time of the morning." Ross pointed out.

"I've been here since you called. The cafe over there accidently gave me an espresso. If you didn't get here soon, I was going to start flying myself. I was terrified you weren't going to make it, I couldn't wait. I kept waiting for the phone to buzz and for you to tell me you weren't going to get here after all. Come one, they're all there waiting for you. Your mom made mimosas." They were all walking towards the exits and the parking garage.

"At this hour?"

"Oh yeah. It's a big deal you coming home, Ross. You have to remember, the last time we saw you was before the shooting. Everyone is eager to see you for themselves and make sure you are okay." Ross didn't know what to say to that. "Your mother had been freaking out with all the closures. She's convinced they are going to close the church at the last minute. I told her earlier it would just be easier to bring the minister to my house and do the ceremony there instead of us all heading over to the church. She didn't think that a wedding held in the same room as a stripper pole gave the right sense of occasion."

"You'll have to forgive her, she's not as classy as we are." Ross said. Jack let the two women go ahead locked arm in arm while he carried the luggage. A smile on his face.

"I've got mimosa's for us ladies. There is probably something stronger if you are wanting that. Jack, do you want something to drink? Do you want wine? There is whiskey in the house thanks to Si. I suppose we could stop and get something else if you want it. They left the liquor stores open."

"At this hour of the day?" Ross pointed out.

"Don't be judgy Ross. There is a pandemic on, you can now drink whenever you want."

"I could murder a whiskey. Thanks Sam." When they pulled into the driveway, Ross was somewhat surprised to hear music and laughter both so loud she could hear them in the driveway. Sam noticed her pause.

"They've been going for an hour and half now. Lord knows what my HOA is going to have to say about all of this. Si has already promised a repeat performance on the stripper poles. Your mother was refusing when I left to come get you, but who knows what they've gotten up to while I've been gone."

"I'm surprised Ruby can sleep with all that noise."

"I sent her to Phillip's mother for the weekend. I cried like a baby when I dropped her off, but it's for the best. If things close down much more, it might be a while before they have her again." Sam said, seeming more serious than she had so far. They got out of the car, but Ross and Jack paused in their step. Neither one was sure they were ready for this.

"He kept his clothes on though, right?" Jack asked. "It's just, Si's been known to go a bit natural when he drinks." Jack asked, wondering how much apologizing he was going to have to do.

"He undid one strap on the overalls, but he couldn't do that and hang upside down at the same time. So, thankfully that is where it stopped."

"Thank god for that." Jack looked at Ross. "I guess we better get in there. It's only going to get worse the longer we wait." Ross was smiling from ear to ear. Much to her amazement, she was looking forward to it. She took a step forward. "Hold on." Sam said, putting a hand on her shoulder.

"What?"

"Firstly….it is so damn good to see you, honey." And Sam gave her another hug. "Secondly, you are going to want some of this." Producing a bottle of wine from behind a potted plant.

"What in the hell?"

"It's after midnight in England." Jack justified. Ross took the bottle and hoisted it, taking a few swallows before handing it back to Sam.

"So our parents are in there, three sheets to the wind at…" Ross looked at her watch. "Nearly ten in the morning."

"Ross, I'm telling you. I don't know what it is, it must be this pandemic, but they are like twenty year-olds in there. Si said something about needing the hair of the dog when he arrived. I thought your mother would get after him, get him some black coffee. Instead, she finds him a glass for the whiskey he pulled out of his pocket. I figured if I was going to have something for the bride to drink, I better hide it." Ross was humbled by how much Sam thought of her needs.

"I'll be surprised if there is any of that whiskey you promised." Jack said. Ross took a few more swallows and then handed it back to Sam who took a decent swig. None of them seemed ready to join the chaos inside the house. Pausing for a moment before opening the door. Sam pushed Ross through the door first since she was the one they wanted to see and then pulled Jack's arm to hold him back.

"I'm glad to see you are wearing a thick pair of pants, Jack." Sam said to his back.

"What?"

"Have you ever seen Belinda drunk?" Sam asked.

"She had a couple of glasses of wine when I came for Christmas. She was very friendly, but nothing terrible. Why?"

"Nothing, it's just Belinda has been drinking for a few

days now. They all have. I don't know what this pandemic has done to the over sixties crowd, but they have gone buck-wild. I know I have told you a few things, but honestly, I have seen things I will never be able to unsee."

"I don't understand." Jack said, wondering how this related to what kind of pants he was wearing. Sam put up her hand and took a deep breath.

"I never told Ross, but at my wedding, Phillip said Belinda and my Aunt Rachel had a few too many and apparently harassed the groomsmen. There was a lot of butt pinching, but also worse things. It made all the groomsmen incredibly uncomfortable. So, I'd keep your legs crossed and stand against the wall if I were you." Sam smacked his ass as she passed him just in case there was any doubt about her meaning. Sam went into the house, leaving Jack confused on the front porch.

35

Jack parked the luggage in the dining room. There was music playing, *Credence Clearwater* if he wasn't mistaken. For as early as it was in the morning, there certainly seemed to be a party going on. Jack walked into the living room to find Ross in the firm embrace of her mother. Not wanting to interrupt, Jack locked eyes with Si as soon as he walked in the door. "Ah, you finally made it." Si came over, arms thrown wide. A whiskey in one hand.

"Jesus man, drinking at this hour?"

"You fight off the germs your way, and I'll fight them my way." Si said, pointing to Jack's mask.

"We need to talk."

"Sure, sure." Si put his arm loosely around Jack's neck and guided him into the kitchen. "Now, there's nothing to be nervous about, son. Just because your last marriage ended miserably, there is no reason to think this marriage will be the same. For one thing Ross is a much better class of person."

"I hadn't even .... Jesus man. It's not about my marriage." Si looked confused.

"Then what is it about? I already told you about the birds and the bees. I know for a fact you and Ross have gone around the mulberry bush a few times." Jack looked around to make sure there was no one else around.

"Why didn't you ever tell me you worked for Interpol?" Si said nothing. The smile had dropped from his face.

"I got to look at your file while I was there." Si said nothing. "You were an informant for them, Dad. Your information led to the break up of one of the largest Asian drug cartels."

"If you know so much, then you know I had to sign a paper saying I wouldn't discuss it until it had become declassified. As far as I know, that has not happened." Si took a drink of his whiskey. Jack stood there in shock.

"Well you can say something now. I have the same security clearance." Si's eyebrows shot up.

"You're working for them? Doing what?"

"We had to join the Spartan Task Force to get the clearance to fly out. Dufort arranged it all. That's why he was able to show me your file."

"Jack, what do you want me to say? You know it all from my file." Si said, standing up straighter.

"Mum and I were sitting at home waiting for you to come home. As if living on the sea wasn't dangerous enough. They would have killed you without even thinking about it. Did you ever think of that? Did you ever think that they would kill you and dump you somewhere and we would never know what happened?"

"Of course." Si said. "Son, why do you think I did it?"

"Because you are mentally unstable?"

"They were selling drugs, boy. I saw kids as young as you were at the time walking onto those boats. They were using them to sell it to other kids. They knew kids would get a lesser charge if they were caught. They were bringing that stuff into my country and using kids to shift it. Selling it to other kids. Getting them hooked when they didn't even know what the stuff was. I wasn't always home. I wasn't at all your games, or school award day. I wasn't there because I was on the boat all the time. Making what money I could to send home to you two. I slept on the boat and ate tinned beans so I could bring everything home to you and your Mum. It was something I could do to make sure it was a safe home. That you weren't being asked to do those things by your mates."

"Dad…." Si held up his hand.

"Because I was always on the boat, I saw everyone who was coming and going. I knew who should be in those docks and who shouldn't be. I could stop those bastards from bringing drugs into my country. And who was going to suspect the old drunk on the boat? Hell, one time the drug dealers paid me to stay silent. Ha. I got your mother a new car that year. I couldn't do much son, but I like to think I did everything I was able to do. Including that." Si slapped Jack's shoulder.

"I have spent almost every day with you for as long as I can remember. More in my adult life than when I was a kid. We have spent months alone, out on the water, in a boat with no one else to talk to. It never once crossed your mind to tell me about all this?" Jack said.

"No." Si shrugged. Jack was about to protest when Si interrupted him. "I signed one of those things, didn't I. Besides. The last thing I need is one of those drug dealers finding out their buddy is in jail because of my big mouth."

"Did Mum ever know?"

"Never. It would have worried her. What else did my file say?"

"Apparently, you're a legend."

"I'm surprised you ever doubted it." There was a pause and then Si added. "I wasn't much of a father Jack. I wasn't there to be one. Your mother was a saint doing it all on her own. You have no idea how many times I worried who would protect you if something happened while I was away. To be honest, there were more than a few storms that had me wondering if the end was coming. When they approached me and I could help, I did. " Si wiped away a tear. A rare thing. "You just wait, son. You'll feel the same way when your day comes."

"Yeah well....that's a conversation for a different day. Sam says you are pretty good on a stripper pole. Where the hell did you learn that?" They walked back into the room with the others. Ross was sitting in a chair with her hair up in rollers and a fresh glass of mimosa while Belinda examined the pink scar on Ross's neck. Ross looked incredibly uncomfortable, but there was nothing Jack could do for her.

"Like I said, I didn't hang out with saints." Si gave Jack a wink. He then said, "Now, if you'll excuse me, I have to go get dressed. It's my son's wedding today. You better start getting booted and suited yourself. Don't want to be late."

"Ross, I'm going to go take a shower." Jack said, to the room in general. "You look great, Love." He said to Ross who looked like she was in her idea of hell with people all around her making a fuss.

When he came out of the bathroom, his suit was hanging up on the back of a closet door. He dressed carefully but quickly. As he was putting his shoes on, he noticed the house was quieter than it had been, and he came out of the room feeling the same quiet. "Ross?"

"They've taken her to the church to get ready." Phillip informed him. Jack got an uneasy feeling. It was at that moment he realized Ross had not been more than a few feet away from him in months.

"When are we leaving for the church?" Jack asked, trying to calm the anxious feeling in his chest.

"Ten minutes. I have strict orders and have been threatened with unspeakable acts if I do not keep to the time table. You aren't to see Ross until she is walking down that aisle. Orders. Here, you are going to need this I think." And Phillip handed him a whiskey. Philip already had one.

"I hope Sam took enough drinks." Jack said, thinking of how Ross was probably hating all the attention she was getting at the moment.

"Judging from the clinking in her bag, she is stocked for the rest of the year."

"Oh my goodness. You look fantastic Roslyn." Belinda said, cupping her hands over her face, tears coming down. Ross rolled her eyes. Her mother was the only person on the planet who was allowed to call her Roslyn. But it drove her crazy. Ross looked in the mirror and smiled. She felt like a bride and it didn't feel terrible.

"Thanks Mom."

"Oh, honey. I've always been proud of you, but today I feel like I could burst." Her mother said, continuing to fuss with the dress. "You've accomplished a lot in your short years and you're very independent. But I'm glad you have found a partner in life."

"It doesn't hurt that he has a tight ass." Sam added, touching up her lashes in the mirror.

"Now, Samantha. What Jack looks like doesn't matter. It's how he treats my girl that matters to me."

"That's not what you were saying the other night Belindy." Belinda shot Sam a warning glance.

"That's enough out of you."

"Weren't you saying just last night that they were going to make beautiful babies?" Sam said. Belinda tried to get upset, but couldn't hide her smile. Ross shot her mother a look.

"You can't stop me from dreaming. If Jack's natural looks help that process along, all the better."

"Mother!" Ross said, blushing.

"Oh Ross, stop pretending I don't know where babies come from. You have a degree in science for goodness sake." Belinda looked at herself in the mirror. "I remember when I first saw your father. It was like something clicked. Something I never knew I didn't have, but once I found it, I couldn't go another day without it."

"Oh my god, Mom! I've never heard you talk like this about Dad." Ross said, floored.

"Oh yes. I thought that man would never ask me to marry him."

"You could have asked him." Sam said.

"I almost had to. He asked me to marry him and a week later I found out I was pregnant." Ross whirled around and locked eyes with Sam. Sam whipped around from the mirror and locked stunned eyes with Ross. Belinda blissfully was running a lint roller over her skirt like she hadn't just dropped a huge bomb. "It was earlier than we had planned, of course." Belinda went on, not knowing the stunned looks that watched her in amazement. "We were always going to get married. That's certainly where things were heading, and we both wanted it, but I was going to go for my doctorate in biology. Your father had this crazy notion he was going to go out and make his fortune and then come back and marry me. As if I was ever going to let him go." Belinda laughed and didn't look around the room until she realized no one had said anything for a while. "What?"

"Mom, you never told me this. You were going to get your doctorate?" Belinda shrugged. Still futzing with the dress.

"That's what you focused on?" Sam said, "Belinda, you were pregnant before you married Frank?"

"It never came up." She looked up at Ross and locked eyes with her. "What's the big deal? You wouldn't think anything of a pregnant bride now. They have maternity wedding dresses. It wasn't that unusual back then to be honest, it's just your grandparents would have had a fit. We just told them you were a week early."

"Damn, Belinda!" Sam said.

"Why are you crying?" Belinda said, looking at Ross.

"Mom, you just told me I ruined your life plan. You had a career you wanted." Belinda looked at Sam. Saw her stunned expression and finally realized what she had said.

"I've really never told you this?" Belinda said. Ross shook her head. "Ross, honey. You didn't ruin a damn thing. Your father and I were over the moon to find you were on the way. Shocked. But over the moon."

"What about your doctorate?"

"What about it? You don't think I would have gone back

and gotten it if I had really wanted it?" Ross's mother had always been a woman who let very little get in her way. Ross didn't have a hard time believing that if her mom had wanted a doctorate after having her, she would have gotten one.

"Why didn't you want it anymore?" Ross said, not completely convinced. "You could have been Dr. Belinda Halloway."

"Because it no longer seemed important." Belinda said, as if this was the obvious answer. Her hands on her hips. "I had you and your father. I was the happiest I had ever been in my life. What better thing could I have done than raise a fantastic human being?"

"Don't you wonder what life would have been like if you had gotten your doctorate?"

"No." Belinda said, matter of factly. "I know what it would have been. I would have spent endless nights working instead of taking care of you. I would have regretted all the lost moments with you and your father, and all I would have to show for it would be a piece of paper and some letters after my name. Not to belittle your doctorate dear. I know what that means to you, Ross, and you earned it with blood sweat and tears. Mine wouldn't have meant that much to me."

"What about your dreams?"

"I got new dreams." Her mother said with steel in her eyes. "Of course I did. It wouldn't make sense for me to still be striving for the same things I did in high school."

"To what? Stay home cooking, cleaning and wiping dirty faces?" Ross said, describing her idea of hell. Belinda looked her daughter straight in the eye.

"No, Roslyn. My dream was to raise a badass woman.

One with brains to match anyone and a backbone to make use of it. You are my dream Ross. You have done everything I wanted to do and then some. The world and the human race are better because of you." Belinda could still see the confusion in their faces. "Listen girls, women's liberation wasn't so that all of us had to go to work and have top earning jobs. It meant we got to choose. I made my choice, and I haven't regretted it for one day. Not one."

"What else don't I know about you and Dad?" Ross said, still stunned. Belinda smiled.

"That's pretty much it, dear."

"Did you know they met in a strip club?" Sam said, smiling from ear to ear.

"Sam-anth-a. You swore you wouldn't repeat that."

"Did I? I'm so sorry Belinda, I had a few drinks that night, I don't remember." Ross's mouth was just opening and closing. Belinda held up a hand to Ross.

"It's not what you think. I worked there.....as a bartender."

"....and Dad?"

"Came in one night with a bachelor party. He wasn't really into that sort of thing, so he sat at the bar all night talking to me. One thing led to another, and there you go. He really was the sweetest man I had ever met."

"That's how she learned how to work a stripper pole." Sam said.

"Sam, you make it sound like it was something dirty. They were nice girls. I made a comment one night after closing about some of the things they did on the pole. They looked so hard to do. They offered to show me a few, that was all. Sam, can you text Jack and see how much longer they are going to be? Close your mouth, Ross. We were young once too with all the things that went with it. Now, let's go out there and get you married." Belinda said, taking her daughter's hands. Ross would have to process all this another time.

36

Jack and Phillip were standing next to the front door. Phillip had pulled their minivan up and they were ready to go.

"Si, hurry up." Jack yelled down the hallway. Si came out of one of the rooms. "Sam texted, they are ready for us. Honestly, the man has never taken this long to get ready in his life."

"Keep your shirt on. I'm coming." Si said, coming down the hallway. "You can't be serious. That is what you are wearing?" Jack said. Si had come out wearing a brand new pair of black overalls. He smoothed down his bib and polished his buckles with the cuff of his crisp white shirt before answering, "I will have you know, I have permission from the bride herself to wear these." Si looped his thumbs through the straps of his overalls to make his point.

"Ross said you could wear overalls?"

"Said she couldn't picture me any other way." Si said. That sounded about right.

"Sam just texted again. The language is getting strong.

We better get over there." Phillip said.

Per the current guidelines, it was a very small affair. Jack, Phillip and Si took up positions at the front of the church with just a few other people sprinkled throughout. Sam had gotten them black face masks to match their suites. Frank had gone back to wherever the women were so he could escort Ross down the aisle. The minister hit the button on the stereo and the music kicked on.

Hidden behind the church doors,Ross heard the music and froze.

"Take a deep breath, Ross. It'll be fine. There are only about five people out there." Sam said, having seen Ross's face drain of blood.

"I thought it would be easier this time." Ross had said it without thinking.

"What do you mean?" Sam said, unassuming. Ross quickly tried to think of a lie. A plausible lie. There was nothing. Sam looked up and saw her friends' face and instantly knew something was wrong.

"Ross.....what did you mean?"

"Nothing, slip of the tongue."

"No, I know that face. What are you hiding?" Ross took a deep breath.

"We didn't think we would get back." She said in a panic. "They were shutting down all the airports. Dufort wasn't even sure he was going to figure something out. We kind of got married over there." Sam said nothing. She just looked Ross in the eyes. Ross waited for the tantrum she deserved. Sam shrugged. "Well then what are you so freaked about?"

Ross wasn't freaked anymore.

"Sam. I thought you would be livid."

"Did you have a maid of honor?"

"No." Sam shrugged. "You're not upset?"

"Ross, honey, it was always going to be a long shot getting you to walk down the aisle. It is nothing short of a miracle that you are standing here right now. So no, I'm not mad. I get it. You were stuck over there, everything is shutting down, no one knows what the next day is going to bring with this thing. I get it. Now. If I ever find out you made up the story about Dufort taking you over there and that you and Jack just did it to avoid getting married here, I'll skin you alive."

"I have pictures to back up my story. And witnesses."

"....and as long as no one else was your maid of honor because I am your maid of honor. No one else."

"I love you."

"I love you too babe, and don't forget it." They were interrupted by Belinda coming back in with Frank. Belinda stopped his wheelchair and put on the brakes. She then moved to foot plates out of his way.

"What are you doing?" Ross asked.

"Your father has a surprise for you dear. He's been working on it since he learned you were getting married." Belinda came around the front of the wheelchair and put her hands out to her husband. On the count of three, she pulled Frank to a standing position. With a smile, he then shuffled over to his daughter and took her arm. Frank had not been able to walk since his stroke.

"He wanted to walk his daughter down the aisle." Belinda added, handing her husband a cane. A great sob escaped Ross. Sam was wiping away the tears from her eyes trying to avoid messing up her makeup. "Damn it Frank, you could have warned me." Sam said. Not giving

Ross any time to recover, Belinda threw open the doors and there was the aisle in question, Jack and Si smiling at the end of it. The music hit the right note, and Ross took her first step down the aisle with her mother on one side and her father on the other. Her best friend led the charge as usual. Then they took another step, and another. Slow and steady. Ross was so fixated on making sure she wasn't moving too fast for her father, they were at the altar before she knew it.

The minister asked Belinda and Frank 'Who gives this woman away in matrimony?'

"Her…..mother…..and…..I …..do." Frank said, slowly but clearly. A surprised gasp went through the room, including Belinda. "Been….working….on….that….too." Frank said, winking at Ross. After that, Ross was a teary mess, and she hardly paid attention to what the minister was saying. She responded in all the right places, and thanks to endless romcoms, she knew what to say, but she didn't take any of it in. Not until Jack pulled a folded piece of paper out of his breast pocket. That hadn't happened the last time they did this. What was he doing?

Shit. The vows. He had already told her his vows. What was he doing? Ross's heart started beating rapidly. Her hands went sweaty and her vision went blurry.

"Ross. Ever since I met you, several things have happened I never thought possible. I have nearly been blown apart. I have been held hostage, and shot." It sounded very dramatic, but it was all true. "In fact, that could be considered our first date." There was a little laughter from the crowd. "I have also fallen in love when I swore to never do such a thing again. And not just a little bit." Jack stopped looking at the paper in his hands and looked Ross in the eye. "You have often wondered where we would live if we ever got to this point. The fact of the matter is, I don't care. I used to think the only place I would feel at home was at sea. Now, I only feel at home when I'm with you. Wherever you are Ross. That is my home. As long as I have you, I have everything I need. I love you Ross. In a way I never thought possible, and I want to say before everyone here, that I always will. Whatever storm comes over the horizon, I want to be with you. *May no Ivy tear us asunder.*" Jack whispered. Ross looked over Jack's shoulder at Si who was dabbing away tears with the palm of his hand. She looked around the church for inspiration and found nothing. The bastard.

There was a long pause while Ross's mind spun aimlessly looking for the words to say what she wanted. Whatever that was. Fuck it. Ross thought to herself. Taking a deep breath, Ross laid herself bare.

"I tried so hard to convince myself I didn't want this. Us. You mentioned our first date. Our second date you came for Christmas." Ross shifted from one foot to the other. "On what could be called our third date, I woke up in a hospital. It was my turn to be shot. I had no idea where I was. The pain was incredible. Yours was the first face I saw, and one thing was very clear to me from the moment I saw that you were there. I was safe. I felt safe. I knew that while you were there, nothing would happen to me. Now, this was not evidence based because, as you have pointed out, bad things seem to happen when we are together. But I remember how safe I felt. I am constantly amazed at how you love me Jack. I don't pretend to understand why. You seem to see something in me I don't see, but I am amazed nonetheless. I want you to know, I will never take it for granted. And no matter what kind of trouble we get ourselves into, you're the one I want with me. You can come too, of course." Ross turned and said to Sam. Jack's hands were already cupping her face before the minister pronounced them husband and wife and gave them permission to kiss.

One of the things Ross loved the most about Jack was his ability to kiss. The one he gave her there, in front of their family, made the angels blush. They turned and faced the witnesses to claps and shouts. Sam did a wolf whistle and clapped the loudest. Feeling the moment, Jack picked Ross up and carried her back down the aisle.

"Don't want you falling on your way out."

"Everyone back to my house for the reception. Minister, you too." Sam hit the button and music played them out. Sam and Phillip dancing all the way. Taking their cue, Frank lifted his arm and Belinda spun underneath it. Si took the hand of the minister who seemed appalled at first, but then caught the spirit with the rest of them and allowed himself to be twirled and danced back down the aisle. They were all still laughing when the doors of the church closed behind them. Leaving the five guests who had managed to make it to witness the wedding wondering exactly what they had just seen.

37

Dr. Fuqin stepped up to the customs agent and handed over his passport.

"Dr. Phillip Fuqin, returning home?"

"Yes."

"What took you to China, Sir?"

"Business trip."

"I'm going to need you to step over here. You have been randomly selected for extra security screening." The hairs on the back of Dr. Fuqin's neck stood up. He searched the agent's face for any sign that this was anything more than what had been said. Not wanting to cause alarms if there was no need. The agent's face was blank.

"Randomly selected?" He inquired. The agent gave a watered down smile. "They are keeping a close eye on the flights from China. Things being what they are right now." This did nothing to settle Dr. Fuqin's nerves. Nevertheless, Dr. Fuqin followed the agent to a small room.

"Please have a seat." The agent asked. Dr. Fuqin sat. All his alarms were going off. At the first sign of trouble he was prepared to make a run for it.

"What kind of screening is this?" Dr. Fuqin asked. Inspector Dufort turned in the chair and said, "I regret to inform you Dr. Phillip Fuqin, a.k.a. Father, that Interpol has put out a red notice on you. You are under arrest." Dr. Fuqin turned and opened the door to run. He was instantly met with five heavily armed guards.

"Come on now, Dr. Fuqin, we have a lot to discuss." Dufort saw the man's shoulder's relax. He knew he was caught.

"I want to talk to him." Lillian said, standing next to Dufort. He had brought her in secretly to see Dr. Fuqin and make sure she still thought he actually was Father.

"That is impossible. I would never allow that. He knows who you are." Dufort instantly said.

"Louis, what are the chances he is getting out of here?"

"It doesn't matter. No one knows you are alive. If you go in there, he will know, which means there is a chance your cover will be blown. I won't allow it."

"You know I am alive." Dufort grumbled.

"You know I would never betray that trust."

"What opportunity is he going to have? Is he going to make a call to the Kremlin from his cell?"

"He could tell his lawyer, and then they tell someone and so on."

"You have a stack of paperwork proving I am Dr. Lillian Kuzlow. Let me do this. Please. I think he will talk to me."

"What makes you think that?" Lillian shrugged like she did most of the time he asked her about her life before the attack. "I will not be able to admit any of it in court." He added.

"I know. But you might be able to piece together some of the story a little better." Louis looked back and forth between the two of them. Lillian had chosen her words well. She knew he wanted to know what happened more than anything else. He hesitated, but then said, "I will be right here. Do you understand me? I'm not going anywhere." Lillian nodded and then entered the small interview room. Louis stayed in the viewing room with the infamous two-way mirror. Dr. Fuqin was sitting sideways to accommodate his long legs being crossed. When Lillian entered the room, he looked up. Severely jet lagged, it took him a moment to recognize her.

"I know you. Where from? I'm sorry, but I'm having a hard time recollecting."

"Cambridge. I caught your lecture on the benefits of genetic modification on select animal and plant species concentrating on hydration and growth time." Lillian casually walked into the room. Fuqin smiled at the mention of his work.

"No wonder I can't remember. That has to be twenty years ago now. Wait." Father held up his hand, thinking. "Dr. Petrov." Louis shook his head. Lillian smiled.

"You do remember."

"It's hard to forget being firmly corrected on concepts of communism in front of your colleagues by the newest hire in the biochem lab." Father said it with a smile. "I'll have you know, your words had an impact. That and working more closely with the Chinese. I still maintain it's a lovely idea, just ruined in its execution."

"I'm the reason you are here I'm afraid." Lillian admitted, sitting down across from him. Father raised his eyebrows, but said nothing. "Through my work, I'm connected to the Spartan investigation. They caught a picture of you in the lab in China. I made the connection in your name and 'Father'."

"Ah, Merideth Mother's ridiculous idea. She caught the English meaning of my name and thought it was hilarious that she was Mother and I was Father. So, they have pictures of the lab in China?" Father smiled at her. Lillian raised her eyebrows and nodded. I suppose it was only a matter of time." Lillian noted that he didn't exactly look disappointed that the lab had been found.

"You look a little different with the eye patch, but it was your blue eye and gray hair that gave it away I'm afraid. Did you lose your eye while faking your death?" Father smiled.

"No, one of the chemicals we use to keep the Shi stable while they grow is highly corrosive, especially if it comes in contact with human skin, or eyes. I'm afraid this was nothing more than a workplace accident."

"They are rather curious as to how you faked your death. Interpol. I assume Spartans played a role?"

"Of course. I wouldn't have been able to do it without their expertise. They created the documents I needed. Found the dead body we used. Planted the bomb that created the fire. They even found a body with blue eyes and gray hair. Always attention to detail. I was very proud of them. Mother, I suppose, should get some of the credit. If she hadn't insisted on using my rather silly nickname on everything, it would have made it a lot harder. As it was, Dr. Phillip Fuqin was able to exist after Genetix with little trouble." He said, looking rather proud of himself. Lillian noticed a certain tone when Father mentioned Mother. Not a favorable tone.

"It's strange to me that the Spartans would want to help you, but they seemed to want Mother gone so incredibly bad." Dr. Fuqin's face turned serious.

"I never could see the sense in treating them like they were machines. You go through all the trouble of creating these amazing creatures. You train them to be the best killers in the world and then you treat them like trash. She was asking for it. In secret, she always thought they would hunt her down and kill her in her sleep. Spent hundreds of thousands on security. They knew where to really hurt her though. They made her confess what she had done. Confessing to the world what Genetix was doing was essentially making her kill herself. There was no way there wouldn't be an investigation that would shut it down. Though, I'm sure part of her was all too pleased to finally reveal to the world her creation."

"Did you speak to her that day? When the Spartans attacked Ikan Hui?" Father nodded his head.

"I saw her right before she killed herself as a matter of fact. Not that I knew she was going to do that. When she called for me, it seemed like it was to tell me what was happening. That the Spartans had taken over the resort. I didn't realize she had erased my contribution to the project so completely until that moment."

"I don't know a lot about what goes into making a Spartan, but if the timeline is correct, you had already sold information to the Chinese and they must have had some part of the lab ready to go by the time Ikan Hui happened. Why betray Mother? Were you thinking of leaving the project?" Father crossed his legs and brushed away something on his knee.

"The Spartan's were Mother's idea. There is no denying

that. I was told in the beginning that all the credit would be shared. We would be partners."

"Mother didn't seem the type to share." Lillian prodded. Dr. Fuqin's face turned dark.

"No, she wasn't. It became very clear she had no intention of sharing the credit. When important people came around, sure they talked to me, but she always proclaimed herself the Spartan's creator."

"Why didn't you say something?"

"Because what we were doing was illegal. If it all went to shit, she would take the fall. Or most of it. That's what I told myself anyway, but I couldn't let it go. Sure she had the idea, but her science had gotten nothing but useless globs. I had made the Spartans what they were, everyone should have been talking to me." Lillian knew she had him, his ego wouldn't allow him to not admit his role in the Spartans.

"Mother already had the military contract when you joined?"

"Oh yes. She knew what she wanted and she knew what she wanted to do with them. Saving the average soldier from being blown to bits. Taking war away from the humans and leaving it to the Spartans. She knew there would be a wide demand for such a thing. Mother was a good scientist, but she was even better at marketing."

"You said her results were nothing more than useless globs. How many tries did it take to get the Spartans as they are now?"

"Once I took over, a few. The first generation looked human, but some of the mutations hadn't gone as well as planned. The second generation was almost perfect. A few tweaks needed to be made, some of the samples had gotten rather warmer than was preferable."

"What happened to those generations?"

"We kept them around to help with the training of the Spartans. They would need to practice their skills. Many of them had specializations. They assisted in that." It was made to sound like they were nothing more than pieces of training equipment.

" You mean they were killed." Dr. Fuqin shrugged and nodded his head as if this was obvious.

"They were mistakes. Not fit for purpose at all. What else were we supposed to do with them?" This was said so matter of factly.

"Did you ever consider the ethics?" Lillian knew he certainly hadn't been guided by them. She wanted to know if they had ever even occurred to him.

"Ah, ethics." Father leaned across the table. "I think the Spartans are a fantastic example of how far we can push science when we untether our minds. When we stop putting limits on what we can do. When we stop giving ourselves reasons to stop, look at what we can accomplish." This was said with the same self assurance Lillian had watched him preach the benefits of communism. He leaned back again. "Of course, I thought about stopping. I knew what they were going to be used for at that point. I should have stopped it, but I just wanted to see the final product. I needed to see that it was possible. That I could make life. And then I did, and they were perfect." He smiled.

"You designed them to be perfect." Louis heard the change in Lillian's voice. Father was starting to piss her off and the poor bastard had no idea.

"I know, but it was amazing that it had all worked." His

face turned serious. "When the military returned them, Mother wanted them killed. Shot as they got off the plane." Father's face turned red. A small vein on the side of his temple appeared. "*My* creations. *My* perfect beings." He took a deep breath before continuing. In a much calmer voice he said, "I'm sure you can appreciate as a scientist how many things had to be thought out and planned for such a thing as a Spartan to come into being. How many little things could have gone wrong that didn't. Thankfully, the board couldn't stomach it. Murder." Father had turned dark. "No one ever asked me. Never asked me what I thought should happen to *MY* creation. Whatever they decided, I would have had to go along with it. That was bad enough, that no one thought to ask the man who had spent endless nights, weeks, months....fucking years making sure the temperatures were perfect. They were hitting their growth markers. That the pods never ran out of the constant supply of nutrients and blood they needed to perform. Fucking Mother was only ever in the Pod house long enough to yell that things weren't moving fast enough. She knew what they were. She knew more than most what had gone into creating them. She knew they were better than a human, they were perfect. And she was just going to kill them." He was practically spitting out the words. White spittle formed at the corners of his mouth. "That's when I decided to leave. Mother had shown there was a future in making soldiers. I wanted to have the say over what happened to my creations." He wiped away the spittle and resumed his look of calm.

"How did you get the information out of the lab?"

"It wasn't all that hard. I gathered a team of like minded individuals. Mother had a way of putting people off if she didn't find them important. I took the leads from the departments. They brought their information with them. No one person, other than Mother, knew all the components that went into making a Spartan. I knew how to make them, but I had no idea how to maintain the machines that kept the Spartans stable while they matured. The chemicals used can only be gotten from certain suppliers. We spent over a year gathering what information we could to make sure that we could deliver Spartans to those who would be able to pay. I have to be honest, when Mother called me into her office that day, I thought it was because she had figured out what we were doing. As you said, we had already landed the Chinese contract. I was weeks away from handing in my notice. Half the team had already left. When she told me she had essentially erased me from the project 'to save me' I really didn't know how to react."

"Like you said, she did you a favor in a way." Father shook his head.

"Mother took my name off the papers because she intended to take the credit. Nothing more, nothing less." Pounding his finger on the table to emphasize his point. "The greatest breakthrough in science in our lifetime and she stole it from me. Newsreel after newsreel had Mother as the creator of the Spartans. Father helped. Not even my real name but the stupid bloody nickname she gave me. *The Spartans killed their creator. Spartans take revenge on their creator.*" He leaned across the table now. "She tormented them and sold them. They killed her because they knew she would never stop as long as there was money to be made. They're smart, you see. The Spartans. They know what they are. They know they were never meant to be a part of the civilian population. They are a pack of wolves who have been released into the lamb's meadow. Even they knew it was wrong, but what else are they supposed to do? Wolves hunt. Wolves kill. It's all they know to do."

"You'll have to forgive me, but you were facilitating the creation of Shi for the Chinese. Are you not doing the same thing as Mother?"

"The hypocrisy is not lost on me. I have become a version of myself that I am not proud of. Who knows, when the Spartans find out, they might come after me like they did Mother. I would deserve nothing less. But the Shi, they are mine. The creation of Dr. Phillip Fuqin. At last the world will know who it really was who created the Spartans. Who made it possible to custom tailor human life." Father turned his cold blue eye to Lillian in a way that made the hair stand on her arms. "You know none of this can be used in court?" Lillian gave a small smile.

"I do know. This was simply for my own curiosity. There is more than enough evidence in your involvement with the Spartans to put you in prison for the rest of your natural life." Lillian got up and headed for the door. "If the Spartans don't catch up to you first."

"It was good to see you again, Dr. Petrov. I'm glad you have found good employment after your death. I know how hard it can be finding good work when you are legally dead." Lillian knew this was meant to intimidate her. Father wanted her to know he knew her secret.

She smiled at him in the completely ingenuine way she had and said, "When you are on the right side of things, Dr. Fuqin, you have the benefit of having friends who will help. It's a pity a brilliant mind like yours couldn't have used its talents in a way that benefited humanity instead of perfecting the worst parts of it." She closed the door before he could add anymore. Lillian and Duffort watched in silence as the guard came and escorted Father out of the interview room.

"He's insane." Dufort said.

"He always struck me as someone that got stranger the more you got to know him." Lillian said. They both watched as he was escorted out of the room in cuffs. When the room was empty, Dufort said, "I have more questions, but that will definitely do for now."

"He will answer them." Lillian said with confidence.

"What makes you so sure?"

"He's caught. It's over. If he is going to let the world know he is the mastermind behind the Spartans like he seems to want to do, then this is his last chance." Dufort watched her. There was a sharpness to her that he hadn't seen since the attack. Her eyes seemed more alive.

"You obviously know more about the original investigation than I do, but was there ever any mention of where the genetic material for the Spartans came from?"

"I had hardly anything to do with the investigation into Genetix, not past how it affected the Spartans. Why?"

"Well, the Spartans range in ethnicity. As far as I know, genetically altered or not, you still need sperm and an egg to make a human. I would like to know where they got their materials. There might be additional charges there since I doubt they got them the legal or ethical way." Dufort never took his eyes off of her.

"I called the head of the team who investigated Genetix as soon as we had Dr. Fuqin in custody. She will be here in a few hours. I'll make sure I get an answer to that question. You are surprisingly good at this. Maybe I should make room for you on the task force after all." Dufort said, not meaning a word of it. Lillian gave a rare genuine smile.

"I have spent more time than I care to think about being questioned by government officials. It was fun to be on the other end of it this time." Not for the first time, Dufort wondered what kind of life Lillian had led in Russia in the short years she had been there.

Dufort stood there alone with Lillian. There were no cameras in this room. Lillian saw the change in his eyes.

"Is there something you wanted to say?" She teased him. Dufort put his hand on the small of her back.

"I think……you are an amazing woman." Lillian couldn't help but smile and with that, Dufort pulled her in. Pausing for only a moment, Dufort leaned in and kissed Lillian. It told Lillian everything Dufort could not.

"I'm still not happy with him knowing who you are." He added, leaned his forehead against hers.

"You'll get over it."

"I doubt that very seriously."

38

"Jack, my boy, can I have a word with you?" Si said. Si had a scotch in his hand that he handed to Jack and then poured himself another one. They were back at Sam's house. It had only been an hour since they had left it earlier and yet everything seemed to have changed. Jack cocked an eyebrow. Something about Si seemed off. He pulled himself away from the party, Si led him out the backdoor. Apparently, it was going to be a private chat.

"What's going on, you're all serious?" Si sat down on the stairs of Sam's deck. He lifted his glass in toast. "Many happy returns." Jack did the same, and they both sat there for a second letting the burning liquid settle. Si said, "What a helluva day son. One helluva day." There was a pause and then he added. "I can't think of when I was so proud of you." If Si had stood up and slapped Jack across the face, he could not have been more surprised. It's not that Si had never said it before. There was the time Jack scored three goals in a single football game. And when he came home with a black eye because he stood up to the kid who was pushing him around, but it was rare. Very rare.

"Because I got married?"

"Not just that. I watched you today. I watched how you carry yourself. How you talk to people. I saw the look in your eye when you saw Ross coming down the aisle. It sounds ridiculous, you've been a grown man for a while, but you're a man I'm glad to know. Not just because you're my boy, but because you are who you are." Si waved his hands around and then leaned over his knees. He wasn't looking at Jack, he wouldn't be able to say what he was saying if he did, and Si wanted to say it. It seemed important. "I don't know, it just struck me today. That and you had the good common sense to marry Ross. She's one of a kind son. Truly."

"You okay? Not like you to go all soft at a wedding." Jack put a hand on his father's shoulder. So rare was it for him to see Si like this, he was at a loss as to what to do.

"Ah, I've been thinking about your mother a lot these last few days. Seeing Belinda and Frank, I think. Or maybe the wedding, or

hell, even the pandemic. Either way, I've been thinking about her a lot more. You made a promise today to love and cherish in sickness and in health. Belinda and Frank are the perfect example of what that means. I never got that with your mother. The closest we got was taking care of each other when we had the flu. And when she had the morning sickness with you. I watch Belinda with Frank, and I wonder if I would be as patient with your mother. I'd give everything I had to find out."

"You would have Dad. You would have done whatever you could just like Belinda does. It wouldn't always be with love in your eyes and a song in your heart, but you would do it. You wouldn't trust anyone else." Jack took another sip of his drink. Not for the first time he wished his mother could meet Ross. Jack too had felt her absence.

"Do me a favor boy." Si's voice cracked. "Tell her everyday. Don't ever let her head hit the pillow without letting her know you still love her." Now he looked at Jack. He needed to know Jack understood what he was saying. He almost looked desperate. "You can't just say it either. Believe me, words can go hollow. You have to show her. Everyday in the smallest way. Women pay attention to that sort of thing. Promise me."

"I promise."

"My biggest regret with Bev was not telling her more. Not making more of an effort so that she knew every single day just how much I loved her."

"You were out on the ocean Dad, it's not like there was a phone at hand all the time."

"It doesn't matter. I think back, and for the life of me, I can't remember if I kissed her goodbye before she left the house that day." Tears were running down the salty old sea dog's cheeks. "And I should have. I should have kissed her everytime she left the house, no matter whether she was going out to the garden or off to the shops." Tears were starting to well up in Jack's eyes as well. "This life you and Ross are living, I don't need to tell you, it has its dangers. You've found out the hard way already. I know it seems exciting now, but it will get tiring eventually. I mean look at that Dufort fella. He can't have much of a home life can he? Do yourself a favor. Settle down and have kids eventually."

"That's a bit rich coming from you. I thought I was an accident, that you never planned on having kids."

"It's true. There were reasons. I wanted your mother all

to myself. I knew I couldn't give up the sea, and that it would be hard to make all that work with a kid." Si wiped his eyes. "But son, it's been the highlight of my life. I know when I go I'm leaving the world better because you are in it, and I claim none of the responsibility. You and your mother get all the credit."

"Blimey, Dad." Jack said, wiping away the tears. Si reached up and pulled him in for a hug. A few sturdy slaps on the back. "I mean it. I didn't want it to go unsaid." Jack downed the rest of his drink and tried to make it look like he wasn't crying like a child. Si pulled a white hanky out of the top pocket of his overalls and blew his nose.

"I would have a few kids already except Ross gets this funny look when you talk about them." Si laughed.

"I've seen the look. I used to get the same look when your mother would talk to me about it. Now that she has found the right man, she might change her mind a little. Keep working on her."

"She actually did mention hypothetical children the other day. I didn't say anything in case she spooked." They sat there in companionable silence for a moment.

"I also wanted to tell you I'm leaving in a while for home." Si added.

"What? You can't. They closed the country."

"I called the embassy yesterday. For residents they are letting us back in, but we have to quarantine in a hotel for two weeks."

"That's going to cost Dad, why go through the bother when you could stay here with us?" Si slapped Jack on the knee.

"I want to go home. I haven't seen the place in a while, and I've got an itch. Harry called me the other day. The fires are getting closer to the house. They are still a way off, but they are closer than they were. If it's going to burn, I would like to see it one more time."

"Dad, you know…?"

"I know boy, you are going to miss me terribly. We can call and Facetime. Not too much mind you."

"I can't believe you want to spend the pandemic without us. Aren't you going to get lonely?" Si gave a wry smile. "You crafty bastard, you are going back out on the boat aren't you?"

"Maybe, nothing for certain. Harry also got the boat up and running. If my plan goes well, I'll go and see the house, then mother nature can do with it what she wants. Head out to the boat and hunker down. I can't think of a more effective way to quarantine than out in the middle of the ocean all by myself."

"He's got the boat up and running?" Jack got a look in his eye, like he was thinking of how he could get back and get the business started again.

"No, don't look like that. You are a married man now and right here is where you should be. Lord knows when this Parid thing is going to end and the tourists aren't going to be going anywhere. It would be suicide to get the business up and running right now. Stay here, with your wife. Keep her safe. Make some babies." Jack made a face. Then a thought occurred to him.

"I'm going to miss you Dad. We've had some adventures the past few years. It's going to seem strange going on one without you. You're a good first mate."

"The bloody cheek! You're the first mate, always have been. No one is captain of my boat but me."

"Take care of yourself Dad." Si looked at him with eyes that looked tired for just a moment.

"Don't you worry about me son. Tough as old shoe leather. Remember what I said? Everyday, everyday." Jack nodded and got up to follow Si back into the house. For a small party, there was still a lot going on. Sam was bringing in food platters from the kitchen. Ross was stuck talking to one of the few relatives who had come. Si walked over to Frank and started talking to him. Belinda was rushing around trying to help Sam. Ross saw him, and with a forced smile on her face, acted like he had called for her, making her way over with purpose.

"Good lord, if I have to hear one more time that this whole Parid thing is a hoax, I'm going to shove that dear old aunt of my mother's right out the door." Ross said, taking what remained of Jack's drink out of his hand and downing it. "What did Si want?"

"Nothing, why?"

"Jack, you two have been out there for half an hour hugging each other and Si looks like he's been crying and so do you. Who died?" Jack took her face in both of her hands and gave her a kiss that made the minister blush and Ross' knees buckle.

"Jack, there are people here." She said, when she could think again.

"He told me to never let you go a day without knowing how much I love you. Through action and words."

"Jack, that kiss wasn't love, it was lust. There's a difference."

"He also told me he's going to head back to Australia."

"By himself? The country is closed. He knows he's welcome at my parents for as long as he needs, doesn't he?"

"The boat is fixed. He's going to check in on the house and then head back out to sea." Ross nodded her in understanding. It was hard to think of Si without thinking of him at sea. Ross turned to look at Si who was now talking to Belinda.

"I'm going to miss him, Jack. I never thought I would say that about someone who makes it a point to walk around in his tighty whities. I've gotten used to him being around. We had some lovely chats in the wheelhouse in the predawn hours."

"Yeah, me too." Jack wrapped an arm around Ross and held her close. He didn't tell her that a pit had settled in his stomach when Si had told him he was going back out to sea. Jack trusted the pit in his stomach, it had never steered him wrong. If something was going to happen to Si, best it happened at sea. That's where his father would want to be. The pit in his stomach was just something he was going to have to get used to. He kissed Ross on the head and said, "I love you."

"I love you too."

<h1 style="text-align:center">39</h1>

It was nine at night. The party had been going for some hours now. They had done all the wedding things. Cutting the cake, first dance, tossing the bouquet. Now it was just the normal crowd. The minister was asleep in the corner, an empty whiskey glass still in his hand. Ross had stuck to champagne, but felt oddly happy and content. Odd, because she was feeling this while participating in a forced social situation. A forced social situation she had been dreading for ages, no less. Ross was sitting at the bottom of Sam's stairs looking out with love at the scene before her. Si was talking with her father, patiently waiting for Frank to get the words out. Her mother, who had let loose a little more than normal, was dancing with herself to the music, a wine glass in her hand, heels kicked off in the corner. Jack was standing in the corner talking to Phillip. Their ties were undone, laying limp around their necks. Their jackets had been taken off long ago. Ross was no longer in her dress. She had just changed into a solid white sweatsuit that Sam had been thoughtful enough to get her. There was a black one upstairs waiting for Jack. Ross had been going to get him and tell him when she decided to sit down and just watch the people in her life.

Sam plopped down next to her, a half filled wine glass in her hand. Sam leaned her head against Ross's shoulder.

"How ya feeling babe?"

"Happy actually. Content even."

"It was a helluva wedding. Not many people, but somehow it seemed perfect for you and Jack. "

"It did, didn't it. Sam, thank you for everything. You did everything you possibly could to make sure I had a great wedding. I can't imagine what you have spent on alcohol, let alone food and everything else."

"It's not everyday your best friend gets married. I'm so glad you are back. I would have done all this and more." They sat there watching the scene for a moment before Sam said. "I'm scared Ross. This virus, it's killing people. A lot of people." Ross turned to look at Sam. Sam felt the normal range of emotions most people feel. But she rarely admitted it. What's more, Ross could not take her fear away with interesting scientific facts like she knew Sam wanted.

"Yes, it is."

"I don't want to die, Ross. I don't want to leave Ruby. I don't want to get sick and have to be away from her for weeks. I know I complain, and I'll admit for a hot second that two weeks of sleeping in sounds great, but in all seriousness, it would kill me. This is a fear like nothing I've ever known and it's there everyday when I wake up. I'm doing everything, wiping down the groceries, wearing masks, hell, I even started putting shoes out in the garage. But it's a virus. I'm not fighting something I can see."

"So far it is only killing the old and the sick. You are

perfectly healthy. So is Phillip."

"My parents aren't." Sam took a sip of wine. They both looked at Frank. Not for the first time, a shiver of fear went through Ross. Frank was already fragile. Parid would outright kill him. "I don't want my parents to leave either. Ruby needs them. I need them. I've had to stop watching the news. It's all anyone can think or talk about. I don't like living like this."

"All you can do is protect yourself and your parents. There will be a vaccine eventually. They are already working on it."

"Come on Ross, tell me it is going to be okay."

"I wish I could, Sam. Viruses change, they mutate. They find out how their host is attacking them and they change. It's what they do, it's just been a while since humans have come across one that affected the population like this one has."

"So you are saying I'm going to have to wipe down my groceries or risk killing my parents for a while longer."

"I'm afraid so. The hope is, that as it continues to mutate, it will become something we can fight off." Ross said. Sam was trying to make light, but Ross could tell she was hiding her true feelings. They both turned back to the scene in front of them.

"If there is one good thing that comes out of this, it's that we will stop taking things like this for granted." Sam said. The room was filled with love. Everyone there had come together to celebrate her love for Jack. She looked at her mother talking to Frank and Si and saw her for the fierce fighter she was. The woman had been single handedly taking care of her invalid husband and had never complained. The woman was just fierce. Si, who made everyone he came in contact with feel special. He pulled them all in with a hug and made them feel like the best version of themselves. Ross's eyes rested on Jack. Never had she been loved the way he seemed to, and while it would take some time to prove, Ross suspected that it wasn't a very common thing. And then there was Sam.

"You're my best friend." Ross said.

"Thank you, Captain Obvious."

"I mean it, Sam. You've always been there. You've never made me feel weird. Half the time you've convinced me I'm not the weird one, it's the world that's odd. You've explained people to me so that they somewhat make sense. You keep me sane. You're the best friend I could ever ask for. And all because we sat next to each other in second grade and you wanted to show me your scab. I love you." Sam grabbed Ross's head and kissed her forehead. Tears forming.

"I love you too. Now stop it, I've cried enough for one day." There was a pause while they wiped their eyes again. Then Sam said, "If there is one good thing in this whole pandemic, it's that you can't leave again." Ross couldn't bring herself to say it out loud, but she was kind of glad herself. It was going to be nice being home for a while. Home with Jack.

The song changed over, and Si got up from where he was and came up behind Belinda and grabbed her around the middle. "Come on woman. Show them what you can do."

"Oh no. Here we go." Sam said. "Come on Belindy, show your new son-in- law what you've got." Belinda was blushing and said no. Then Frank said, "Shake…… it…….babe." Belinda went up to the pole, threw a leg around it and did a rather adept spin.

"Oh my god!" Ross said, in horror. Her hand flew to her mouth.

"I told you." Sam said, getting up and pulling a wad of ones out of her back pocket. Ross got up too. Jack came to stand next to her.

"What did you say your mother did for a living?" Jack asked.

"I'll explain it all to you later. She's doing rather well. Especially considering she's wearing a pants suit." At that moment Belinda unbuttoned the jacket of her outfit and shimmied it down her arms. Swung it several times around her head before letting it go. It flew into the face of her husband who was whistling at her and throwing his own ones. The song ended with a round of applause and Belinda collecting her money. She went over to Frank and said something. He laughed and said something back to her, which made her gasp and give a little slap to his arm. Then Belinda kissed him.

"Your parents are rather adorable together." Jack said in her ear. Ross couldn't remember the last time she had seen either one of them smile so much. It was still a shock to her to see her father in a wheelchair. Looking at them now though, they were okay. Life wasn't perfect. Far from it really, but they had each other. Looking at Jack, she knew what that could mean in bad times.

"They are rather adorable, aren't they?"

"Come sit next to me dear." Si said, patting the sofa seat next to him. "It was a great day, wasn't it? You looked fantastic." Ross leaned over and kissed his cheek.

"I'm glad you were here."

"Wouldn't have missed it for the world."

"Jack says you are going to go back home. You know you

don't have to. Mom and Dad are happy having you around, Mom says you're a big help."

"They have been lovely, but I do need to go home. Like I told Jack, I haven't been in a while, and for some reason, I feel the need."

"Plus the boat is in working order again." Ross said. Si nodded, "Plus the boat is working again."

"When do you leave?"

"Day after tomorrow. I've already made my reservation to quarantine for two weeks. It's all settled."

"Take care of yourself. I mean it." Si squeezed her shoulder.

"You too. Maybe settle down, have a few kids." Ross's eyes went wide.

"Si, not you too? I mean I expect this sort of thing from my mother, but not you. I just got married! Can we give it a minute?" Si gave one of his rare genuine smiles and a barky laugh.

"When you get to my age, Ross dear, you start to think of what you are going to leave behind. I will leave behind one house. Bought in nineteen sixty-five for a quarter of what it is worth now. A boat which, thanks to my friend Harry, is good as new. Stories too colorful to be told at my funeral. A few pairs of overalls in various states of decline, and Jack. Now you and Jack. He's the joy of my life, Ross, other than Bev. I couldn't be more proud of the man he is, and for a large chunk of my younger life I was convinced I didn't want children. Thankfully, Bev knew better, she usually did." Si looked Ross in the eyes. "You are a smart woman, you have a good heart and bravery like I have never seen before. You too are going to have a few good stories to be told about you at your funeral, but I'll tell you something for nothing, Ross. It all pales when you see your child grow and exceed you in all your best qualities."

"What if I raise a really smart serial killer?" Ross said, putting out there one of her fears about having children. Si laughed.

"Well, that too is a legacy, I guess. It's a roll of the dice. For what it's worth, there is no evidence of insanity in my family tree. Alcoholism. But to my knowledge, we have never killed anyone who didn't deserve it."

"Thank you, Si, for explaining to me why I should have children." Si looked confused. "Everyone else has made it sound like my duty as a woman. Like it would be a crime to let these ovaries go to waste. Or some other nonsense reason to bring a person into the world. You actually listed reasons. Thank you."

"Does that mean…?"

"Oh, I'm still not agreeing with you, but I appreciate you treating me like a thinking human and not a breeding machine." Si pulled her towards him, and Ross rested her head on his shoulder until Jack (in an attempt to escape her mother's wandering hands) came and got her for another dance.

An hour later, Ross was feeling rather drunk despite only having two glasses of champagne, the rest of Jack's Scotch, and three glasses of wine. "That would be the jetlag." Jack said. He was now wearing the solid black sweat suit Sam had gotten him and feeling the four beers and two Scotches he had downed.

"Maybe we should go." Ross said.

"You go tell Sam we are going to head home, I'll go grab

our things." Before either one of them had gotten very far, the next song came on and Si took a running jump at the pole, his momentum spinning him around it. He then bent over, showing his overall covered bum to the crowd and did a fairly good 'pop 'n lock'. Looking over his shoulder, he unbuckled one of his overall straps before spinning on the pole again, the loose strap flying around him. Taking his clip on tie off, he threw it into the crowd and then, to the amazement of them all, leaned backwards and came down the pole upside down.

"The man's insane." Jack said.

"That's it, Si. I'm cutting you off." Sam yelled out to him. "You have to watch them. We've had a few near misses with the landings. They get a few drinks in them and they think they are twenty-two again. The last thing any of them needs right now is a trip to the emergency room." Ross gave a sideways glance at her friend. Sam was starting to sound more and more like a mom.

"Where in the seven seas did he learn how to ride a stripper pole like that?" Ross asked.

"While the sea is definitely his natural habitat, you'll find that Si has survived this long because of his natural ability to adapt to his surroundings. He does this by picking up the culture of wherever he is. Including strip clubs, apparently." Jack explained. "The man is going to break something."

"Let them have their fun." Ross leaned into Jack. He put his arm over her shoulders. Tomorrow they would all wake up with hangovers and discover the hard way none of them could digest alcohol the way they once had. Belinda would have to go back to playing nursemaid to Frank. Sam and Phillip would pick Ruby up from her grandparents and once again be getting up early to feed her. Life would go back to normal soon enough. Or what passed for normal. "Let them have their fun tonight."

"Come on dear, I've got our stuff together in the dining room." Jack said, his motives for getting Ross home were not entirely pure. Ross went up to Sam, "Do you think Phillip could give us a ride to my apartment?"

"You aren't leaving now." Sam said, rather emphatically.

"Why not? We are exhausted. It's almost midnight."

"You haven't taken a turn yet." Sam said, nodding at the poles. Ross stood there stunned, she was far too tired to think of an excuse that Sam would accept. Sam handed her another glass of champagne and said, "I have the song picked out and everything." Ross looked at Jack for help and he merely shrugged. With no graceful exit available, Ross downed her champagne in hopes that it would have the ability to make her forget her dignity. Sam turned around and put the song on. Ross knew from the first beat which song Sam had picked out. "I haven't heard this song in at least a decade." Ross said.

"Middle school dance, remember?" Sam said, smiling from ear to ear. For reasons unknown to science, Ross, who did not have a musical bone in her body, could not keep her body still when this song was on. For that reason, Ross had not played it, had flat out avoided it, since becoming an adult. Ross was ashamed to find that after all these years, it still had the same effect on her. Annoyingly, her head started to bob, and then her shoulders started to move and before she knew it, she was dancing in the same ridiculous way she always did when she heard the song. Sam, of course, standing there egging her on. Jack stood in shock as Ross began singing the lyrics, and when the beat dropped, jumped onto the pole, hooked her leg around it and pointed out over the crowd as she spun.

"That's my girl!" Sam yelled and whistled. If Ross had been paying any attention to the other people in the room, she would have seen appalled looks on her parents' faces as they asked themselves the same question Ross had asked when they had their turn. Where had she learned to dance on a pole like that?

Ross did a couple low ground spins and then decided to try her party trick. Taking a page from Si's book, Ross tried to hang upside down on the pole, but it was harder than it looked, and she half fell to the ground (though she was pretty sure she made it look intentional). By the time the song ended, Ross was laying on her back with her legs wrapped around the pole.

"Do it Ross! Do your thing!" Sam shouted. Ross then did a handstand using the pole to lean on and blurted out the periodic table alphabetically. As had been the case most of her life, there was no one there to tell Ross if she got it wrong and as tired as she was, Ross couldn't be sure herself. Sam sat a cup in front of her, and when Ross had finished, she rolled to a sitting position and drank the shot. The crowd went wild. When she had stopped spinning, there were more people in the room than there had been before. The next song cut out, Ross landed on the ground, looking at the stern face of Dufort standing behind Jack and her parents.

Ross squinted to make sure she wasn't seeing things. Dufort smiled and gave her a little wave. Everyone else turned to see what she was looking at. No one said a word. Slowly a small grin slid across Dufort's face and he said, "Dr. Halloway, if you could, I would like a word." The

wedding party slowly turned to look at Ross who was still sitting on the floor leaning against a stripper pole.
"Sure."

40

"What the hell are you doing here? How did you get here? Everything is shut down." Ross said. Getting herself up off the ground with as much grace as she could muster.

"I assure you, international policing is still happening." Dufport's grin was still in place, "I'm afraid something has come up that requires me to interrupt your party. If I could have a word with both of you?"

"Listen here, these two just got back from being with you, they almost missed their wedding because of it. So, whatever mess you have, go fix it yourself." Si jumped in, getting closer to the inspector than was necessary. Si was drunk, he was giving the impression he could still land a punch if he needed to.

"I understand." And Dufort did understand. "I understand today is important. I would not have come if it wasn't necessary."

"They are all like this." Si said, turning to Jack. "It was the same in my day. They turn up out of nowhere and expect you to drop everything. Don't do it son. This is your wedding day. Don't let them ruin it." Si said, looping his thumbs through his overalls and glaring at Dufort. Dufort preferred to talk his way out of fights, and he was rather good at it. While Si's reputation preceded him, Dufort was certain he could land a good punch if he needed to.

"What the hell could be so important that it couldn't wait until tomorrow?" Jack asked, not caring if his father threw a punch at Dufort.

"There have been developments in the situation we discussed earlier." Dufort's face turned serious. Ross nodded. Her head was fuzzy and she was still trying to figure out if this was real or a jet lag induced dream.

"Speak English man." Si said, shaking his head. "What development? When did it happen? Who was involved? Stop speaking in bloody code."

"With the Spartans I'm assuming?" Ross asked. Dufort nodded.

"Not these damn Spartans again." Belinda asked, joining the conversation with Frank in his wheelchair. "Ross, what is going on? My daughter wants nothing else to do with these Spartans." She informed Dufort who was almost invisible behind the wall of their parents.

"I'm sure the inspector wouldn't have come out here if it wasn't important." Ross tried to sooth. Belinda may have sounded calm and reasonable, but that was how she got you. Ross could tell from the way she was standing that if the inspector didn't play his cards right, he was heading straight for a Belinda ass chewing.

"Are you that inspector?" Belinda asked. "The one who helped Ross after she was shot?"

"Yes." Dufort said, suspicious. He felt like he was being lured into a trap.

"The one who investigated the attack on my daughter's

research trip?"

"Yes, that was me." Belinda's back went straight and she took a step toward the inspector.

"I would like to thank you for all your hard work. I'm sure you will have some understanding of how important a day this is considering my daughter was fighting for her life not that long ago. While you have no doubt come a long way and at great expense, I think it would be best for everyone if you let Ross and Jack out of whatever scheme you have. Surely you have better qualified people to handle whatever it is. My daughter would like to get back to her life, and after all she's been through, I think she deserves a little peace and quiet." Dufort's eyebrows went into his hairline. It had been a long time since he had been told off so nicely. "Interpol is a multinational organization." Belinda continued. "Now, I am well aware of how smart Ross is, but surely, in the whole wide world, there is someone else out there who can help you with these Spartan things. She's still healing." Belinda was standing extremely close to Dufort now. Shoulder to shoulder with Si. Definitely not staying six feet apart. Dufort was having to lean back to keep distance.

"In......short........*fuck*.......*off*." Frank said, from his chair.

"Come on Belinda, why don't I take you and Frank home? It's getting late." Phillip offered.

"I'm not going anywhere." Belinda said, not taking her eyes off Dufort. "Ross is not going anywhere. Do you understand me? She and Jack deserve their happiness and you, sir, constantly calling on them to help you figure out the Spartans, is not part of the picture." Dufort was stunned. He had found himself in many tense situations, but never had he had the parents of an agent come between him and the agent.

"Mom, I can handle this."

"Ross, I'm serious. You deserve this, don't let them talk you into anything."

"Dad, why don't you go with them?" Jack said, but if he was looking for help from Si, he was mistaken.

"Hell no, I've still got security clearance. I want to know what is so damned important you can't leave these two alone to get on with their lives."

"Actually, this is a higher security level than you have." Dufort informed Si. "I had Jack and Ross's security level raised just for this mission. It will be taken back down afterwards. This is for their ears only."

"Inspector, I'm not sure this conversation is going to happen tonight." Ross said, too tired and a little too drunk to argue with all of them. Si gave Dufort the two fingered salute. Frank gave him the one digit American version.

"Take that you bastard."Si said, smiling at Frank's support. Dufort nodded.

"A pleasure meeting you, sir. Madam." Dufort addressed Si and Belinda. Dufort turned to leave and Ross said, "I'll walk you out." Not wanting Ross to be left alone with Dufort, Jack said, "I'll go with you."

"You really do pick your moments, don't you?" Jack addressed Dufort as they were walking out of the house.

"It's one of the skills they train you for at the academy. I am sorry, I knew you were getting married, if there was anything I could do about the timing, I would have done it. We got this information as you were leaving. I have spent the time between then and now confirming things. I didn't want to come for you, your presence has been requested."

"By who?" Ross asked, as they were walking out to the front porch.

"The generals."

"Well, they will just have to get over it. It's my wedding night." Jack stated firmly, putting an arm around Ross's waist.

"I just want to get something clear…what has happened? Did the Spartans back out? Did you find Father? I'm assuming there was a problem or you wouldn't be here." Ross asked.

"Ross, for the love of everything holy, it's our wedding day." Jack pleaded.

"I'm not going to go, I'm just wondering what happened, that is all." Ross looked at Dufort expectantly. Dufort looked around. Looked at the heavens for guidance. He had barely slept since Jack and Ross had left Porton Downs. Things had been happening so quickly.

"We picked Father up at Heathrow as he was returning from China. While he is refusing to name who he was working with, he is cooperating in every other way."

"The strange name thing with him and Mother?"

"Mother's idea. Apparently she thought it was cute, or something."

"I always thought that was a bit weird." Jack said, god help him, now he was interested.

"So he was selling the information? So other countries could build their own Spartans?" Ross asked. Trying to keep it all straight in her drunk mind. Dufort lit a cigarette. Taking advantage of the fact they were outside, and let out a long, slow stream of smoke.

"Not just the 'recipe' as you called it. They will come and

set up your lab for you, get it running. Train your staff. The whole package." Dufort waved his hand around, making a smoke circle. Ross wrapped her arms around herself, the thought made her cold. Jack stood there in stunned silence. "The Chinese got greedy. Wanted him to stay and expand the lab. Create a larger generation in a shorter time span, but they wanted it for the same price. Father...Dr. Fuqin had to get tough with them before they would let his team leave."

"So there are Shi's out there?" Ross asked.

"Oh yes. What Dr. Fuqin has told us matches up nicely with the Spartans intel they just got back to us. I have to say, if they weren't such frightening fuckers, I could get used to how quickly they follow orders. The Spartans have done their own intel. Even managed to get most of the intel without going to bloody China. They have someone in place now. Anyway, the lab is much larger than expected, and we recently found out that this was not in fact the first generation of Shi they have produced." Dufort said. There was a pause while that information sunk in.

"How many then?" Ross asked.

"We don't know."

"What do you mean you don't know? What did Father tell you?" Jack asked, irritated.

"He was rather vague on the specifics. He told us the Chinese had been pleased with the results to a point, but that they wanted more and they wanted them faster. To the point where he thought they were going to push the technology to a disastrous end."

"Bloke chose an interesting time to develop a conscience." Jack said.

"What did the Spartans think?" Ross asked.

"They couldn't be sure either. They said the training program seemed rather advanced, it is possible there are a few generations out there at this point. So, a few hundred. Three hundred at the most. We are trying to contact our agents in the Chinese military to see if the Shi have turned up there. We are thinking they were developed for defense just like the American Spartans originally were. The information is coming in quickly."

"What do you want us for then? I can't see how we could possibly be useful." Ross said.

"We have run into a problem with the communication between us and the Spartans." Dufort said. Taking another very long drag on his cigarette.

"What's that?"

"They will only speak to you from now on." Dufort watched Ross's expression as the words hit her. Ross's adrenaline went up. Her mouth dropped open. Jack came up off the post he had been leaning on.

"Don't be ridiculous." Jack said. "What the hell for? Why does it have to be her?"

"In short, they suspect a trap with us. I suppose you can understand where they are coming from, can't you? They have little reason to trust the military. I've been hunting them since the world learned about them."

"Then why accept the job?" Ross asked. "They could have just not called us back." Dufort smiled.

"Because they had gotten word of the Shi and want them gone as well. Getting paid an insane amount of money to do it was all the motivation they needed."

"Inspector, it's my wedding day. I'm exhausted from the last time I went with you to 'a secure location'. I want to go home. To the home I haven't seen in almost a year. I want to sleep in, and then do nothing. Surely the Chinese and the Spartans aren't going to bring the end of the world in the next twenty-four hours......are they?"

"Probably not." Dufort said, a little stunned. He was used to people following his orders immediately.

"I can Zoom call the meeting surely? I don't need to be there in person, do I? Afterall, there is a pandemic going on."

"Given the nature of the meeting and its security level, the meeting can not be trusted with a Zoom call." Dufort said, managing to sound offended at the very idea.

"Give me one day to get a decent night's sleep and visit my apartment, then I will go where you want."

"The hell you will." Sam piped up, bursting through the front door behind Jack and stomping down the steps to stand in front of Ross. "You have been gone for six months. You were supposed to be gone for a week. You can't do this to me Ross. You can't just leave again and not know when you are coming back. *If* you are coming back." Sam's eyes were wet with tears that she wouldn't let fall. Ross had never seen Sam this angry with her. She was stunned into silence.

"This is an issue of global importance." Dufort said, feeling he should help.

"Fuck that, I don't care." Sam retorted, turning her fury onto him. She was a little drunk, or she would have said that differently. The sentiment would have been the same. Just said nicely.

"Excuse me....?" Dufort said.

"Every time she leaves, something terrible happens. About two years ago, we left to go on an all expense paid trip to this fantastic five star resort and literally nothing has been the same since. Ross is staying here, with the people who love her, and she is going to get back to the life she had before those damn Spartans decided to have a fucking revolution."

"Sam!" Ross said, in shock.

"No, she is not going any damned place with you. Now, you can either go back and tell the generals and the Spartans and whoever, these Shi are to figure it the fuck out, or I would be happy to tell them for you. The choice is yours."

"Sam, please."

"I'm sorry, Ross, I know you are a grown woman, and I usually leave you to make your own mistakes, but I've had it. I have been a nervous wreck for too long! You are going to stay here, you are going to have a normal fucking life where there is no chance of you dying before we are ninety-seven and causing problems in the nursing home like we have always planned. There is a global pandemic on, she's not going anywhere." Sam was now in the yard between Ross and Dufort.

"I'm afraid Dr. Halloway signed a contract and is a member of the Spartan Task Force. If she does not come with me now, she may face charges." At this Ross and Jack piped up with their indignation.

"Excuse me?"

"Where the hell was that stated?" Jack asked.

"How are you going to charge her if the mission is so secret?" Sam retorted. "Charge her secretly? Put her in a secret jail?"

"Something like that, yeah. Who is this woman?" Dufort asked Ross.

" Mrs. Samantha Bowling, best friend of Ross, wife of

Phillip, and mother of Ruby. Not to mention the owner of this house from which you are about to be booted. Who the hell are you?"

"Inspector Louis Dufort of Interpol."

"Big…..fucking…deal."

"Mrs. Bowling, I don't think you understand the significance….."

" What part are you not getting? She's not going anywhere with you." Sam looked at Ross, "She quits, all right? There, she no longer works for your taskforce."

"That's not how this works." Dufort stood there, not exactly knowing what to do.

"You would throw us in a prison if we don't come with you?" Ross asked. Dufort rolled his eyes and took a deep breath. Civilians.

"It's one course of action." Dufort answered. Jack took a step towards Dufort that made him jump.

"Sam, go back inside the house." Ross said.

"Ross?"

"It's alright Sam, I'm not leaving, I'll be back in a few minutes." Sam turned on her heel like a stubborn teenager and stomped back into the house. Dufort, who had just stomped on his spent cigarette, popped some nicotine gum into his mouth. Ross let him enjoy it for a moment as she sat down on the front walk. Jack stayed where he was, ready to act should Ross attempt to leave or Dufort try to arrest her. "How's Lillian?" Ross asked. Dufort looked at her side-eyed, suspicious at the change in subject.

"Better than the last time you saw her. The long days take their toll. Identifying Father seemed to put a spark back in her. She even interviewed him."

"I'm surprised you allowed that." Ross said, smiling,

knowing perfectly well Dufort would have a hard time denying Lillian anything.

"I have enough evidence to charge him, find him guilty, and keep him hidden away in a facility where no one has ever heard of civil liberties for the rest of his life. Lillian thought she could get some information out of him, help connect the dots, and she did." Ross nodded.

"I'm not going with you Inspector. I'm sorry. I wish I could be the person you need me to be, but I'm not." There was a pause, and for a moment, Ross wondered what Dufort was going to do. He was absently toeing the ground in front of him.

"I am perfectly aware that neither one of you chose this life. You were in the wrong place at the wrong time. The fact stands though that you, on multiple occasions now, have gotten the better of Spartans. I don't know how you did it, but you did. It's a fact. A fact that has not gone unnoticed. Whether you like it or not, you are an expert in Spartans. Both of you. You possess a skill set that can be useful to humanity."

"Where do you live, Inspector?" Ross asked.

"What does that have to do with anything?"

"Answer, please."

"I have a one bedroom in Belgium."

"How often are you there?"

"Right now, a few times a year."

"When was the last time you were home for Christmas?"

"Dr. Halloway, I know where you are going with this."

"Then you know why I am not going to go with you. Go back and tell whoever you need to that I politely decline. The Spartans will do what they do, the generals will do what they do. But I can't live like this."

"Is this you 'fucking it up'?" Dufort asked.

"In a way, yeah. This is me reclaiming my life. The Spartans have already been too big a part of it." Dufort nodded.

"There is a good chance they will reach out to you again with something. They will threaten to arrest you. Again, you have a skill set useful to humanity." Ross waved him off. Duffort knew he could keep it from happening.

"I'll find another way of fucking it up. I've had lots of practice fucking up."

"Well, congratulations Dr. Halloway, Jack. Sorry to interrupt the day."

"Don't be sorry, it was good to see you."

"Oh, I almost forgot. A little something to start your life together." Dufort handed them another envelope.

"Another plane ticket?" Ross said, joking.

"No, your payment for your services thus far. I went ahead and had them make it out since I figured there was a good chance you weren't coming. Saved it going through the mail."

"Payment?" Jack said, coming off the post. "I thought it was more for King and Country and all that." Jack looked down at the check Ross was holding, and his eyes almost popped out of his head. Dufort saw the reaction and smiled.

"Don't be silly. Consulting pays rather well, especially when it is urgent. I would never think of not compensating you both for your time." Dufort was smiling when he got into his car and drove away. Jack and Ross, still standing on the porch, now wondered if they were making the right decision.

41

When Ross opened her eyes the next morning, the first thing she saw was the fan overhead. Ross was lying completely still on her back, watching the keychain hanging from the pull showing the organic chemical compounds of Magnesium. Sam had gotten it for her when she had graduated from her master's program. Ross had asked her *why magnesium?*

I had no idea what it was, Ross, I just knew it was sciencey. The center of it was mirrored, and the late morning light flickered across it, casting rainbows on Ross's ceiling. It was the same scene Ross had awakened to hundreds of times before. To the point where, for one instant, Ross thought maybe it had all been a very elaborate dream. Maybe she hadn't gone on the research trip with Nils yet. She and Sam had downed a couple of margaritas. That would explain the headache. Maybe she had been so worried about the trip and Jack that it all manifested in the strangest damn dream. That would mean she hadn't been shot, Jack hadn't taken her away to hide her on the boat, and hadn't proposed.

Then someone rolled over next to her. Ross turned to see if it was Jack and felt the stiffness in her neck. So, it had all been real. Right up to the wedding and Dufort's late night visit. Ross sat up, and the pounding in her head let her know the glasses of champagne and wine had also been real. She looked over to ask Jack if he wanted coffee, but something about the way his mouth was hanging open made her think he would rather sleep a little longer. Slowly and gingerly, Ross got out of bed and made her way to the kitchen where she brought the coffee maker to life. Carbon, her cat that her neighbor had returned last night, jumped up and head butted her.

"It's good to see you too, little man." Ross found herself smiling to herself as she moved around her kitchen. The events of the evening before replayed in her mind, and she wondered what reason Dufort gave to the generals for not flying away at their request. She was glad she didn't have to be in the room when he did it.

Aspirin taken, coffee in hand, and cat following behind, Ross made her way to the living room where she crossed her legs and sat on the couch. The place was silent, and Ross sat there and absorbed it for a while. It had been a long time since she had been this alone. Then she turned on the TV. Ross turned on the news. Parid-21 was still spreading like wildfire. Images of tired hospital staff dressed head to toe in gear followed by white body bags flipped across the screen. Stats that seemed hard to believe were thrown around. There was no mention of Spartans or the Shi. Ross didn't feel bad about turning Dufort away the night before. That didn't keep her from wondering what was happening. The thought of there being a new type of Spartan out there ran cold fear through her, so Ross shivered and decided she wasn't going to think about it.

Getting up from the couch, which got her a terse look from Carbon, she went out to look out her window. The sky was a flawless blue. It was almost hard to imagine that there was anything wrong underneath it. Dufort was a lovely man, but he had brought a side of the world to Ross that made it impossible to ignore. Ross looked down at the nearly empty streets and tried to imagine what they had looked like before she left. So much had changed, and at the same time nothing at all. Dufort's parting words were spinning around in her head. *You have a skill set that is useful to humanity.* Was that true? Or was Dufort blowing smoke up her ass to get what he wanted? You could never be sure with him. Ross bit her lip. How were three very brief conversations with Spartans enough to make her an expert?

"Penny for your thoughts." Jack surprised her, and Ross jumped. Jack was standing in the doorway of her bedroom. Hair gorgeously shuffled. A light layer of stubble covering his jaw. The only thing that kept him from looking perfect was the fact that he was squinting to keep the light out of his eyes.

"Aspirin and coffee are on the counter."

"Cheers." Jack poured out the coffee black and drank half of it. "That's better." He came up behind her and looked at the empty street below. "Seriously, what are you thinking?"

"Just replaying the past few days. Mainly Dufort's visit last night."

"Bloody man. What did he think we were going to do? Throw up our hands and hop in the car."

"I'm not sure he had a choice. I got the impression that he was there simply to say he had tried."

"I was scared to death you were going to try and convince me to go." Ross repositioned herself to lean on the window.

"No, I can't say I'm not curious as to what is going on, but no."

"You sound like you thought about it."

"I honestly can not see how they don't have other people to handle this. They keep on saying we are experts, but if that is true, it's not saying much."

"Ross? What are you thinking." Jack said, trying to figure out Ross's train of thought. Ross smiled, knowing full well her thoughts were hard enough to follow when you weren't hung over.

"I'm thinking, I am really glad to be home. I am really glad to be married, and though it was lovely, I'm never doing that again. I am thinking that I shouldn't feel this content when there is so much wrong with the world. I am thinking about getting back to work in the lab and what I'm going to research. I've had six months to think of new research."

"But...." Jack asked, knowing that was not all Ross was thinking.

"I'm also wondering if I can ever get back the life I had. Or if that has been some sort of dream I've kept hold of to get me through."

"What are you saying Ross?" Ross reached out and looped her arm through his and around his waist. Leaned her head on his shoulder and said, "The old Ross was naive. Smart, but naive. Naive to think by coming back here, the fact that there are Spartans and Shi out there would mean less. That I would be able to put away the fact that I had been shot. That the nightmare from that night would somehow go away." Ross shook her head. "I'm a different Ross, and I am going to have to learn how to deal with that." Jack pulled her closer. There was silence for a moment before he asked, "But you still aren't going to really join the task force...right?"

"Of course not. I've got Lillian's contact info, I'll just pump her for information." They watched the clouds in the sky for a moment. The sinking feeling was still in his stomach, and now he didn't know if it was because Si was going back home, or because Ross obviously was not going to be able to let the Spartans go completely.

"Listen, you were worried about where we are going to live right? I had a thought last night." Ross looked at him curiously. "What about this, we give ourselves three months. We stay here in lock down, see where this Parid thing is going, and then we decide what our next move is. How about that?"

"What do we do in the meantime?" Jack lifted an eyebrow. "Jack...seriously."

"Well, we have that check from Dufort we can cash. Even if your lab shuts down, between that and the money we got for looking for the boys, we should be able to get by easily for a few months." Ross nodded. Jack pulled her head in and kissed the top of it. "What do you think? We'll live an ordinary domestic life for a while and see how it suits us." Ross thought about it. Her going to the lab (because it was impossible to think that she wouldn't), coming home to Jack and Carbon. They would eat and talk about their day and then sit and watch stupid TV until it was time to go to bed. It seemed so simple. So boring. Extremely ordinary. It made her smile.

"Absolutely we can do that. Abso-damn-lutely."

Other works by K. Patteson:

<u>**Ross and Jack Series:**</u>

Trouble On The Water

Book 1

ISBN: 978-0-578-67787-3

Trouble on the Ice

Book 2

ISBN: 978-1-7359525-1-2

<u>**Standalone Books:**</u>

Ghost Island

ISBN: 978-1-7359525-0-5